Pack Leader Down

Pack Leader Down

Nathan B. Tracy

YAV Publications

Asheville, North Carolina

Copyright © 2010 by Nathan B. Tracy

LCC Number: 2010907719

ISBN 978-0-9790221-8-0

Published by:

YAV Publications
Asheville, North Carolina

YAV books may be purchased in bulk for educational, business, fund-raising, or sales promotional use. For information, contact Books@yav.com or phone toll-free 888-693-9365.

Visit our website: www.InterestingWriting.com

3 5 7 9 10 8 6 4 2

Assembled in the United States of America
Published June 2011

The Pelican

CONTENTS

Chapter 1   —   The Ledge 9

Chapter 2   —   The Warning...13

Chapter 3   —   Yellow Pine 22

Chapter 4   —   Sailing South...26

Chapter 5   —   The Pelican..29

Chapter 6   —   Bait Shop Attack 35

Chapter 7   —   Foiled Attack 40

Chapter 8   —   The Grouper Digger..46

Chapter 9   —   The Storm 50

Chapter 10 —   The Shot...53

Chapter 11-I — The Tunnel..58

Chapter 12 —   Storm Driven...62

Chapter 13 —   The Pack...66

Chapter 14-I — Dog Breath and Bugles 73

Chapter 15 —   Shell Mound..76

Chapter 16 —   Reconnaissance 80

Chapter 17-I — Higher Ground 84

Chapter 18 —   Bad Guys Advance...93

Chapter 19 —   The Drug Lord's Camp 96

Chapter 20-I — Happy Hunting Ground...101

Chapter 21 — The Dogs Attack..105

Chapter 22 — The Wolves..108

Chapter 23-I — The Arboretumist 111

Chapter 24 — Fat Man Down..114

Chapter 25 — The Snake...118

Chapter 26 — I, Me, My, Mine IS, IS 122

Chapter 27 — The Aeroplane Returns 125

Chapter 28-I — The Plum Tree and Politics 131

Chapter 29 — The Wolves Close In 136

Chapter 30 — The Awakening..140

Chapter 31-I — To the River...144

Chapter 32 — Metamorphosis...149

Chapter 33 — Where Does It Come From 152

Chapter 34 — It's Hard to Trust Attack!..156

Chapter 35 — Truth and Contention 161

Chapter 36 — Rest Stop 164

Chapter 37 — It Depends on the Mission 167

Chapter 38-I — Tombstone...170

Chapter 39 — Nearing Solid Ground..174

Chapter 40 — No Tracks in the Sand 177

Chapter 41-I — The Pack Returns 179

Epilogue 183

Author's Comments...201

Glossary of Nautical Terms..205

Dedication

To my wife, Martha
She raised my biological children, was a foster mother to over fifty
children over twenty years, and the adoptive mother of Amanda and
Anthony

Nathan Bartlett Tracy II and his wife Amber
Nathan Bartlett Tracy III
Austin Tracy
Toddington Shipley Tracy and Mary Tracy
Emily Tracy
William Tracy
Lark Bliss Holden (Tracy)
Whitney Holden
Forrest Holden
Lois Collier Moffett (Tracy)
Savannah Moffett
Amanda Dawn Sumner (Tracy) and Steve Sumner
Ayden Sumner
Tristan Sumner
Anthony Patrick Tracy (unmarried)
Sandy—biological mother of Bart, Todd, Lark, and Lois

CHAPTER 1

The Ledge

"Cut your power and swing left," Cowboy screamed toward the pilot station at the top of his lungs. He was aft, working on the tarp covering the fish hold hatches.

Rushing forward, he screamed again, "Do it! Cut power and turn full to port—that's left to you, stupid! ass." He was running through the crew quarters and could see the pilot station on the other side of the galley. It was empty. Then he saw the captain, who was supposed to be conning the vessel, pouring coffee in the galley. The next words were too vile to record.

He ran toward the pilot station, shouldering the captain out of the way in the galley, spinning him around in a shower of scalding coffee.

He entered the pilot station at a run. As he reached the spoked wheel, he came to a stop, grasping a spoke with his left hand just as the channel marker slammed against the starboard bow. Then the vessel stopped suddenly as her forefoot struck the ledge. Cowboy was thrown against the wheel. The governor on the V 12-71 GM engine kicked in, feeding power to the propeller, skidding the vessel forward with the sound of grinding timbers and torn metal. Then the stern settled with a crash as the rudder struck, and the propeller thrashed against the ledge. The spooked wheel spun violently as the rudder struck the ledge and twisted as the rudder shaft was pulled from its guard. The spinning wheel caught on Cowboy's clothing, lifting him off the floor and tossing him to the overhead.

Shuddering from stem to stern, the vessel ground to a stop. The impact threw the captain forward from the galley, sliding him into the pilot station on his belly. He scrambled to his feet by grasping Cowboy's belt, whose shirt was still tangled in the spokes of the wheel. He hauled himself erect

9

while grasping the transmission control and jerking it into neutral. The big diesel engine was revving because the shaft had snapped and released the load of the propeller. He pulled the throttle to idle.

Cowboy untangled himself from the now stationary wheel and leaned against the bulkhead, holding his bruised side and trying to work the fingers of his damaged left hand. He turned to the captain and slapped him hard with the back of his right hand, cursing violently. Then he planted his yellow cowboy hat firmly on his head and polished each beige boot by rubbing it on the back cuff of his Levi's.

There was a crunching and grinding sound as the current swung the vessel clear of the ledge.

"We're making water!" a crewman hollered from aft. "The shaft log has broken open and water is pouring in!"

Holding his side and limping, Cowboy made his way aft at a run. "Get the engine pump on line," he shouted. "Pull up an engine-room bilge hatch and check the bilges to see how much water she is making."

He shouted again at a crewman emerging from the engine room.

"Get your tail to the bow and drop the anchor before we get washed aground. Everyone, listen up! With the cargo on board, we will all be in jail by morning if the cops come looking. Let's do what we need to do quickly."

The captain, who was supposed to be conning the vessel, limped aft with blood running from his nose. "Look, Cowboy, I didn't know about that hazard marker. This is my first time up the Anclote River as captain."

"Listen, jerk, you may be the temporary captain of this vessel, but if I ever see you again, you will be a dead man if we don't get this boat unloaded tonight. King may kill you himself. He doesn't like screwups, so make yourself scarce, if we ever make it to the dock."

"Cowboy," a scrawny-looking crew said quietly, "I've seen a glimpse of a big, black boat pulling away from a dock over there." He pointed to the north side of the river. "I mostly come to tell you that the pumps are keeping up with the water, but we have a bellyful already."

"Is the cargo dry?"

"Yes, sir, it's all OK, except maybe in the lazarette. If the bow lifts much, all the water will flood aft and possibly flood the cargo."

"See to it that everything stays dry," he growled.

Cowboy scanned the darkness and made out the low silhouette of a forty footer moving in front of the lights on shore, blinking them out for a moment. It didn't show any navigation lights. Then he saw a glint of a thin gold stripe that went from stem to stern. It was King's hopped-up vessel.

Cowboy found the captain with the bleeding nose in the galley washing his face in the sink. He hunched his shoulders and appeared frightened of the approaching man. "Your name is Gill, right? You sure aren't a first mate or a captain, and I'm not calling you one."

"Gill, you better be competent with the anchor and a towline if you hope to live. Get forward and rig a towline to a boat coming alongside.

Rig the anchor line to the cathead and get someone to man the clutch while you handle stuff on the bow. Keep the engine at idle so we will have electricity and engine power to the winch."

The man responded by running to the anchor chute, elbowing the other crew out of the way and knocking out the keeper pin and shoving the anchor overboard. When the line went slack, he let some run out and then pulled a loop back to a snatch block and then ran the line to the cathead of the winch and took a turn. He handed the line to the other crew who stood near the clutch handle of the winch.

Then he dropped down through the forward hatch and climbed through the opening into the anchor locker. He pulled out a coil of one-inch nylon and tossed it to the deck. He followed, making the bitter end down on the Sampson post, adding several half hitches to the tail. Panting and still bleeding, he waited for the word to pass the towline.

King brought his vessel alongside and tossed a light line to Cowboy.

He was red faced and scowling with anger, threatening to shoot the entire crew. Cowboy kept his right hand on a bulge under the left armpit of his windbreaker. His damaged left hand lightly held the painter from King's boat, after taking a turn on a cleat.

"Cowboy, I'm holding you responsible for this screwup. If we get caught, you are going to die one way or another. Here is what you do, and you better succeed. Get his boat unloaded and then get it hauled someplace, and get it power-sprayed in and out and from one end to the other before dawn.

"The plan was that this boat would be out in the gulf by dawn and the crew using the pumps to wash it down. Now we change plans. I want all of the crew out of town as soon as we unload. How you get them out is up to you. Pay as much as you need to keep things quiet. You stick around and make sure the boat gets cleaned out. After that you can take off. Screw up again and you are history.

"One last thing, if that insurance adjuster, Bart Casey, gets wind of this, I want him floating out to sea, face down. You got that?"

King finished his instructions and took the towline. The trawler's anchor was winched into the anchor chute and stowed. At just above an idle, the forty-foot go-faster used its thousand horsepower to pull the shrimper slowly to an old dock, unseen, in a pitch-black lagoon.

A large U-Haul was backed to the edge of the dock, the driver not daring to put any weight on the rotten planks. The driver and his helper, along with the crew from the shrimper, began transferring the cargo.

King backed his boat away and hid behind some brush on the riverbank, watching through his binoculars. Another shrimp boat was standing by to tow *Lazy Boy* away. As the loaded truck pulled out, King eased the black boat into the channel and quietly made his way toward Clearwater Bay.

CHAPTER 2

The Warning

Bart Casey slowed his car down to keep the dust rising from the dirt road to a minimum. The dark waters of Anclote River were on his left, and across the river was a large modern restaurant perched partly over the water. The business center of Tarpon Springs was a single line of old buildings two blocks long. They faced the road which followed the river, edged by seawalls and docks.

Restored sponge boats lined the dock near the seawall, adorned with strings of sponges and brightly colored buoys rigged to the short masts like Christmas decorations. An old diving suit with a brass helmet swayed above the deck, the lead shoes stretching the old material.

There was a lot of bright blue and very red paint on the old vessels, as well as radiant white glistening on the work-worn hulls. It was an effort to capture the romance of fifty years ago. The brightly painted hulls reminded Bart of several heavily made-up ladies that he once saw sitting on barstools in Las Vegas. The display was a bit too garish for his taste but appealing to the camera-toting visitors.

Bart was known in most marinas and boatyards in the area as an excellent marine insurance adjuster and marine surveyor. He carried an all lines insurance adjuster license and was an active member of a large marine surveying organization. The combination of his adjuster and surveyor credentials was unusual, qualifying him to handle almost any marine claim from yachts to shrimpers to tankers, barges, tugs, sailboats, powerboats, or cargoes. His marine surveyor credential proved his ability to investigate, estimate damages, and report without prejudice on almost any marine casualty. He was technically up to date but loved the older vessels, especially the ones made of wood. His competitors didn't understand wood construction and its problems and were afraid of the legal implications, leaving the field wide open to him.

Bart remembered the real workboats, weather-beaten and covered with machinery, stained with oil, and bleeding rust from deteriorating fasteners. After a good catch they were laden with sponges, with hundreds drying in the rigging. A sponge exchange across the docks offered bins of sponges of many kinds and quality, selling wholesale to the traders and retail to the usually badly sunburned tourists. That was the era before imitation sponges, when men washed their cars every Saturday with the real thing.

Bart turned his eyes back to the gravel road, slowing in a wide spot and steering his car near a high chain-link fence. Even before he turned off the engine, two German Shepherds and one huge Doberman were bunched behind the gate, barking and not looking friendly. Over their heads, fastened to the gate was a large sign with the words painted in red letters, "Marine Repair-Keep Out—Guard Dogs."

Bart spoke to the dogs and they backed away slowly, still barking. He visited the yard every few weeks so they were at least acquainted with him, even if not satisfied that he had the right to be there. One was showing a lot of teeth and the hackles at his shoulders were raised. Bart didn't recognize him. He usually got along with dogs easily, but the Doberman wasn't responding in a friendly manner.

"It's OK," an unseen man shouted. "Let the guy in and we'll eat him later if he causes trouble." Laughter followed. The dogs drifted back behind piles of old propellers, nets, damaged trawl doors, stacks of rough-cut two-inch lumber, old winches, outriggers, and a thousand other things. The relics created a visual foreground for the large shrimp boat that was on the left-hand marine railroad and a smaller one about sixty-five feet in length was beside it on the ways to the right.

In order to make repairs or paint the bottom of large boats, it was necessary to "haul" them. This yard used railroad tracks that went into the water to a depth of ten or twelve feet. A dolly was rolled down into the water under the belly of the vessel. A winch then pulled the dolly and the vessel out of the water. Large timbers were placed under the vessel to hold her steady and prevent further damage.

Other commercial fishing boats were moored at the "marine repair" docks that followed the river. Three shrimpers were rafted together, all of them over seventy feet long and twenty feet wide, their masts and outriggers pointing toward the sky.

The big dog, a bulky Doberman, was still snarling and circling around Casey, keeping piles of junk between himself and Casey just as the German Shepherds were doing in a slightly friendlier manner.

Bart scanned the area and then noticed a figure standing on the bow of the large shrimper on the ways. A winch cable was attached to the bow. Wooden blocks chocked the wheels of the dolly. The deck of the shrimper was at least eighteen feet or more above the land, accessed by an aluminum ladder leaning against the hull.

The speaker was standing on the bow with his legs obscured by the high bulwarks that circled the decks of the shrimp trawler. Casey grinned as his eyes followed the lines of the vessel. He loved the utilitarian look of shrimp trawlers.

The high and upswept bow handled rough water, the low amidships facilitated the hauling of nets, and the high stern protected it from waves from the rear. The full rounded belly held the fish-holds, the huge diesel engine, and tanks holding many thousands of gallons of diesel fuel, The heavy timbers of the keel and skeg gave the vessels a strong backbone and protected the bottom from rocks or coral heads. These trawlers were designed for utility, not for aesthetics.

"Hey dogs, shut up. This guy Casey is OK. Casey, that big dog is new and doesn't know you, so act real casual. Come on up. Once he sees you with me, he'll calm down."

The ladder bounced under Bart's weight as he climbed upward. He smiled back as he climbed above the dog pawing at the lower rungs he had just left. He finally made it to the top, climbing over the bulwarks and dropping to the deck. He went forward around the pilothouse to the bow.

Pete, owner of the boatyard, was the king of this domain. He had one hip against the bulwark and one foot on the anchor chute that held a huge Danforth anchor, the chain dropping through a bronze hawse pipe set into the deck and into the chain locker below.

"What brings you visiting today?" Pete asked the question with a welcoming grin on his leathery face. His last name was Greek and about twenty funny-looking letters long. He was just "Pete" to Bart and the non-Greek patrons of the boatyard.

"I'm here to look at *Lazy Boy* over there on the other ways." Bart nodded in the direction of the smaller shrimper on the other side. Its name was stenciled on both sides of the bow. "Someone called the insurance company about an hour ago and said she had been damaged. I see she is still dripping, so you must have just hauled her."

"I hauled her first thing this morning because she was taking on water through her shaft log. I called the owner, and I guess he called the insurance company. She hit that big rock ledge in the channel, bounced her skeg over it, and caught the prop and the rudder. The impact bent the prop and snapped the prop shaft, and that tore out the shaft gland and then bent the rudder shaft clear out of the guard."

"Nobody has hit that rock in a long time, not since they put that buoy on it," said Bart.

"It was dark, Casey, about 2:00 a.m., and they was in a hurry and making a swing without lights to unload onto that old dock that's about falling.

The captain is from down Keys and has only been here once or twice. The jerk at the wheel was having a cup of coffee in the galley. The owner is laid up and real bad off sick, so he let his first mate take over as captain for a trip or two."

"I guess you have a story to tell about them running without lights, using the old dock, and unloading in the middle of the night and a jerk at the wheel."

"I've got nothing to say, Casey. It's not healthy these days to ask too many questions."

"If you don't mind, Pete, I'll go over and climb around some. I can look at the shaft gland and make an inspection tour of the inside. The insurance company asked me to look around and give them a report on her general condition as well as handle the claim. She hasn't been surveyed for several years."

"We're friends," Pete said, as he took off his baseball cap and fingered the bandana tied at his neck. He smoothed his wet hair and put the cap back on with the bill to his back. His dark complexion and prominent nose was signature Greek. He was of medium height, thin and muscular wearing a wide leather belt, the buckle fastened at his hip. He was obviously worried about something. "If I was you, I'd just look at the bottom damage and forget about any inspection of the inside. If I was you, I wouldn't even look up after you checked the damage." His voice did not have the sound of humor in it as it usually did, and the serious tone matched his frown-creased forehead.

"You sound very serious, Pete. What's up?"

"Let's just say, the crew unloaded cargo late last night and hasn't had a chance to clean up the ice holds, bow spaces, lazarette, and such. Getting towed to that old dock, unloading, keeping her pumped out, and towed here has kept the crew busy. They just left an hour or so ago—if they all left. I think one crew member is across the road in that old, derelict fifty footer that's rotting in the pepper berry bushes. The dogs keep looking over there and staying near the fence."

"Can you explain why they would offload on that old dock, in the dark, and why would they want to clean the bow spaces, lazarette, and such? Sounds like their cargo may not have been shrimp. Nobody puts shrimp or fish in the bow space or the lazarette. Now I see wisps of spray in the air around *Lazy Boy*, so you already have guys pressure-washing the fish hold and probably everything else."

"We had them cleaning up at first light, just after one of those shrimpers rafted down there pulled her in. I'm not explaining anything, Casey, but I will tell you this that you going on that boat will be real dangerous. You might like to know that somebody—not saying who—may have seen your friend King waiting near that old dock for the *Lazy Boy* to come in. It's said he left quick after a big U-Haul truck pulled in and they offloaded the cargo."

"Nobody puts fish in a U-Haul truck. Now I'm getting your message, Pete. You know I really would love to tie King into something illegal. He has killed at least four people so far, two of them kids."

"I understand your feelings, Bart. I know a lot about things going on—mostly about local boys trying to make a living, and with the shrimp off as they are they may be doing a bit of illegal stuff. But they are just guys. King is seriously bad and dangerous. Some say he is big time and may be tied to the rough guys in Tampa."

"I hear you, Pete. And maybe that guy in the bushes over there is going to report everything he sees and hears, and if he has seen me get too nosy, I might not make it home. That really makes my belly hurt. How do you know for sure he's there?"

"One of the guys on the boat, after unloading, rode it up here to give me my instructions to clean up *Lazy Boy* and to give me a bundle of cash.

They had called me at home at about 3:30 a.m. He had on a beige cowboy hat and beige-colored boots. I have seen him before and it's said he is second in command of King's operations. He's the field man that does the dirty work while King keeps out of sight. They call him 'Cowboy.' Well, the dogs were acting anxious, and when I glanced up I just caught sight of a part of one leg and a beige boot as he sneaked into the cabin of that derelict. For just a flash, I saw him peeping out of one of the portholes and I think I saw part of his hat. I wouldn't even glance that way, Bart,"

Pete said quickly.

"It's hard not to look now that you have told me about it." Bart chuckled. "I take it he is making sure no one gets on board except your guys, or if someone does to get word to King or take care of it one way or the other."

"You got it, my friend. If you go on board that boat and find funny stuff you are as good as dead—believe what I say. You're on thin ice already—as I am sure you know, because of all of your snooping around about King."

"You know I had the claim on King's go-faster that chopped up the two fishermen down in the Narrows. I had to ask around a lot because no one would give me a straight answer," Bart replied.

"I know that, Bart, but I bet that King doesn't know you are working the insurance claim for *Lazy Boy* hitting that rock. My bet is that when he finds out you are here; he will figure out that you are still hunting for evidence for his killing those two guys with his souped-up boat. Casey, the word is that he's serious about putting you down and out of action one way or another."

"How about you? You know a lot more about what goes on than I do."

"I guess I am ashamed to say it, but I know a lot of stuff, but everyone knows I keep my mouth shut and that I mind my own business. I wouldn't even be telling you if you weren't in so much danger. My men won't say a word, and for all I know they may even work for King once in a while.

That's why I hire them. They are true professionals when it comes to not knowing anything about anybody—when asked."

"I sure would like to call the DEA and let them check the *Lazy Boy* and tell them about King being here."

"Look, Bart, you don't know anything for sure. You personally haven't seen, smelled, or heard a thing. The captain and crew are long gone. All that will happen is that the boat will be confiscated and the owner will be ruined. He has troubles enough with his health and is a real nice man and has been thinking about selling the boat. I've been fixing and maintaining the boat since the day he bought it. I don't think he has any idea what his boat has been used for."

"No one will be arrested," Pete continued. "Nothing good will happen, and I will lose a darn good job fixing and redoing the whole boat—which I have already been paid for in cash—by somebody other than the owner.

If you blow the whistle, the owner, who is a dying man, won't have a refurbished boat to sell so that his wife will be able to keep eating."

"You know how to lay it on a man, don't you? I still don't feel right about it but I see your point. The bad guys would all get away. The good guys all lose and I would probably get shot in the process. And as you pointed out, the poor prospective widow would starve to death."

"That's the way of it, and I need to tell you, Casey, one of my guys heard that 'someone' is willing to pay for you to have an accident—the more serious the accident, the more the reward."

"That's scary news, Pete. I never thought that just nosing around about King would cause that much response. For the first time I am actually afraid for my own life. You know, Pete, I have been planning for months to take some vacation. I'm going to sail down to the Keys for two weeks starting this weekend. Now it looks like I'm running away."

"That may be a good thing, Casey. Go for it!"

"OK, Pete. You know best about this kind of thing. Call my assistant, Billy, if anything comes up while I am gone. He's the best guy for shrimp boats."

"Don't sweat it, Casey. I'll be working on *Lazy Boy* for a month or more. I got paid plenty and need to take enough time to look like I earned it. When you get back, we can sort out the cost of repairs caused by the grounding that the insurance company owes. Take your time."

Bart laughed along with Pete, but was still privately wrestling with the morality issue and the appearance of running away. On the one hand, he wanted to call the authorities, while on the other hand, he realized that it would cause more problems than it would resolve. He promised himself to think about it on his cruise to the Keys.

"Here is what I would do," Pete said with a hand on Bart's shoulder.

"I'd climb down, walk over to the *Lazy Boy* and just look at the damage to the shaft and such, and take a few pictures. They want me to pressure-clean the whole boat inside and outside, repaint inside, and repaint all the rigging, topsides, and hull. Once she is all cleaned up, you can come back and do your inspection, and no one will worry because there won't be any evidence of whatever went on."

"It sounds like a practical move," Bart said reluctantly.

"When you are through inspecting the underwater gear, give me a shout and I will climb down and walk you to the fence to act like I am protecting you from the dogs. When we get to the gate, you tell me loud enough for that guy in the bushes to hear that you are taking off for a two weeks' vacation. I wouldn't mention sailing down to the Keys. He will report to King or someone that you didn't go inside the boat so you couldn't have seen anything, and on top of that you are going on vacation.

It may take you out of their gun sights."

"OK," said Bart, "but how about you? They must know that you know what is going on."

"Don't sweat it, my friend. I have known enough to put half the town in jail and have never said a word. Everyone knows that I have friends that know what I know and that killing me will just take the lid off a lot of stink. Both the honest and the dishonest know that I will do a good job for a good price and they know I just mind my own business, like I told you. It's a standoff and it works. You have to do business different today than what we did before drugs."

As Pete opened the gate, a pickup truck came to a stop in the center of the dirt road. "Hey, Pete," the driver called from his window, "anything exciting happening?"

"Hi, Glenn, you stopping in front of my gate is the biggest news I can think of," said Pete. "It's not often that Mr. Concrete, Glenn Keys, stops to chat. This here is a marine insurance adjuster, Bart Casey. He's got an insurance claim on that little shrimper over there."

"I'm not sure it's smart being this guy's friend, Casey." Glenn laughed at his own wisecrack. "Well, Pete, you promised me a ride on your shrimp boat before I retire and move to North Carolina and turn from being a Cracker to a Tar Heel, hillbilly, mountain man, or whatever. Whatever they call me, I will still be just a red-neck working guy that lucked out."

Glenn grinned and his rugged face glowed in spite of his ruddy complexion and rough skin—cooked by too many years of hard work and sunshine.

"Whereabouts in North Carolina, Mr. Keys?" Bart asked.

"Near Lake Junaluska—just north of Waynesville, Mr. Casey. But Mr. Keys was my father, I'm Glenn."

"Glad to meet a neighbor, Glenn. I'm Bart. I have some land up in Fines Creek, about seventeen miles north of Wal-Mart, a few miles off 209."

"Wal-Mart, that's the local meeting place," Glenn said with a chuckle.

"And I can see 209 from my place."

Just then his CB radio squawked. Glenn said, "We have a big pour about to start—thick slab for a commercial building. Glad to see you guys, but gotta go. Look me up, Bart." He waved, put the truck in gear, and left in a cloud of dust.

"That's one fine gentleman," said Pete. Then he raised his voice so that the man in the derelict could hear. "Have a good vacation, Casey. I envy you going out of town for two weeks." Pete winked at Bart. "Sorry, I couldn't let you on the boat today, but everything will be ready for you to inspect in about a month, so take your time."

Bart turned his back to the derelict and spoke in a quiet voice.

"Someone is spending a lot of money on an old wooden boat, Pete."

"Someone hit the jackpot last night with the cargo from *Lazy Boy*,"

Pete replied in a low tone, as he turned to shake Bart's hand. "Listen, I know that after that talk we had last year about you praying for me, that it's my turn to start praying for you. Don't expect much because you know I don't have a very good connection yet."

"Pete, once you are connected, the connection is fine, so keep on praying."

Bart opened the door of his car and started the engine. Before closing the door, he nodded to Pete with a smile and mouthed, "Thanks, friend," then made a U-turn and headed home.

CHAPTER 3

Yellow Pine

The phone was ringing and the dogs were barking as Bart was getting out of his car in his driveway. He shouted a "hello" to the dogs, unlocked the door, and ran to the phone on the kitchen wall.

"Bart Casey," he answered as he took a long gulp of air.

"Casey, this is Pete. I hope we didn't talk too long and got Cowboy's suspicions up. That's why I didn't tell you this stuff."

The dogs were barking at the back door with feet up on the glass door, wondering why Bart hadn't let them in as he always did when he arrived home.

"Pete, give me just a minute so I can let my dogs in before they break down the patio door."

"Go to it, Casey, and I will open the bottle of champagne that I intended to share with you, and will probably drink it all by myself."

Bart chuckled and put down the phone. As he unlocked and opened the door, two dogs were on their back legs and leaning against him. He leaned forward and the huge chocolate Lab slurped his cheek. He roughed up his hair and stooped lower so that Kate, the golden retriever, could have her slurp. He hugged them both and urged them into the house, and in their exuberance, they nearly knocked him down in the process. He poured food into their dishes, and they forsook him in favor of food. Now, at least, he could talk to Pete without the two dogs climbing on him.

"OK, Pete, sorry about that."

"I heard you pour the dog food so you will have about ten seconds before the food is gone, and the Lab will probably swallow the bowl too."

"Well, it takes a dog man to know that kind of inside information," Bart said with a chuckle.

"Look, Casey, I could talk dogs all day, but what I have to tell you is more important right now. Don't ask me where or who, but I found out a few things. That unloading at the old dock, in the dark, with a U-Haul truck was early 1970s stuff. The only reason they didn't get caught was that no one would believe anyone would do such a thing today."

"That had me suspicious too, Pete."

"I got the answer. They never planned to do such a thing. They never even planned to unload anywhere around here. Oh, before I forget, it was Cowboy hiding in that old boat in the bushes. After you left, I got food for my dogs and fed them over where I park my old truck. I kept watch by adjusting the side-view mirror. Sure enough, out popped Cowboy, dusting himself off and heading up the road toward that old convenience store by the bridge. He was probably going to call for a ride."

"That's one question solved. Now tell me about this unloading thing."

"Right, just thought you needed to know for sure who the players are. Well, they was to offload down west of Everglade City. There is about fifty miles of swamp from there to Cape Sable—the camp could be anywhere in the Everglades. They keep most of their stuff down there and then send it out on small boats or boats like grouper diggers and such.

They couldn't get the *Lazy Boy* to their camp to unload. Let me tell you why before you ask.

"Well, you probably noticed that *Lazy Boy* looks a bit different than most of our gulf shrimpers."

"I did for a fact, Pete. I was thinking about that on the way home. She is higher in the bows and built down to the keel with a lot of dead rising, more like a deep draught sailboat."

"You got it, Casey. I guess I've taught you pretty good." Pete hooted.

"She was built on one of those little Georgia islands that had a stand of yellow pine and an old sawmill. Well, the old man died and his son inherited the sawmill, but his son's wife didn't believe in cutting down old, growth trees. So they compromised. He decided to quit selling pine boards and to build shrimp boats, and she decided to let him cut just enough timber to build them. That wood was so hard and had so much pitch that you couldn't drive a spike into it and worms couldn't eat it. You had to drill every screw hole."

"We're talking of Atlantic Ocean boats, not Gulf of Mexico boats," Pete said. "Most are built to handle more weather and waves than we get in the Gulf."

"So where are we heading with this?" asked Bart.

"Very simple. This was the first time they had ever used *Lazy Boy*, and them being drug haulers and not super marine experts like you and me, they never gave a thought to draught. She was about three feet deeper in the water than gulf boats and went aground a mile or so from the camp.

They knew they had to get the load off quick, so they steamed to Tarpon Springs because they knew this area and knew about that old dock."

"And," said Bart, "the first mate, who was then the captain, didn't know the Anclote River so he put the vessel on autopilot and made a pot of coffee in the galley."

"That's the story, Casey. Oh, just so you know it all, Cowboy was the one who paid me to clean up the boat. He was scared that King was going to off him, so paid me plenty for me to do it right, and right then. He had the captain, first mate, or whatever with him. The guy had a broken nose that was still leaking blood. He asked me to call the insurance agent for him so that the damage could be fixed for the owner. He knew he was out of a job but wanted to do the owner right. Actually, I put the thought in his head by telling him that I knew the insurance agent for the boat.

He said for me to call so I did at about 7:00 a.m. I've known him for years. I also just happened to mention your name to the agent. Of course, he knows you, but I was trying to make sure that this thing didn't come unglued by involving some guy that I didn't know."

"You have been a busy bee this morning," Bart said. "I still feel that we should tell the DEA or someone, but like you said, we would all be in trouble, and King and his crew will escape scot free—the cargo is gone and the U-Haul is gone. You and I would probably be handcuffed and put in jail, your yard and my stuff seized, the *Lazy Boy* seized, and no one will even get near King. We know a lot of drugs flow in and out of the Everglades, and all we know about King's outfit is that it is west and south of the Everglades City in the Thousand Island area. Everybody knows that there is stuff in that area since the days of the pirates."

"You got it," said Pete. "Don't forget your experience with our wonderful drug investigators. They had you on their list for six months and about destroyed your reputation by asking everyone on the waterfront about your activities."

"Yes, and just because I left my business card on the bridge of a trawler that they later found loaded with pot and abandoned in a river near Savannah, claiming that one of my surveyors was seen on the shore and signaled to the boat that there was a trap. Six months later, an agent called me and told me that they had cleared me. That was the first I even knew that I had been a suspect, but it did explain why so many people stayed real clear of me. Even guys I thought were friends later apologized and said that the Feds had handled the investigation on the assumption that I was guilty of running drugs, and told them so.

"They never found my so-called employee and were left with just my business card on the bridge of a boat that I had surveyed for a buyer and who paid in cash like most fishermen do. There wasn't any good identification of who he really was. I just had a name on the telephone and an envelope with my fee in it. Later, he called back and I told him about a few things to fix and that the trawler was in very good condition.

He didn't want a written report, said thanks and that was that."

"I want you to know that I did my part in setting the Feds straight but they didn't think much of my opinions," Pete said. "Well, Casey, after this conversation, I am going to drink your half of this champagne. I've already had my half. Good sailing, my friend, and give my regards to the hounds."

Bart hung up the kitchen phone. For years it had seemed strange to him that a rough, old sponge diver and owner of a shrimp boat repair yard would drink champagne. Most rough guys drink scotch, bourbon, and some kind of whiskey. He wondered why Pete had a refrigerator always stocked full of champagne. An old sponge diver told Bart that Pete was supposed to have been married in a big wedding and that he had ordered a truck full of champagne. He caught the bride talking about his money, so he didn't show up for the wedding and had been drinking champagne ever since. It made a good story, whether truth or fiction.

CHAPTER 4

Sailing South

The breeze of the land became undecided—puffing, dying, puffing again—as mid-morning wind is supposed to do on the West Coast of Florida. The sails hardened, causing a stir of water around the outboard rudder and stiffening the pull on the tiller. Then the sails sagged, flopped lazily, and hung quietly. A sudden slant of wind from the west filled the canvas and slammed the boom outboard against the main tackle. The new onshore wind steadied, driving the small vessel up to hull speed—an exhilarating four knots, about as fast as a long-legged guy can walk.

Who cared about speed? The temperature felt perfect and the sky was a deep blue, accented with puffy white clouds. The breeze pressed steadily against the sails. There were no phones or pagers, no secretary, friends, or employees. He could sail or anchor up or do whatever he wanted to do—including nothing. He did kind of wish that he had gotten his VHF radio fixed but the parts hadn't come in. So he was on his own and hoped that he wouldn't need the coast guard.

He smiled and stretched out in the cockpit, his movement encouraging his dogs to sit up and lick his face. Dutch, a huge chocolate Lab with a head the size of a football, tried to nuzzle his hand off the tiller to get scratched. Kate, a strawberry blonde, a "golden retriever," nibbled his arm to demand her share of attention. Soon she would start retrieving stuff and it was fun to see what she would show up with. With most things, she nudged you to let you know that she had something and then backed away to see if you would try to take it from her. The other things she dropped at your feet or placed in your lap.

Dutch gazed at Bart with his huge eyes, an amber-colored outer ring and a yellow ring around the deep black pupil. Actually it was more complicated than that. His eyeball was an intense white with a dark ring, then an amber ring, followed by a yellowish band, and finally a dark black purple. They would be scary eyes if you were feeling guilty about something. When he stared at you, it was with an intense and penetrating watchfulness.

Dutch was tall and bulky, weighing at 125 pounds rather than the eighty-five pounds that the breed was supposed to weigh. Eating was important to Dutch. When you were eating in his presence he would sit patiently, gazing at you while drool dripped in a steady stream from both sides of his ample jowls. His long, thick tail was as hard as wood and could unintentionally sweep the dishes off the table or beat a plant into rubble.

The dogs were very different, one from the other. Dutch acted deliberately and only moved fast when he had to or occasionally wanted to. Kate, on the other hand, was spring loaded. Everything she did was bouncy or quick. She always held her head high—eyes alert and searching.

Her thickly feathered tail stood upward, its reddish tresses turning to gold at their ends when caught by the sun. She exuded health, youth, and activity. She made Bart laugh.

Life was great. Bart Casey was in a mellow mood. Escaping the office and its responsibilities lifted a weight from his shoulders. There was never an end to insurance claims, marine investigations, vessel surveys, and reporting. Then there was the task of managing the office, handling the finances, and writing and supervising dozens of reports to the people or companies that hired his firm. Now that he knew that he was being hunted, those business concerns looked small in comparison.

Bart routinely handled the sinking, burning, and stranding of vessels. These investigations often required days and nights spent in salvaging the remains from the bottom of the bay or gulf and pawing through the ruined vessel to establish the cause of the loss. Sometimes there were problems with yacht owners and repair yards that were sometimes hard to deal with. Most yards were honest, but he had learned that you had to ask a specific question to get a specific answer. Owners seldom volunteered any information and often had no compunction of feeding you a line if you were willing to swallow. Actually they were lies, but always excused with the thought that the insurance company had taken their money and now they wanted to get some of it back. All of that was relatively easy.

A threat to your life was different. Bart was accustomed to problems, but this thing with King was personal. It was hard to understand.

Handling marine cargo claims was also a part of his business. Many required hours or even days on board the ship as it discharged the cargo.

Once he spent thirty hours on a vessel unloading in Savannah because one of his men became suddenly sick. He had found a large piece of cardboard on the dock and used it as a shield against the icy wind sweeping down the Savannah river.

Cargo claims were usually complicated to handle, required a lot of documentation, and were subject to sleights of hand by stevedores, longshoremen, and warehouse managers, and truckers were great at obfuscation. Forget getting any truth from the longshoremen and forget any trucker and warehouseman.

You just flew by the seat of your pants trying to collect information.

Luckily, most insurance companies were excellent, and their claim managers were people of integrity, contrary to public perception. They usually understood your problems and often offered to help in various ways, but they did require long and involved reports that took hours to formulate. A good report was an adjuster's or surveyor's best defense against criticism, usually coming from the parties that were not inclined to want the truth reported. Armed with a good report, the insurance company could fend off most of the arrows aimed at you. Unfortunately, that would no longer help Bart in the King situation because they had closed their file. He was totally on his own.

Bart was struggling to free himself of thoughts about the threat from King. He gripped the long tiller and sat on the high side of the cockpit as the breeze filled the sails and heeled the vessel. As he brought back his thoughts to the boat, the sails, the pull on the tiller, the gulf, the sky, and his dogs, the world became a much nicer place to live.

The weather report was right for once. The weather maps on his computer at home showed a nationwide high-pressure system with nothing brewing in the Caribbean or off the coast of California. Except for summer thunderstorms generated by the heating land, it should be good sailing for a week or more, except for a small disturbance south of New Orleans.

It had been a long and unusually cold winter with many Floridians speculating whether spring would ever arrive. It had, and it was very pleasantly warm during the day and mild at night. The mosquitoes and gnats had yet to appear in their usual numbers. It was a "Camelot" time for a few brief weeks.

CHAPTER 5

The Pelican

Bart's boat was thirty-seven years old, built of wood with loving care by Osgood Boat Works in St. Petersburg, Florida, and maintained by them for many years while it was owned by a local doctor. Sometime in her life she was fiber-glassed on the exterior and bottom, and from stem to stern and port to starboard. No fresh water could seep into her inner parts and that was the reason she was reasonably sound. Her name, *Pelican*, was stenciled down the sides of the bows. She squatted on the water like a pelican, hence, her name.

She was only twenty-four feet on deck but rigged to thirty feet with an up-raked bowsprit. There was a bronze collar fitting on the end of the bowsprit to which was attached a chain bobstay ending at a fitting low on the stem. Chain bowsprit shrouds were attached to the bowsprit collar and to the sheer of the vessel, both port and starboard. A forward stay was shackled to this same collar and ran up to the head of the mast. It was this heavy arrangement of the bowsprit that gave the little vessel the appearance of a small sailing ship and allowed her to carry a large jib and a sail much larger than most boats her size. The bowsprit was held to the deck by a heavy array of bronze fittings and wooden backing blocks.

Pelican was built with a high clipper bow, a low bulwark surrounding the deck. Her sheer and deck dipped downward to amidships and then flared up slightly at the narrow stern. She was unusually beamy amidships with a trunk cabin, an ample cockpit, and a barn-door-sized outboard rudder managed by a long, heavy tiller. A solid steel "horse" arched over the tiller and was embedded in the transom. It was the anchor for the main sheet tackle and the overhanging boom that regulated the position of the mainsail.

The vessel was nearly flat bottomed amidships with some dead rise both forward and aft with a skeg slotted to receive a centerboard that stowed in a narrow centerboard trunk in the cabin. The trunk was built down the middle of the cabin, separating the bunks from one another. A table leaf was hinged to each side to make up a dining area.

She was sturdily built and carried a tall wooden mast and long boom.

Her sloop-rigged sail area was large for her size.

Bart was single now but not from lack of interested lady friends or his own libido. The wife of his youth had "moved on," and the kids had left the nest. It was a time for dogs.

He had a good grin, an even disposition, and folks said that "what you saw was what you got." He considered that a compliment.

He was also a political conservative, believed in a literal interpretation of the constitution, a Christian, dogmatic about morality and principles, and pragmatic when it came to completing the assignments he received.

He told his employees that they could do anything, not illegal or immoral, to get the job done. The office motto was "Tell it like it is and let the chips fall where they may."

His business card cited him as a "marine surveyor" and an "insurance adjuster." To "survey" meant to check carefully. That's what he did on ships, yachts, fishing vessels, barges, tugs, ocean cargo, and anything else that floated. A surveyor didn't even know if an insurance policy existed.

He just determined the facts, the condition, or the amount of damage or injury and reported his findings. Someone else took it from there.

As an adjuster, he applied the insurance policy, paying what it said to pay and excluding the things it excluded. Most things were cut and dried, making some people happy and some unhappy. He had no control over what the policy said. Many people were very upset because they had no idea of what they had bought. Many purchased less expensive policies and were unaware of their limitations. The adjuster became the enemy.

Cargo was difficult to survey or adjust, because of the number of corporations, charters, owners, and insurance companies involved.

The documents were often inscrutable, completed by people of many nationalities and degrees of clerical competence. The origin of the casualty could be months of time and thousands of miles of sea removed from his entering the investigation. The cause of the damage and the amount of financial loss coupled with the complications of admiralty law turned any casualty into a puzzle of only one color. Then you had to write it up with an archaic marine boilerplate full of salty language.

The trick was to couch the report so as to persuade your principles, without apparently offering an opinion—in theory. In reality, because of a lack of knowledgeable people in the insurance companies, you needed to make the coverage decisions and gently tell the recipient what to do.

This fit nicely with his long-standing all lines adjuster's license and his membership in a well-respected marine surveying association. With his knowledge of boats and cargo, he could easily switch from marine surveyor to adjuster in order to finalize the claim. It made him unique in the business.

The profession of "surveyor" began in the late 1500s when Lloyd's of London was started in a coffee shop by a group of men who individually offered to insure a portion of the risk to insure sailing vessels and their cargoes. A casualty could occur halfway around the world but information traveled slowly. Ship owners would appoint men at various ports of call to respond to any casualty, to investigate, determining the nature, cause, and extent of the loss, to handle salvage, repairs, or the sale of damaged cargo, and then to send a report to the ship owners or Lloyd's. The collections of investors did the rest.

The surveyor had no knowledge of who the actual owners were, who "insured" the vessel, or for how much and under what legal language. The surveyor would send a detailed and unprejudiced report so that someone else could sort it all out and make payments for repairs, cargo, etc.

Bart wasn't about to be restricted by archaic procedures and regulations, or conforming to nonsense. He believed in ethics, hard work, and honest reporting.

Above all, he believed in dogs. He liked other animals, but the honesty and faithfulness of dogs inspired him. Their line of thinking was straight and uncomplicated. They understood loyalty, even unto death when necessary. They had some emotion, such as love, joy, fun, forgiveness, and, of course, jealousy. Their emotions are not the kind that confuse the issue or interferes with duty.

Sure, they were all different in many ways, responding differently to stimuli, but the essential "dogness" was the same. Some dogs know their limits, but most hounds have no limits when it came to essentials. They know when to retreat not to run away from trouble, but to stay alive to continue the task, the fight, or the duty before them. Their wholesome approach to life deeply affected him. When one of his animals died, it was a deep loss and a time to grieve.

Over the years, he had migrated to mostly hounds. He liked their earthy smell and their laid-back attitudes. When the name of a departed dog came to mind or was mentioned to him by family, a lump would form in his throat and his eyes would mist over. He had cried over every one of them in the times of sickness, injury, or death. He remembered the good times too, and they stirred his emotions deep down in his belly.

Bart was not thinking about his danger, his business, his own attributes, or the inward workings of his dogs as he sailed slowly southward. He was hardly thinking at all, except to pet and play with his dogs, to feel the vagaries of the wind, and to make the needed adjustments to the sails.

The day was slipping by slowly as he proceeded south with the uncertain final destination somewhere in Florida Keys. The distance was determined by the wind and by how long you wanted to sail. Exact planning didn't jibe with sailing. One was the antithesis of the other, unless you relied on your motor to keep your schedule for you. The *Pelican*'s motor was so small that it made practically no impression on schedules.

He looked west toward the evening sun—unfiltered by the clouds hanging on the far horizon or on the thin sea mist; the sun was still burning in the nearly cloudless sky. It was still well above the water but settling toward a shimmering sea, the water a silver carpet spread out for its exit.

Soon the colors would deepen to orange and red, the clouds lying on the horizon, changing color as the sun dropped lower.

This was his first sunset since leaving Indian Rocks. He had sailed about thirty nautical miles, so he pulled into a pass leading to the Inland Waterway south of Tampa Bay. Anchoring well out of the channel in the lee of a sand spit, he watched the last of the red sunset as he shuffled his feet in the mud behind the mangrove line. On feeling a clam beneath his feet, he would reach down and dig it out. "Red sun at night is a sailor's delight"—the old saying portended a good day tomorrow.

The dogs romped in the shallows near the sliver of sand, raising flocks of protesting birds ready to rest for the night. The huge body of Dutch pushed frothy waves as he ploughed through the water. Kate preferred the shallows, where she could pick up speed in futile hopes of catching a bird. By twilight, Bart and the dogs had dried off, and the birds were settling down in their mangrove perches. They were finishing off his dinner of very tough Quahog clams. You couldn't chew them; you just swallowed them, which was definitely dog style. He was sipping coffee, the dusk of evening settling around them.

He first heard the engines and then saw the vessel blasting through the pass. The jet black hull of a 38 Cigarette-type boat crackled the air with its unmuffled engine noise, throwing a tall rooster tail with the power of three reengineered 350 hundred horsepower outboard engines. It swerved directly toward the *Pelican*, deliberately passing on the wrong inside of the channel marker. Bart was alarmed. It looked like the speeding boat would hit his small vessel in the side.

The water shoaled quickly, so the driver swerved the vessel sharply but too late. The rooster tail turned to mud as the stainless steel cleaver props found the bottom. He quickly reduced the power and went to neutral.

The driver tilted the engines enough to clear the bottom and idled back toward the channel, while he leaned his hip against the wheel, looking at Bart through binoculars.

Bart knew the boat. It didn't make him afraid, but it did make him concerned. Originally, it had a red shark's mouth painted on the black bow with the name *Intimidator* painted in large red letters down both sides of the hull. This boat had been in an accident when it had run over a small fishing boat, and it had chopped up the two fishermen with its three cleaver props in Indian Rocks Narrows. After the killing of the two men, the black boat made it to the front page of the paper three days in a row, but the owner's name and face didn't appear anywhere.

The public didn't know who the owner was but all the marina owners knew; it was Johnny King who became even more of a pariah on the waterfront. King had lots of money and used it to avoid justice.

Somehow, none of the authorities did anything except impound the boat making it impossible for Bart to inspect it for the insurance company.

He had been hired to investigate but hit dead ends everywhere. Even the families of the dead men wouldn't talk and soon moved away with their neighbors, believing that they had received an insurance settlement. It hadn't happened; it was hush money paid by King.

Bart was the insurance adjuster and the company had paid no one. It was an obvious cover-up, and all the claims went away quietly under the influence of cash from somewhere. Bart was frustrated but finally closed his file—officially, at least.

He personally wanted the guy to go to jail for manslaughter, but the guy hadn't even had a hearing and the police and marine patrol files were closed and sealed by a judge. Some said that King was under investigation by the DEA or other organization, and they didn't want their case compromised by an insurance investigation or a lawyer. A lot of people knew how Bart felt and quietly agreed with him that King needed to be in prison for any one of the several reasons.

The claims manager of the insurance company was ambivalent. On the one hand, he was happy that his company didn't have to pay any claims, but, on the other hand, as a citizen he wanted justice done.

King was driving the black boat as it idled back into the deeper water of the channel. The red shark's mouth was gone and the name *Intimidator* was painted out too. In its place, a thin gold line like a lightning bolt streaked down the length from bow to stern. As the boat entered the channel, King revved up the engines and raised his fist to Bart, index finger extended. The bow of the go-faster rose as the props took hold under the revving engines. The boat made a tight turn, blasting toward the pass and out into the Gulf of Mexico.

King had found him. He was either intimidating him or trying to kill him. Bart was angered by the encounter and lay awake in the cockpit for several hours trying to figure out what was in King's mind. He had a second coke and moved down to a bunk in the cabin and finally slept fitfully, with Dutch contending for the narrow mattress.

CHAPTER 6

Bait Shop Attack

He awoke with the sun well on its way toward the zenith. The cabin was already becoming hot and there was a slick of sweat on his face.

The dogs were in the cockpit so he joined them, stripping off his clothes and lowering himself into the shallow water. The dogs followed at his call; they had dog smiles as they turned to him for attention. A great blue heron that had been standing motionless in nearly a foot of water, his long sharp bill pointed downward in hopes of spearing breakfast, suddenly leapt into the air and ponderously swooped across the waterway for the quiet of the other side.

Bart decided to sail down the Inland Waterway rather than go out into the gulf. He knew that there was a small marina about ten miles ahead, not far from another pass to the outside. He intended to buy some bait and try fishing on the way south. A horseshoe crab scuttled past as he hoisted Dutch into the boat while Kate clung to the rudder. Bart helped her into the *Pelican* and then he followed. He fried some canned meat with an egg, sharing a few bites with the dogs that were ignoring their dog food.

About noon, he put in at the marina. It was in a small cove on the mainland side of the waterway, with a narrow entrance surrounded by mangrove on the west and south but lined with docks and boats on the east and north. Most of the boats were modest fishing vessels or older yachts. The bait shop was built of rough, sawed boards, now mostly gray and warped. The roof was rusted metal and the covered porch had a motley string of chairs. The docks were far from straight and level.

Water squirted from the overflow of the shrimp tank, forming a constant small waterfall. Pelicans roosted in the mangrove on the west

35

side toward the waterway; the brush was white with droppings. Some birds squatted in the branches while others sat on pilings, and a bold, old pelican walked around in the small parking area near the bait stand.

Large black anhinga stood on pilings with outstretched wings, drying in the sun.

He had dropped the sails and the boat was nearly at a stop. Off to his right, behind the mangrove, was a narrow sandy beach. The favorite animal of his childhood, the fiddler crab, a thumb-sized little crab that lived in the sand was out by the hundreds, scurrying around on some important business. He watched them for a few minutes, each proud little soldier holding up one large claw, a macho gesture often challenged by another tiny crab. Kate saw them and barked. In a second, the tiny beach was cleared, every crab hidden.

Bart started his tiny outboard and snuggled the *Pelican* up against the dock and made her secure, fore and aft.

Bart looked around and grinned. This was the old Florida of his childhood. No doubt this had once been the home of a fisherman and his family, with racks for drying mullet nets. Now it was a tiny store, bait stand, and marina.

Bart was in the back of the store drinking a cold soft drink with the dogs around his feet acting uncertain about the strange environment but sniffing the goodies' rack looking for a treat. Suddenly, a sleek, black vessel roared into the mouth of the small marina making a skidding turn with engines screaming. The air vibrated with the sound of power as sheets of water arched through the air. The wake struck moored boats and jolted them against their mooring lines. The violent waves snapped lines, throwing boats against the docks and into one another. Within seconds, the black hull lunged from the marina and into the waterway while the violent wake continued to rebound around the marina basin.

The dock master stood in his doorway screaming and shaking his fist at the retreating boat, while flocks of seabirds squawked and circled in the air. Dutch was pressed against Bart with lips curled back, white fangs showing. Kate was behind the counter with a frightened look on her face, tangled in a confusion of fishing gear.

Bart ran to the dock shouting uncomplimentary things as he ran to see if the *Pelican* was damaged. Her tall spar was still arcing through the air as she rolled on the rebounding wake. Water was pouring from her cockpit scuppers and the bilge pump spewed water from its through hull fitting. Dutch stood on the seawall, stiff-legged with his shoulder muscles bunched, his hackles raised, and his white teeth bared.

The dock master lunged for his telephone, swearing and red faced.

He smashed the phone back on the hook almost immediately and turned to Bart.

"It won't help to call," he said with clenched fists. "By the time the police or the marine patrol gets moving that hair ball puke will be fifty miles offshore or nearly back to his den in Clearwater. You seen that boat before, mister?"

"Yes, and I know him," Bart replied with a grimace on his face. "I handled a claim for his insurance company. The truth is that he tried to get me last night when we anchored up in shallow water near the mangrove. He found the bottom and swerved off and gave me the finger, a real thug."

"He's the guy that killed those fishermen, wasn't he?"

"He's the one," said Bart, nodding as he spoke. He scowled as he answered. "In my opinion, he is a dirt bag. I was the insurance adjuster."

"You don't sound like you like him," said the dock master holding his hands, palms up.

"No, sir, and it looks like the feeling is mutual.

"There were also two kids killed while swimming up in Clearwater Pass where the channel runs near the beach. There weren't any witnesses that I could find," said Bart with a lowered head. "And no one even admitted seeing a boat. Some guys on the beach thought they heard a noise of big engines but no identification at all. I think they were honest, but I also think it was him. The kids were the sons of parents who worked on a long-liner boat owned by King that some say was hauling drugs.

"There wasn't any claim made for the two boys, and I wasn't officially involved. I have been snooping around because I think the two killings were linked."

"I'm sorry I came in here and got you involved," Bart said, as he looked the owner straight in the eye.

"Well, mister, I guess you know for sure he's into hauling drugs," the owner said in a lowered voice, even though no one else was in the store.

"I couldn't prove it but there is talk about it. I was crew on a friend's shrimper and saw his boats two or three times. I saw one that my buddy said that King was using a few days ago, offloading about 3:00 a.m. in Tarpon Springs, with no lights. Once I saw the black go-faster offshore of the Dry Tortugas near a freighter. The guys on the shrimper said they think he deals by going out to a mother ship. He's so fast he can get out and back while it's dark and not get identified. It's said he sometimes uses grouper diggers and shrimp boats." He leaned toward Bart as he spoke.

"When did you see him unloading in Tarpon Springs?"

"Just a few days back. My wife filled in for me here, so I could make a few extra bucks working for my buddy on his shrimper. Actually, I didn't see the guy, but my buddy said that the trawler was one that King has been using lately."

"That fits with what I suspect but we can't use it to get him arrested.

Do you want me to leave?" Bart asked. "I hate to cause you trouble. I just stopped by to get some bait. I figured he was just giving me a hard time last night. Now I'm getting worried. He must have been told that my boat was not in my slip in Indian Rocks. I could only sail north or south, so it would be easy to find out which way I went. In an hour, he could have gone far enough to know I didn't go north."

"Well, you don't have to go anywhere till you're good and ready," said the dock master emphatically. "If he comes back, I intend to pump some lead into that hull and maybe him," the owner said, as he pulled out a pump shotgun from behind the counter and jacked up a shell. Kate was just emerging from behind the counter and at the sound of the gun action she took another dive into the fishing gear. Both men laughed.

"I've got an old twelve gage double-barrel shotgun back there somewhere. I would be proud to lend it to you."

"Thanks. I have guns at home and thought about bringing one but decided that I didn't even want to think of the need to defend myself. I guess I still don't. I appreciate the offer."

"You are welcome here anytime. Don't give a thought about what King did here."

"Thanks, but be careful," Bart said, touching the dock master on the shoulder. "This guy is dangerous. The two fishermen he killed were illegal Cubans that had worked on grouper diggers. I think they had hauled drugs for King but I couldn't prove it. The two kids belonged to Mexican parents that had worked on long-liners. I figure they had heard too much and had to go. Their parents haven't been seen in a long time, so the kids were living with grandparents. Their friends and grandparents got awful nervous when I interviewed them."

"You think he murdered those people too?" asked the marina owner, with his eyes squinted in a frown.

"I can't prove it so far," answered Bart, "but I'm still trying. I've been asking a lot of questions and I must have hit a nerve. He seems to be seriously after me. By the way, was there a towboat with the shrimper when it was unloading?"

"Yes, sir, the shrimp boat had hit a rock in the channel "

"I know about that but it doesn't prove anything. I hope he slips up soon! Look, let me help tie up those boats that broke loose."

"Thanks, but I have a kid that works as the dock master for ten bucks a day and all the soda pop he can drink. He'll be here shortly after he mops up the floors of the restaurant up by the highway. They give him dinner to bring here and an old duffer lets him live on his boat to keep it's pumps going. The worms have about eaten the whole bottom. It just floats by habit. He's a good kid but not too bright."

Bart fished out a twenty-dollar bill and handed it to the marina owner.

"Sounds like a good kid. Please give this to him."

"Thanks, I surely will, but I will give it to him just a few bucks at a time or he will waste it or lose it. Thanks again."

The cockpit of *Pelican* was still wet as was the sole of the cabin, but their gear was dry. Bart checked the mast and rigging for any signs of damage. He gave a turn on each turnbuckle to make up for any stretching.

Everything was OK, except for the rudder. It had no lockdown so the wake had lifted one pintail out of its gudgeon.

Bark heaved up the heavy rudder, settled it back on the top gudgeon, and tried the action, and everything was working well. He liked the word "pintail"; it was much more salty saying "pintail and gudgeon" rather than "hinge." Abaft was salty compared to "behind" and "beamy" a nice way to refer to the width of a woman or anything else. He chuckled, and the dogs looked up with a smile, wagging tails. They liked him to chuckle or smile. To them, it meant that things were going to be just great. He waved to the dock master, started his tiny engine, and motored out of the marina into the Intercoastal Waterway.

There was a slight breeze so he set the jib to give the engine some help until the breeze freshened. The dogs stood on the bow side by side to watch the way ahead.

CHAPTER 7

Foiled Attack

That afternoon Bart and the dogs were down at the pass at the north end of Pine Island, and carefully and slowly pulled through the sandbar-strangled pass with the centerboard up and the rudder touching bottom. Poles placed there by fishermen, and not by the coast guard, marked the shifting way through the pass. He made it through on a slow outgoing tide and then anchored both fore and aft in two feet of water behind a long sandspit protecting him from the wiles of the Gulf of Mexico.

They were stopping early because it would be very late if they continued to the next anchorage. Bart had caught several jacks on the way down and was busy cleaning them on the beach as a small fire of driftwood was heating up. The dogs were on a futile mission to catch a sandpiper or a seagull.

Gulls circled overhead hoping for a handout of fish guts and a pelican stood near the boat expecting a few fish heads to swallow whole. A ghost crab skittered by at the side of his vision, moving from one hole to another, and looking like a blown leaf or a piece of fluttering trash. The steady onshore breeze was keeping the no-see-ums and the skeeters at bay.

Bart ate the fish along with some fried potatoes and a can of peaches.

The fish and the potatoes shared the same frying pan and tasted about the same, but the dogs who shared the feast didn't care a bit and went on to lap up the grease from the frying pan after it had cooled down. The dogs were happy and delighted with the afternoon. Bart agreed as he stretched out on the warm sand for a nap.

Just before sunset, the blasting sound of King's boat died near the pass. The black boat drifted a minute in neutral as Bart watched him from a distance of about hundred yards, while King checked the markers and apparently decided against trying to run the pass. It was nearly low tide and the disturbed water over the sandbars was a clear warning against entering.

Suddenly, the engines blasted the air with sound, the bow lifted high as the propellers bit the water, and then settled as the vessel leapt back into the gulf.

Less than an hour later, Bart heard the rumble of the three big engines in the Intercoastal Waterway to the east, several hundred yards away. King had gone north to the next pass and entered the Inland Waterway and then traveled south. *Pelican* lay in a skim of water behind a series of mudflats and oyster reefs. He could make out the shape of the boat, but the figure of King was indistinct. The vessel lay quietly for a few moments and the afterglow of the sunset reflected from King's binoculars. Then the roar returned as the vessel accelerated, turned, and headed back north.

The sound faded for a minute as an island came between them, and then returned and slowly died away. King had made another try and was no doubt frustrated again by the shallow draft of *Pelican*. When he left, he was moving at top speed with little regard to the "no wake" speed limit. Bart pondered the question of what would happen if they were caught in open water.

Bart could hear the occasional snap of shrimp floating out as the tide receded. Un-stowing his shrimp net with the telescoping handle, he took a strong light and walked over to the pass. Finding a place where the current swung near the beach, he shone the light, catching the fiery eyes of drifting shrimp. Carefully he dipped the net, letting the sock drift out with the tide. Slowly maneuvering the hoop of the net, he scooped up several dozens of shrimp.

Later he and the dogs shared boiled shrimp as a bedtime snack. He slept fitfully and awoke tired but with a plan. They left the anchorage early with a nearly full tide flowing through the pass and into the gulf.

It was going to be a marathon of sailing. It was his plan to sail all day in the gulf and then keep going all night and part of the next day. The timing was bound to confuse King. There were dozens of little inlets where Bart could be anchored, hidden from the gulf. King would have to check them all.

On the fourth afternoon, Bart was in the gulf with the "Thousand Islands" on his port beam. They had sailed all of the previous day and night. Now he needed to let the dogs run and relieve themselves. They had each left him a package on the foredeck that morning, both looking very guilty but wiggling with unexpended energy. At least he could squat on the bulwark like the sailors of old and do the necessary. As a matter of fact, a lot of shrimp boats and grouper diggers still had no facilities, and you fended for yourself in all kinds of weather. The reason was simple; toilets took gallons of pressure water and a large hole through the bottom of the boat for the waste pipe. Bart was visualizing a dozen or more sinkings related to toilets.

He knew that lots of boats sink because of flush toilets or pump toilets.

Hoses rot, pipes break, through-hull flanges snap off, toilets back-siphon, and pumps fail. These were problems easily avoided by simply having no toilets. The old sailing ships had boards to sit on in the fore-chains and the spray of rough water kept things clean. On some sailing ships, the officers or passengers had a privy with a box chute that dropped things down into the bilges to create a very foul-smelling situation for the sailors that lived below decks. Bart had elected to have no "head" on his boat.

The wind remained steady, pushing *Pelican* along at hull speed. Bart's arms and shoulders ached from tending the tiller and his fanny itched and was growing allergic to the cockpit bench. He sat on a life cushion but it didn't help. His neck was sunburned, and his eyes were burning from the constant breeze.

The sailing was great, but now he was aching, sweaty, tired, and ready to anchor up. He often told prospective sailboat buyers that they had only about four days a year to enjoy sailing. The rest of the time it was too hot, too cold, too windy, too rough, or too calm. Once in a while, things worked out for a perfect sailing day. This had been one of them.

A friend of his once said to him that the mind could absorb only as much as the butt could endure. His buddy was referring to boardroom meetings but the principle was the same. His bottom was numb, and he had reached that point where his brain was turning to mush, completely overcome by his sore and itching backside. He searched the shoreline to find a small waterway into the mangrove where he could tuck in the boat and spend the evening reading.

They had not been attacked by the black boat the night before and he had begun to relax. No doubt, King had been looking for him in the Inland

Waterway, not expecting Bart to cruise offshore all night. The waterway had ended at Fort Myers and the rest was outside sailing, whether he liked it or not.

Bart had not planned an ambitious voyage. At the rate they were traveling, he might not reach Key Largo before he had to turn back at the week's end. According to his dead reckoning, he had averaged less than three miles per hour and he only had three days of southing left.

There were more of the thousand islands ahead of him, then Cape Sable, Flamingo, Florida Bay, and then down to Key Largo. He stood up to stretch, holding the tiller between his knees. He pulled his damp shorts away from his skin and then sat down on the cockpit bench.

Dutch whined and shoved his huge nose under Bart's arm. He was dark amber in color with wavy hair down his spine that sparkled in the sunlight. His buddy, Kate, danced around for her turn to nuzzle. She had been saved one day prior to execution at a dog pound and always displayed her appreciation. Dutch loved her, and it helped him shed some fat by playing with the tireless Kate.

Right then, Dutch was hot and ready for a swim. So was Bart. Bart had to admit that there was no cool or comfortable place on the little boat, except for the bunk, and that was a bit too short and much too narrow.

Dutch thought it was just fine but didn't want to share it with Bart.

Realizing that the breeze would eventually turn offshore, he used what little headway he had and turned inland toward the shoreline of mangrove. The tide was low but was about to turn toward land, so he planned on it to help push him along and give him some deeper water as he neared the mangrove line.

Bart was trying very hard not to think of much of anything but his discomfort. After remembering the threatening acts of the *Intimidator* and the sound of its engines, he had feelings of dread.

The *Pelican* was barely moving, the wind had died, and the tide dead low and about to turn. Nothing was happening, so thoughts he didn't want to think about started to intrude. Bart left the tiller and went below opened a warm coke and grabbed a bag of chips.

Playing with the dogs by making them do tricks for chips helped, but the thoughts returned.

He remembered that Johnny King had sneered when he introduced himself as the insurance adjuster for King's insurance company. King had thrown back his head, laughed, and said, "Have at it, buddy. I don't want to make a claim for my damage and don't expect anyone else to make one." King showed no remorse for killing the two men when Bart began to ask about the accident.

His response was to smirk and pull a business card out of the breast pocket of a black silk shirt and hand it to Bart. "The King" was printed in large red letters on a black card. Phone numbers were at the bottom of the card. King stood as tall as he could make his five-foot-eight-inch frame stretch. He crossed his arms across his chest and sneered.

Bart put a sheet of paper on his clipboard ready to take a statement.

King was vague and wandering as he told Bart what had happened. His business was "investments" with no clarification as to what kind of business or where his office was. He implied a lot, but really offered no solid facts. He spoke of sudden crosswinds, a phantom boat that forced him into the fishermen, a steering problem, a changing tide, his girlfriend falling against him, etc.

His story was vague and as changeable as the wind. Nothing was his fault. When Bart pressed him, he became disagreeable, refused to sign anything, and told Bart to go see his attorney. Then he told him to get out of his house. He clicked on a device and the iron gate in the iron picket fence around his place clicked open. Bart made a good slow exit just to aggravate him. It was a macho thing.

It got worse. King's attorney called the insurance company to complain about Bart being antagonistic and rude to the insured and incompetent to handle the claim. That made the claim manager of the insurance company mad. He liked Bart and recognized the earlier attempt to discredit the adjuster.

About a million "smart" attorneys and high-rolling insured had tried that before. In response, the claim manager told Bart to pull out the stops and "get the sorry hair ball." Unfortunately, the words in his support didn't do much good in helping him nail King. Bart finally closed the file as all the potential claims went away.

Now he was upset just recalling the incident. The whole reason for this vacation cruise was to forget about Johnny King. He brooded.

Dutch licked his face and Kate snuggled into his leg. They read his mood and wanted him to forget it and play with them. He tried and nearly succeeded.

Pelican was being pushed slowly landward by the barely rising tide.

Bart tied a life preserver to a light line and tossed it away from the boat.

He stripped down, pushed the dogs overboard, and then jumped in behind them. The water was bathtub warm but relaxing. The dogs swam around and then tried to climb on him. He put their paws on the life preserver, but they didn't stay still for long. The water was only waist deep for him as he gently let his feet sink to the loose bottom. He watched several small stingrays scuttle away in tiny clouds of stirred-up muck. He decided to return to the boat before he stepped on one of the rays and got a spike in his foot. He finally hoisted the dogs onto the boat and followed them up by using the rudder as a step. The dogs shook and sprayed the area with water. They were happy and frisky with the cooling evaporation.

On getting dressed in a thin shirt and shorts, Bart felt comfortable.

He started to make coffee by reaching into the cabin and turning on the alcohol stove by feel and putting on water to heat. Alcohol stoves are slow, so he used a wide bottom pan and only enough water to make one cup. He fed the dogs, and by then the water was hot so he turned off the stove and poured the boiling water in a cup over a heaped tablespoon of ground coffee.

He fished the binoculars out of their shelf inside the companionway.

Relaxing in the cockpit and sipping coffee, he scanned the mangrove swamp ahead of him, painted white with pelican poop in places. Birds moved in the branches and in the air, squawking their awareness of an intruder. Then he scanned the horizon. Three sailboats were hull down, only their sails visible in golden hues as they caught the late afternoon sun.

Northward and well out to sea, a shrimper was moving southwest and would soon be out of sight. Swinging his glass to the north, he sucked in his breath to steady the glass as a tiny spot appeared to be moving toward him. The sky to the east was murky and the distant rumble of thunder came and went. Then in the distance, a steady sound could be heard and the black dot had grown larger. He could see the white of broken waves at its bow and a feeling of dread filled his stomach. He knew that sound.

CHAPTER 8

The Grouper Digger

Dutch was standing in the cockpit with his huge red paws on the companionway slide, his long body stretched and his powerful thighs supporting him. His head was turned northward, looking at the dot and listening to the sound. Kate was afraid and just peered over the bulwark with her chin on the cockpit coaming; ears cupped forward, tail held out straight behind her. Bart sat on the starboard bench of the cockpit with a hand on the tiller. He felt cold fear strike his belly like a lance. He turned his face upward and asked for deliverance for himself and his dogs.

The black boat circled out into the gulf, turned, and came straight in toward the *Pelican* at full throttle. Bart was sure that the *Pelican* was too big a target to intentionally hit, but the man was a maniac. Bart grabbed the main tackle with one hand and reached for Dutch's collar. Kate had leaped into the cabin and disappeared under something.

The engine thunder vibrated the air and the deck of *Pelican*. Bart felt it in his belly along with the tightness of fear.

"We need angels, sir, real soon," he muttered. At the last second, the black hull veered sharply, sending a wall of water over the boat's side, drenching both Bart and Dutch with water and mud. King had tilted his engines because he knew the water was shallow. *Pelican* rocked backward with the impact of water and then her stern lurched upward with the wake. Her bows plunged downward, the main tackle hard as steel as it held against the whipping mast. Then she rolled and rocked at the same time, the shrouds going hard on one side and then the other.

The black boat made a tight U-turn and thundered back into the gulf.

It turned again and headed toward *Pelican*, seemingly intent on ramming the sailboat. Suddenly, it veered off and raced back to sea. Bart was watching it recede when a voice shouted from his south side.

"Ahoy!" shouted the voice, which startled Bart who was intent on watching the black hull recede. He looked south and was shocked to see a forty-two-foot grouper boat only a hundred feet away. A man was standing on the bow with a rifle in his hand.

"You OK?" the man shouted.

"We're fine, thanks to you, but my evening cup of coffee got washed away," Bart replied.

"Well, how about you drop your sail while I put some lines on you and raft up to this old grouper digger. Then come aboard and have some dinner with us. We got some freshly caught grouper. Bring your dogs.

My name is Hubert Snow. This young 'un is my son Todd. My wife Mary is in the galley."

"I'm sure glad you showed up when you did. My name is Bart Casey.

Glad to make your acquaintance. This brown dog is Dutch and the blonde is Kate."

Bart, the captain, and his son sat on the fish box nursing hot cups of coffee in their hands. The dogs sprawled on the deck after a thorough inspection of the vessel. The smell of fish frying came from the small galley forward. Dutch kept an eye on the cook.

"Casey, I know that there black boat but mostly just see it at night when we're fishing offshore. I don't want to speak ill of no one but that there one is a real bad customer." He looked down while considering what to say.

"We had been anchored up behind that little island back there to do some fixing on our bandit reels and such. Salt water and fish slime really clog them up. Got to have them work else you have to hand up the fish and that's mean work. I'd rather push a button and have the motor reel in the line and hopefully a few groupers.

"Besides, my wife wanted calm water for a change so she could rest some. I heard that boat a coming and peeked out and saw you and it, and got underway thinking it might be a dope deal and we wanted to scat.

When I saw it start to happen, the way he aimed right at you, we figured you was in trouble and come on over."

"Captain Snow, you have my everlasting gratitude. You may have messed yourselves up by helping me but you sure saved my two dogs' lives and my life."

"It was the Christian thing to do, Casey."

"Let me tell you something," Bart said with a serious expression. "You may laugh at this but as he was heading toward us I prayed for angels to come and help us. Then you show up out of thin air."

"Angel is one thing that I have never been called. It could be my wife 'cause she is the reason we're here."

"I noticed a Bible on the table in the galley a few minutes ago. You must be a Christian."

"Yes, sir, she more than me, and I got the feeling you are too."

"Yes, sir, I am."

"How come you to be out here?" Captain Snow asked. "These islands hold a lot of trouble and it's best to stay out a few miles to avoid getting involved."

"I don't go very far offshore because my boat is getting old and too much rough water could pull her apart. I was just going to duck into the mangrove to sleep and be gone by first light."

"I don't aim to pry and you don't have to tell me but I'm curious why that guy wanted to sink you."

"I'm an insurance investigator and a marine surveyor and had some dealings with that guy. He killed two men with his boat up in Boca Ciega bay, well, actually in Indian Rocks Narrows, and may have killed two kids in Clearwater Pass. I've been snooping around for some time. He's got a multimillion-dollar house on the bay that looks like a fortress. I can't seem to find a job or a business to account for his money. Some say he was just a boat mechanic living in an old derelict yacht just a few years ago."

"Well, that explains things. He was out to sink you, and I'd bet that if he could have got you in the water he would have chopped you up with his props."

"Same as he's done before," Bart replied. "I don't have any proof that this guy killed intentionally, but just my nosing around has stirred him up. I received two phone calls with heavy breathing and a threat to my life—'If I didn't keep my nose out of other people's business, etc., etc.'

That was just last week. Then three times he has tried to get to me, but I spend the nights in shallow water because of my draft. So far I haven't done much relaxing."

"He's a bad one," said Captain Snow.

"Dad," said the son, who was about twenty years old, "tell Mr. Casey about us selling our catch to that fancy grouper boat out on the hundred fathom line. It may fit in with what's going on."

"I'm not sure it fits in but I'll tell him," Captain Snow said. "Bart, we had a good catch of groupers and were about to head home when this forty footer came up to us while we were just drifting. It was a real clean boat and hardly looked used. It had bandit reels set out and had a long line reel. That's kind of strange to have a setup for both groupers and swordfishes. Anyhow, the deck machinery looked hardly used but not serviced at all. It was all gummed up with salt and rust."

"They wanted to buy our fish," Todd interjected.

"That's right," said Snow. "And they offered more than we could have sold them for up in Fort Myers. My wife says I was wrong, but I sold them and Todd and me helped offload into their hold. They had an ice machine and filled us back up. It was a darn good deal, but when I saw their hands I knew I had done the wrong thing. They had soft hands. Look, how rough and ugly mine are—Todd's too."

"What was the name of the boat?" Bart asked.

"The *High Liner*," Todd replied.

"I know that boat," Bart said. "It docks at Madeira Beach and always has a load of fish. I hear that the fish house likes it because the fish is always fresh, not like some that have been on ice on the boats for weeks."

"Most of their fish come from the likes of us or from that big Jap factory ship that cruises the gulf. I doubt the crew of *High Liner* even knows how to set out a long line for swordfish or rig them bandits to fish for groupers."

"They was dopers plain as can be," Mary chimed in. "I'm not faulting Hubert. Them would have more than likely shot us and taken the fish. He did the right thing but maybe he did it for the wrong reason, but never mind. Come in for dinner now."

"Well," said Captain Snow, "we have to act dumb and blind out here to survive. These drug times are hard on an honest man. The evil ones always seem to have the advantage because they got no feeling for right or wrong. It strains my religion but I got no choice but to keep digging groupers or else sell my boat and move on. All we know is fishing."

Snow and his family sipped coffee with Bart until well after dark and then Bart and the dogs went aboard the *Pelican* to sleep.

The morning sun was on the horizon when Bart cast off from Captain Snow's grouper boat.

"Thank you, captain, for a pleasant night and thank Mary for the great breakfast. I won't need to eat again for a week. Lord keep you guys."

"Keep safe, Casey, and watch over them dogs. Good sailing."

CHAPTER 9

The Storm

The brisk offshore breeze stiffened the sails as *Pelican* headed south.

Captain Snow and his family were headed west to the hundred fathom line to fill their hold with groupers.

Pelican stayed on a starboard tack, making leeway but still making hull speed well offshore of the mangrove islands. Bart eased the main sheet to relax the sail and let out the jib sheet. The leeway eased as the vessel surged ahead proudly.

The day was a scorcher with a flat blue sky. The wind had changed mid-morning and now the breeze was rising from the west as if with a purpose. Bart scanned the sky, feeling that somewhere inland the heating interior of Florida was breeding an electrical storm that was sucking in air from the gulf. The big storms reached up thousands of feet and could deliver more punch than the *Pelican* could take. If he saw one thunderhead building up, he planned to get near land, lower all sails, and put out a heavy anchor.

The rising wind testified that a hungry storm somewhere inland was sucking in fuel. As if in confirmation, a distant rumble drifted from the east. Bart pulled the tiller to windward and the *Pelican* turned to port and headed toward land.

He scanned the shoreline looking for a safe harbor but it was an unbroken wall of green mangrove with a few coves and a few small peninsulas. His chart showed miles of shallow water and mudflats.

According to the tide tables, which he had cut out from the *St. Petersburg Times*, the tide should be close to its lowest level. He didn't do well interpreting official tide tables. His power squadron instructor would be embarrassed to learn that one of his students took shortcuts and got his tide information from the local paper. Why not use a slide rule, take a sun shot, and leaf through tables in a heavy stiff-backed tome. You know, the Navy way.

The onshore wind would keep the tide in longer than usual but when the storm arrived and the winds changed directions, the tide would go to dead low. It was comforting to know that if you grounded on a low tide all you had to do was take a nap and eventually the tide would come in and you would float off.

The *Pelican*'s high bows would catch a lot of wind unless he could get into the lee of the mangrove and anchor by the bow. He didn't want her to wallow and surge because of her heavy mast and ancient bones.

He needed to get inshore fast, so he started the tiny outboard, set his sails wing for wing, and headed landward with gusto, a bone in the teeth of the tiny yacht. The dogs stood on the deck in front of the cabin with noses pointed toward land.

The water was ruffled by the wind so it was difficult to see the deeper water even with his polarized glasses, but slightly to port seemed to be the deeper area with shallows on both sides. With good Polaroid and flat water, you could pick out the different colors that spoke of the water's depth. *Pelican* didn't need much water. Her centerboard bumped on the bottom so Bart cranked it up. A few minutes later, the bottom bumped into a sandbar and then slid across into deeper water.

As the boat neared land, Bart dropped the mainsail, lashing it to the boom, and then gathering the jib, lashed it to the bowsprit. As the engine pushed the vessel forward, he opened the fore hatch and pulled out a heavy line and the big Danforth anchor. He let the engine push the boat into the mangrove, dropped the anchor beside the bow, ran the line through a cleat, pulled a loop back into the cockpit, and paid it out as he backed away. When enough rode was out, he took a turn around a cleat and dug the anchor into the mud. He let the anchor line slide through his hand as he reversed the engine, dropped the smaller Danforth as a stern anchor, and put the engine in forward to set the anchor and center the vessels between the anchors. He took some of the slack out of both lines and made them fast to cleats. Then he shut down the engine and tilted it up, slipping a cover over it.

He had done all he could and was ready for the storm. It was lingering beyond the horizon but its heavy clouds were over them. Mrs. Snow had given him some table scraps in an empty butter tub. He found his crab trap, baited it, and lowered it over the side. He could see the bottom, and watched while the blue crabs inspected the bait and then he would jerk the trap close and haul the crab aboard. He caught several as the dogs watched intently and dangerously pushed their noses into the large pot that held them, claws up reaching, hoping to catch a dog. Bart put the cover on the pot. He soon had five large crabs and the alcohol stove had a steaming cauldron of water on it. In went the crabs, and later, satiated by melted butter and crab meat, Bart washed his hands in the salt water, washed the pots, and sloshed down the cockpit sole where the dogs had worked over their portion of crab pieces.

As they were finishing cleaning up, the first puffs of wind came with that cool wet threat of the storm to come. A spattering of huge drops fell, so they all tried to get through the companionway at the same time, but first Kate and then Dutch made it through, and Bart followed. He slid the hatch cover closed and put the bottom board in the companionway opening.

Dutch leaned heavily against him panting, as thunder rumbled and the sky darkened. Kate was looking for a place to hide. Wind-driven rain suddenly pelted the tiny yacht, causing it to lean to starboard. Bart sat on the bunk. Kate came out of hiding to snuggle against him on one side while the hulk of Dutch pressed on the other side, both with their noses under his arms.

The winds lashed hard against them, causing the bow to swerve both right and left, surging against the bow anchor. The anchor line was bone hard, stretching straight with the pressure; then the thunder crashed following blue bolts of lightning as the torrential rains cascaded down upon them. Bart sat on the starboard bunk with Kate hiding under his knees and Dutch sitting on the bunk beside him, pressing hard and hiding his head under Bart's arm. Bart could see through the opening at the top of the companionway and watched the wind and rain smoking the small world around them. They huddled dry and hopefully secure in the tiny cabin. Grand togetherness!

After the storm passed, the tide returned and the little vessel sat calmly in the quiet lee of the mangrove swamp. Bart cooked; they swam, staying clear of the mangrove and the alligators and moccasins that lived there. A few seagulls came by to investigate but left without a snack. Bart refused to think of the black boat and instead read his novel and sipped a stiff drink. Night came and the crew slept soundly in the rain-cooled air of the cabin. They had no visitors.

CHAPTER 10

The Shot

Refreshed by a good night's sleep, Bart awoke early, started his coffee, measured out food for the dogs, and then sat in the cockpit enjoying the sound of birds, the smell of low tide, and the feel of the fresh new sun. Beside the boat, two horseshoe crabs scuttled by, kicking up mud and looking like huge armored spiders. Then there was a trail of muddy water as a hermit crab marched by, his front legs pulling his awkward shell home. Bart dipped the net into the water, scooped up the crab, and dumped him out carefully into the cockpit.

Kate approached the shell. The animal had completely withdrawn and shut the door behind. Bart kept the dogs away and finally the animal emerged. Kate jumped back and Dutch was ready to attack. It scurried a few feet over the strange surface and then disappeared back into the shell it was using for a house. If it grew, it would need a larger shell. Bart chuckled and dropped the crab overboard. It stayed hidden in its shell for a few minutes and then emerged and scooted away.

Later, Bart stood in the cockpit with his leg holding the tiller amidships. It was another bright, clear tropical day. Dutch stood with his nose thrust toward the wind, while Kate lay atop the cabin in a sphinxlike position keeping a vigilant eye on every movement Bart made. Her long strawberry hair stirred in the breeze and turned from red to blonde as the hair moved. It was mid-morning and the wind grew increasingly fitful as it wanted to turn into an onshore breeze. The jib lost its draw and flapped as the loose mainsail jerked the boom back and forth against the tackle.

Bart loosened the starboard jib sheet, put a turn around a cleat, and held the bitter end. The jib began to draw sufficiently. He positioned the boom amidships with a hand on the uncleated main tackle. *Pelican* carried too much sail for her size so he had to be careful in changing tacks. When the wind made up its mind to blow onshore, he set the sails and loosely cleated down the lines, bracing his feet on the coaming and handling the tiller.

With a steady wind, there wasn't much happening. He tried not to think as the dogs napped. He was glad for the steady breeze because Dutch was passing gas as he slept. Kate was on her back with hind legs spread wide and front paws together on her chest. She was held in place by the cabin on one side and the bulwark on the other.

Their luck in avoiding King the previous evening was no doubt because the storm was violent. King had no doubt seen the high anvil-headed clouds that spoke of violence and wind. He was smart to stay home and not chance the 150 miles of open water between Indian Rocks and the place where *Pelican* was likely to be moored for the night.

Late in the afternoon, as Bart scanned the distance in front of the vessel, he noted some rile-looking water well ahead. Opening the cockpit bunker, he pulled out a rolled sea chart and scanned the coastline. He had only a limited idea as to where they were but studied the land for clues.

Returning to the chart, he noticed a small inlet that they had passed a mile or so back. Now he noticed the long tongue of shallow water jutting well out into the gulf dead ahead of them.

He steered to starboard and made a course to go around the shallow water. When they passed it, he set a course landward, following the channel behind the mudflats. He liked to keep half a mile of sea room from land but close enough that he could motor to land in a few minutes if another storm suddenly popped up over the horizon. It wouldn't be necessary to be so careful with a newer boat but he had to pamper *Pelican*.

Right now he was ready for a swim and so were the dogs. Mooring up close to the mangrove in the lee of the mudflats would give him calm water and possibly some clams on the flats.

Bart dropped the jib, gathered it together, and made it fast to the bowsprit with a length of shock cord. Then he untied the main halyard easing down the main sail and letting it drop into the cockpit. He felt the centerboard drag in the mud, left off gathering the sail, and pulled the centerboard pendant to bring the centerboard up into the centerboard trunk and made it fast. He felt the lower end of the outboard motor scrape the bottom so he turned and unlocked the outboard, tilting it up to raise the propeller out of the mud.

Pelican had nearly stopped but now began to ease toward the mangrove with the new pressure of landward wind.

He heard the rumble before he had started to tilt the motor. Glancing to the west, he noted a gray wall in the distance with the tops of high black clouds just visible on the horizon. This was a frontal storm moving eastward across the gulf. That wasn't the rumble he had heard. The black boat was headed south not far offshore. It was aimed at him again.

Pelican's mainsail was down in a heap, drooping over the boom. There wasn't time to lash it to the boom.

The dogs became agitated, Dutch leaning over the cockpit coaming and Kate watching with her head just showing from behind the cabin of the tiny yacht. All three of them knew that they were vulnerable. Time was running out, and Bart realized that there was virtually nothing he could do. They were still several hundred yards from shore and the black boat would be upon them in seconds.

Long swells came from the storm moving through the gulf. The main storm cell was north of them but sending out the swells. The black boat was leaping into the air and crashing down with sheets of water flung from its bows. A gust of wind rippled the water around them and a cloud moved over the sun, turning the water to a steel gray. The black boat lunged like a pit bull intent on fighting.

This dog didn't growl, it roared. The sound reverberated in the breeze and the cleaver props threw a rooster tail of blue water into the air as the bows split the waves, throwing sheets of white both port and starboard.

Dutch wanted to attack, straining forward over the bulwarks and growling.

Kate was skittish, not knowing whether to hide or to join her family in some kind of battle. Her love got the better of her and she slinked out of hiding and took her stand beside Dutch. Bart was afraid, but ready to fight. He grasped a boat hook in his hand like Ahab, ready to harpoon the white whale.

"God help us" was all he could say. He hoped that the *Intimidator* would slow, or turn away, but neither happened. It plunged straight toward them.

A plume of dark mud and weed suddenly blasted from the stern of the black vessel as the three cleaver props dug themselves into the mudflat.

Pieces of metal arched into the sky as the cleavers battered their way to destruction against a buried oyster bar. The bow slammed down as the boat came to a sudden stop as the lower end of the engines became buried in mud. King was standing at the helm with his eyes on Bart. As his boat came to a sudden stop he continued onward, over the low windshield, past the bow, and into the shallow water.

The center engine belched smoke as the pistons continued their high-speed work, but without the cooling water from the mud-plugged intake, it overheated and the pistons melted into the cylinders. The port engine puffed steam and quit. The starboard engine smoked, stalled, and shut down.

The driver emerged from the water struggling to his feet. Blood flowed from his skinned nose and his knees and shins caused by his flight over the windshield. He faced Bart across a hundred feet of mudflat, shaking his fist and shouting as he struggled back to the black hull. It was the "King" just as Bart had expected. He climbed into his boat and disappeared. When he reappeared, he held a rifle in his hand. He took aim. He changed his mind and put the rifle down.

Bart didn't have time to react to the raised rifle but relaxed when he saw King lower the gun. It was probably a bluff.

King cranked the three engines but only one responded. He reversed the transmission and revved the engine unmercifully in reverse. He activated the trim motors and all three engines began to rise, loosening the vessel from the bottom. It moved backward, flowing mud out from under the bow. Slowly, it backed out from the flat with the one operating engine vibrating violently. Once free of the flats, King attempted to steer for the gulf, apparently intending to circle around the flats and attack from deeper water.

The vessel hardly responded, vibrating badly and belching smoke.

King knew the effort was futile. He put the engine in neutral and then shouldered his rifle. Bart didn't even have time to respond.

The first bullet smacked into the cabin bulkhead next to Bart. He lunged for the companionway but tangled with Dutch. Kate was on the bulwark with a vicious snarl. The second bullet struck Bart in the left temple, spattering blood and hair against the cabin bulkhead. He fell backward into the cockpit, hidden by the sail, unmoving.

King put down the rifle and studied the sailboat through his binoculars.

He saw the blood-spattered bulkhead with clumps of bloody hair slowly sliding down the side of the cabin. A head shot. He didn't know that he was such a good shot.

The brown dog was out of sight, nuzzling his Leader under the sail.

The red dog snarled in King's direction. He raised his rifle and fired just as his vessel nosed into the mud and stooped. He missed and the dog was gone. Reversing the sputtering engine, he backed away and then turned and limped northward on a course toward a distant cove in the mangrove.

CHAPTER 11-I

The Tunnel

The flash of light was blinding. To me, it was like being inside a floodlight when the power was turned on. Every nerve ending in my body from head to foot glowed and tingled while a gentle electrical current flooded through my being. The current slowly subsided as the blinding light faded. Then there was blackness, total; but to me it was a comfortable blackness.

The lights came up similar to the stage lights for a play. First was the dim outline of a path and a feeling of wideness on both sides but with blackness above.

Then the path became a path of bricks, laid in herringbone order with edging. My vision widened and brightened as vivid colors penetrated the gloom. Clumps of azaleas in crimson, pink, and white emerged with their own internal light while gloom prevailed everywhere else. Then tall, wild flame azaleas emerged from the darkness in bright orange and flaming red, rising above the lower plants. A large live oak was draped with wisteria vines, lush with purple blooms.

The dogwood emerged, most a creamy white with an occasional brilliant white. Then the pink dogwood came into view with a magnificent color that made me stop and wonder at the handwork of God. Pink dogwood was my favorite from my earliest recall. Pink dogwood awed me.

Behind the dogwood were banks of rhododendron and mountain laurel. White lacy blooms of mountain sarvice trees, as the natives called them, appeared in the background, with red bud, flowering plums, and behind all the towering flowering pear trees in the shape of a candle flame but not so sharp. Wisteria looped in the branches of another giant oak, dropping long lines of vine with vivid clusters of purple flowers. Beside

58

it stood a towering magnolia tree, closely decorated with hundreds of blooms the size of a plate. Iris, daisies, black-eyed Susans, tulips, and other plants edged the walkway. A huge lilac with clusters of bloom leaned over the side of the path, infusing its scent through the garden. I stopped as another smell more delicate than the lilac came to my nostrils.

I stooped down and parted the low creeping plants, and there was the delicate pink of the tiny and elusive trailing arbutus.

The muted lighting remained but each tree and bush seemed to have its own internal lighting, burning through the gloom. On either side of the path like a planted border, hundreds of flowers of every kind lighted the path with their florescent blooms. An open space was matted with bluets and white violets. A tiny stream flowed over and around smooth rocks and beside it was a bed of tiger lilies. They grew by our brook when I was a kid and for some reason they were among my favorites.

Ahead was a glow, like the distant glow of a city drawing me forward.

I walked effortlessly, my feet touching the ground but my body nearly floating. The garden exploded around me in color and form. I thought of my father who would have marveled at the beauty and placement, recognizing the order and symmetry and the immense knowledge that had been poured into it. Dad would have sat down in the chair he carried around while watering his garden and just soaked in the glory of this magnificent garden. Then the thought struck me that just maybe he was here tending this garden, just as he had tended his before he died.

I don't get this, I thought as I regained my ability to think rather than just be stunned by the beauty. In all the books and magazines I have read, the newly dead walk down a long black tunnel with a blinding light at the end. At the end was where they met God, an angel, or whatever was going to escort them to their just destinations.

I guess I'm dead, I thought to myself without too much alarm. I would rather be alive but if you had to be dead, this sure was a nice place. But why the flowers and why the blue sky and green fields that I see at the end of the garden? Shouldn't it just be a bare tunnel of whirling lights ending with a photographer's flash? Then a formal welcoming committee should appear, bringing to mind my faults and omissions, a scolding with austere faces, and then a ticket punched for my trip to the next station—up or down. My musing stopped as things began to change.

The garden receded on my right and a pink two-story stucco building appeared. It was shaped like an H with two wings facing forward and between them a tropical garden with a mosaic-crusted three-level fountain spouting water, situated in the middle of the garden patio. Each end of the forward-facing wings had a stairway going to the second floor and the railings and wall were draped with bougainvillea: lavender, coral, and red colors of clustered flowers backed by the lush green of leaves.

I studied the child playing in the fountain with a toy boat. Blond curls framed his face. As he turned I knew him. It was me at age three or four.

I looked back toward the front and saw the swinging sign above some lounge chairs: "Venice Myakka Hotel." Beside the highway was a road sign, "US 41." I recognized the nearly car-less "Tamiami Trail." A black man in a white linen suit stood by the edge of the road holding a lantern.

He waved at the occasional car to entice them in for a room or dinner. It was 1936 and the depression was deep.

Movement on my left caught my attention and I turned. There stood a large three-story New England farmhouse near a huge barn and other outbuildings. An ox yoke hung from a heavy pole sunk deep into the ground. On the yoke were the words "Tall Timbers Art Colony." Glancing up I saw the cupola of the barn, and on its top a large weather vane in the form of a woman riding sidesaddle on a galloping steed with its mane and tail streaming in the wind.

A wide-roofed porch followed across the front of the house and on the steps sat a dog and a boy. A horse stood near the steps, the reins of the bridle looped over the newel post.

The horse was Penny, the dog was mine, and the kid was me. It was 1943, the year that the house and barn burned to the ground. Unknown to me then, that page of my life was soon to end.

Then on my right stood a large three-story wooden building with various jutting and wings and wide balconies over rooms below. A huge spreading ewe bush sprawled on either side of the wide front door. Behind the Steel Hill Inn lay a deep valley with Lake Winnisquam winding through the hills for miles, dotted with islands. Beyond the lake lay Laconia, NH, and behind it Mt Belknap. To the north I could see a glimpse of Lake Winnipesaukee and the White Mountains.

Expensive cars were parked in the circle of the driveway, their owners living in luxury on the golf course, riding horses, swimming, or just relaxing in recliners on the decks.

A tall, thin black-haired man stood with his arm around a short chesty woman with blonde hair. They were my parents. Standing beside them stood a gangly kid that was obviously me. It was 1943 and I was eleven years old. The Inn was our new home and Dad was the manager.

The last to appear was another large barn with connected outbuildings.

The barn was obviously finished for human occupancy with wide granite steps, glass doors, and many glazed windows. It was situated on another hilltop, surrounded with fields and forest. The view was pleasant but not spectacular, blue mountains in the background. This was "High Mowing School" in Wilton, New Hampshire. It was a progressive boarding school based on Rudolph Steiner. The eighty boys and girls were mostly rich and aristocratic. I wasn't either. To me it was just school and a home for seven years.

Kids were ranging around on all sides of the oval of grass inside of the circular drive, girls were sitting on the steps of the building in pleated skirts, boys tossing footballs or baseballs or just horsing around. This building had a large weather vane too. The vane was a prancing horse above four arms with large N, E, S, and W letters. The horse swung above the compass points, pointing into the wind.

I studied the kids and sure enough I was there twice, once as a kid aged eleven riding a bicycle and again as a grown youth of eighteen tossing a football. Sitting on the wide granite steps were eight girls watching and smiling. I scanned their faces and knew each one of them—they had all been girlfriends at one time or another—several, more than once, and three of them deeply loved. Years of memories flooded into me and I saw many fleeting episodes. Then the vision and the memories faded and the end of the garden was at hand.

I stepped into the field, stunned by the bright light and the beauty.

The trees were scattered over hills and valleys, huge magnificent trees hundreds of feet high. Wild flowers of every kind bloomed in the sun. The myriad of grazing animals were unafraid, some coming toward me in welcome with heads high and smiles in their eyes and on their faces.

I was suddenly extremely tired so I sat down in the knee-high clover, careful not to disturb a clump of daisies and several purple trilliums. There was a trailing arbutus near me. I leaned forward to smell the delicate perfume. The lights dimmed as I lay back, drifting off to sleep.

CHAPTER 12

Storm Driven

Lightning cracked as the sky grew purple. A blast of wind vomited out of the towering cloud, pushing *Pelican*'s bow into the mangrove.

The mangrove scraped along the vessel's sides with scratching sounds and then released her into a small lagoon with deep black water moving inland, pushed by the tide and the pressure of wind. Then the wind and rain exploded into the swamp, driving the *Pelican* before it.

Kate was frightened and nuzzled Bart, and when he didn't respond she scrambled into the cabin and hid under the tiny galley, trying to nestle under the pots and pans. Dutch cringed with the explosions of thunder, remaining pressed against Bart and tending the still-bleeding wound.

On the black boat still disabled in the gulf, King was blinded by the storm. He had lost sight of the sailboat because of the heavy sheets of rain that lashed the seas around him. His one remaining engine was vibrating enough to shake the boat and the vessel was barely making headway. He turned into the wind, shutting down the sputtering and vibrating engine.

Turning in the direction of the shooting, he screamed obscenities into the gloom. "Nobody messes with me and lives," he shouted.

He couldn't see the sailboat and that worried him. He hoped it would eventually drift out to sea and take the dogs and the body with it, but knowing full well that the wind was driving it into the mangrove where it would surely be snagged and held by its rigging. He knew that he had to find the sailboat before someone else did because he would be the prime suspect. The sailboat, the dogs, and the body all had to disappear, and soon.

The rain finally slackened and moments later the sun burst through the clouds. The offshore wind followed after the storm and King was drifting slowly out to sea.

"Let it drift," he muttered. The farther away he was the better he liked it. He picked up the spent shells and tossed them overboard with the rifle.

Then he scanned the gulf and the shoreline, looking for the sailboat. It wasn't in sight and that bothered him.

Then he called a buddy on the boat's radio to come and tow him in.

He went below to shower and change his clothes. He felt really good in spite of his ruined engines, bloody nose, and other scrapes and bruises. He mixed a strong drink, taking it to the pilot station and lighting a cigarette.

It was the first time he had given thought to what he had done. With one good shot he had solved a lot of problems, but had created even more.

He knew that he had made a mistake, shooting Casey and letting him and the boat disappear. He had to find him, bury the body, and destroy the boat and the dogs. The grouper digger had recognized him too, he was sure. He would have to make sure they never made it back to land.

There were too many loose ends and he was tied to all of them.

He thought back to those days only a few years ago when he was a boat mechanic and living in an old derelict near Blind Pass. He had enough money to party and otherwise he didn't have a serious thought in the world. Then he had decided to go big time by selling his soul to the thugs in Tampa. They still owned part of him and would soon be expecting him to smuggle more drugs as soon as the last load was sold. They were never satisfied and he could never hope to get out of their clutches unless he pulled off a really big haul. When they heard about this mess with Casey, his life wouldn't be worth a plugged nickel unless all the loose ends were snipped away.

I'm the "King," his psychotic mind flared for a minute. Then reality intruded. *Actually I'm an indentured slave and a murderer. But h*is depraved mind switched on again, *just a few more kills and I'll be free. Then I'm going to disappear.* He didn't know that he was also a prophet.

As King drifted with the tide awaiting a tow, the *Pelican* drifted aimlessly in the maze of pools and waterways for hours. She pivoted to release a snagging branch, and then continued to flow inland with the tide. The offshore wind hardly touched the boat because of the dense mangrove and cypress hammocks that sheltered the area. The incoming tide pushed the small vessel further into the swamp. Then she stuck fast with her forestay tangled in the limbs of an ancient live oak with huge outreaching limbs. The ground was higher, white banks of sand and shell sloped up from the black water.

Dutch remained at Bart's side, cleaning the oozing wound, with his tongue, gently licking and whining occasionally. His amber eyes were wide and frightened, as he lay stretched out against Bart's body. Kate had abandoned her fear as a sense of duty prevailed. She was busy retrieving.

She had dumped a shirt on Bart along with sneakers, socks, and two pencils. She was agitated and restless. Her pack leader was down. Then Kate took over as nurse to let Dutch get some sleep.

Darkness settled around the small vessel and her crew. Night sounds surrounded them and cicadas by the thousands screamed at a high pitch in the oak trees. The water stirred slightly, a mullet jumped and splashed, something grunted on land, and bats by the hundreds darted through the air. The dogs were nervous but watchful. Dutch couldn't sleep but watched Kate as she cleaned the crusted blood from Bart's face. Then his attention was drawn to the grunts, splashes, and croaks. There were sounds in the swamp around them that Dutch had never heard. Kate kept watching the darkness too as more sounds filled the night. Dutch never relaxed his upright hackles or his bunched-up shoulder muscles. He didn't understand the sounds either, but was ready to fight.

The sun came up in a cloudless sky, filtering down through the branches of the great old oak. *Pelican*'s bow rubbed against the sandbank, her spreader and forestay snagged and held tightly by the oak. Her stern was away from the bank in deeper water. To their right was a mat of hyacinths, floating green leaves with purple flowers. Two widely spaced eyes stared at the boat, the gator's body submerged, eight feet of it hidden under the hyacinths. The water swirled as a giant garfish, looking prehistoric or like a menacing spaceship that might have challenged the *Enterprise*, swam by near the surface. Dutch took a step back, not knowing what the monster was.

As the sun swathed the decks with its warmth and brightness, Dutch was on his feet nuzzling Bart and giving his little growl that usually told Bart to let him out for potty duties. Bart didn't move. Dutch went up the side of the cabin to the bow and made a powerful leap to the dry ground.

As he landed on the shore, the bristles of hair rose on his shoulders and down his back as he stood stiff-legged and snarled with a mouth full of white teeth and lips pulled back over pink gums. He faced a pack of dogs standing in a semi-circle. Kate leaped beside him and bared her teeth.

A large, black dog stood stiff-legged and ready to attack if necessary.

The circle of dogs bared their teeth. Their bodies were tense, their shoulder muscles bunched, the hair on their backs was hackled, and their tails stiff and unmoving. These dogs were ready to spring into action. They knew what they had to do and nothing was going to stop them.

CHAPTER 13

The Pack

"First one who tries to get past me gets killed. Get it?" Dutch growled.

"Me too," said Kate, taking a step backward but looking mean. "My name is Kate and I can fight."

"Whoa guys," growled a huge black dog. "Dutch, it's me, Buster. I knew Him before you and love Him just as much. I'm here to help. We all are. I didn't recognize you at first."

"Hold on, buddy," said Kate. "I don't know you so don't make a move. If you do, all you are going to see is a golden blur with teeth."

"It's OK, Kate," said Dutch. "I know this guy and he is a friend. Wow! Buster, you gave us a bad scare. I was faking it but would have taken you on anyway if you were enemy. You look great, black and shiny and big enough to put me down like you did when we were playing."

"Thanks," Buster replied, "but at 125 pounds you were hard to handle. I just pretended that it was easy."

"Is this the guy you keep telling me about?" asked Kate.

"Yes, he was my best buddy," said Dutch with a grin.

"Dutch, old friend," said Buster, "we were sent here to help Leader and somehow get him out of this swamp. I'm not the strongest, the smartest, or the fastest dog in the pack but I've been put in charge of all these guys and gals beside me. You're in charge of you and Kate, but I'm sure that we can work together. Every one of us knew him, but Chinook, that big black husky over there, probably knows Him the best of all of us, but he's not into leading. He was a wheel dog on a sled team and was into pulling and not leading."

"Everybody, listen up," Buster said. "When I was chosen to come here as your leader I was briefed on a lot of stuff. For one thing, none of you has had much direct swamp experience. Cookie has some by instinct from her parents but the rest of you don't know much about the Everglades.

First, remember that our mission is to save Leader. This swamp is full of all kinds of small animals like opossums, coons, wild hogs, rats, turtles, giant toads, muskrats, and believe it or not lots of cats. Now here is a rule that must not be broken—we don't chase small animals.

"You may not know this, I didn't, but there are crocodiles here as well as alligators. They are very quick and very vicious. There are lots of python snakes, some twenty feet long. They wrap around you and squeeze and then swallow. They are very sneaky and hide underwater or in the marsh grass and grab you.

"There is very little dry ground like this sand hill we are on. It is mostly just shallow water with sharp coral rock underneath. The way you tell high ground is by the trees. The cypress can grow in the water and the palms can grow in swampy places, but the oaks, the royal palms, and the gumbo limbo trees need high ground. The pines need the driest places.

"Of course, you know the mangrove is mainly near the salt water but the pepper berry bushes grow everywhere. There's lots of cactus, some with a million spikes and some like daggers. Make sure you know this stuff. If you are a scout, the only way to find high ground is to look for the right trees. Wow, this leadership job is tough. I haven't said that many words in my whole life." Buster went down in his sphinxlike position.

"I'm glad you are here with all that knowledge, Buster, and all this help from the pack, because Leader is hurt badly and has lost a lot of blood. Kate and I have been cleaning the wound and keeping the bugs off but we better get to doing something quickly," Dutch said.

"Water," said Camper, a very fat basset. "He needs water. He always gave us lots of fresh water."

A tall tan and red dog stepped forward. "I'm Red Rider, His name for me. A war was going on and I was sent to be a helper for a medic. I had to find wounded guys. I just lived with Him for a year or two but He was a real friend. He would almost climb into my doghouse to pet me."

The tall dog stood rock still as he spoke. "My real owner, that I hardly knew, sent me off to war so I know wounds. We need to give Him an IV and some antibiotics, but we can't. I agree that all we can do is try to give Him water and keep the wound clean like Camper said."

Buster looked at Kate. "Are you a retriever, Kate?"

"Yes, sir," she said, as she demurely sat down with a wide smile on her face and her golden tail swishing. She liked the looks of the big guy.

"Can you retrieve Him some water from somewhere?"

"I did already, along with a bunch of clothes and stuff. Trouble is how to get the top off the plastic milk jug that he keeps the water in, and how to get it into his mouth."

"I got an idea," said a tall, brown and white basset hound with a long Roman nose and ears nearly to the ground. He sat down beside Buster, his body erect and nose held high. "We can lick it in. Once He dropped a sheet of plywood on His big toe and it swelled and turned black and got infected. I licked it every day for a long time while he sat in a chair on the patio. I cleaned out the infection, took off His toenail, and kept it clean. He healed up just fine, so licking is a good thing and I have a big tongue. By the way, my name is Rocky." He looked steadily first at Dutch and then at Kate and smiled as his tail slowly wagged, brushing the sand.

A little basset hound giggled. She was small but very basset-looking with white, brown, and black spots. Her nose was white and freckled with brown spots. "I'm Twinkles," she said with a grin. "We all know about your tongue, Rocky."

"OK, guys, this is an emergency," said Rocky, a bit embarrassed by Twinkles. "I was named after some movie guy that beat a Russian giant so I'm going to do something."

With that he jumped onto the bow of the boat and ran down the cabin side to the cockpit. He took one look at the bloody wound and almost lost heart. He crouched over Bart and began to lick Bart's lips. At first, they were crusty and dry, but he moistened them and kept on gently licking.

He stopped and looked at Buster who had joined him.

"You know," Rocky said, "when I was a pup He took me sailing a lot in this boat. He tried to keep me away from the edge of the deck, but the water looked so good that I leaned over the side and fell in. I thought I was a goner, but He turned the boat around and reached way down, just barely reaching my collar, and fished me out of the water. We went to an island and I chased birds but kept stepping on my ears and flipping over.

Then when I went out to the boat I couldn't get back in. What I'm saying is that the sides are too tall. We need to get it closer to the bank."

Buster considered what Rocky had said. "OK, everybody," Buster growled, "we need to get the back of the boat closer to shore so we can get in and out easier. Moose, you are the biggest by far, so work with Chinook and get the boat moved in. You little guy, Frankie, start scouting the area. Chihuahuas are quick but maybe not quick enough to avoid a snake strike, so be careful. Don't be a hero. Besides, you are little enough to get through almost anywhere in this hammock. Look out for gators lying in the brush."

"Yes, sir," Frankie replied, jumping straight up and down, his huge brown eyes protruding out farther than usual and his tail wagging like a windmill in a gale.

"The rest of you guys form a perimeter. We don't want gators, coons, snakes, vultures, or anything else alive that isn't a dog."

"Buster," Dutch said, "I am a mountain dog and know coyotes, bears, and such but there is a thing over there in those flowers that is just two eyeballs."

"That's a big gator," a light brown basset said. "My name is Penny and I know gators. They are mostly underwater and the more space between their eyes the bigger they are."

"Look," said a tall, heavy, brown basset, "it's moving up that channel away from us. You can just see the tip of his nose and his eyes and a swirl of water behind. I think he figures that the boat is too big to eat. He didn't have his nose out of water so he probably never smelled dogs."

"OK, guys, let's get to work," said Buster. "You big guys get this boat moved in."

After a chorus of "yes, sirs" the pack was making sure the area was free of hostiles.

Chinook and Moose jumped into the water to try and move the boat.

Red Rider stood in the stern of the boat as a lookout.

"Leader is moving," shouted Rocky.

Dutch and Buster leaped simultaneously, shoulder to shoulder from shore to the cockpit. The boat shuttered and moved under the impact.

Bart was moving his arm and touching his lips. His eyes fluttered open and he looked into three sets of wide brown eyes. The amber and yellow eyes of Dutch turned on a faraway light in his brain. A faint smile touched his mouth.

"Quick," Buster growled. "Dutch, get that lid off the milk jug while I put his hand on the handle. Rocky, give him a few more licks."

It worked. Bart pulled the jug to his lips and drank deeply. He reached and touched Buster on the nose and then his hand dropped; his eyes closed and he was still.

"Guys," Moose called from the water behind the boat. He was dog paddling and making a froth of muddy water. "When you hounds jumped on board, the boat moved and pushed me under. Ever see the bottom of a swamp?"

"You better shut up, Moose," said Buster with a smile, "or all the gators for miles around will come in for a furry dinner."

"And I'm in here too," Chinook growled with a smile on his face. "I like nice, clean snow a lot better than bay bottom muck."

Buster called Red Rider and told him that Leader had moved, taken a drink, and passed out again. "What do you think?" he asked.

"It's a good sign. He may come and go like that for days. We need to keep Him warm and in some shade."

"Hey you dummies," said a yellow cocker spaniel prancing and yapping. "Why are you out there swimming around trying to push that boat? You're gator bait for sure."

Buster turned a cold eye on the cocker who was looking disgusted.

"You got a better idea how to move the boat, Igor?"

"Yes, sir, grab that rope hanging from the boom and throw it to me."

Buster complied. Igor grabbed it and with skidding feet pulled the boat up close to shore and then ran around a tree with the rope several times.

Chinook and Moose emerged from the water, shook water and mud all over Igor, and then ignored him. Dutch and Buster chuckled.

"Anybody else have any idea how to care for Him?" asked Buster.

"I have. My name is Bonnie Lass," said a big solid basset that didn't look like one at all. Her head, ears, nose, and front legs were brown and her body black; her paws were a mix of brown and white. "I am Harry's mate and Twinkles' mom. When I was real sick and just wanted to lie still on the deck of our house, he covered me with a blanket every night. I'm too fat to jump into the boat but our cocker friend, Igor, looks like he has enough energy to tug a blanket. He can get Kate to find it for him and the two can pull it to the cockpit and ready for when it cools down."

"You heard the lady," Buster said. "Igor, get Kate and drag a blanket into the cockpit."

"I've done a lot of sailing on this boat, so I can show you guys where He keeps stuff," said Rocky.

The dogs had done about all they could do, so most of them stretched out on their sides in the sun or in the shade and slept. There were whines, twitches, and running legs when someone was having a good or a bad dream.

High in the giant oak that shaded the island, Spanish moss swayed in the breeze. Wild orchids nestled in the crotch of limbs and resurrection fern was thick on the limbs; the rain had given it moisture so it was green and healthy.

Cookie, a muscular looking brown dog, stayed vigilant on the outer perimeter. She got up and trotted back to where Buster and Dutch were sitting. "You know," she said, "my parents were hog dogs—they hunted wild razorback hogs. They were tough and kind of mean. What I'm saying is that I have a hunting instinct and a darn good nose. I'm thinking I smell men, just faintly."

Buster called Rocky over. "Rocky, you are a hound like us. Let's all concentrate and see if we can smell what Cookie thinks she smelled."

The four of them sat on their haunches with noses high in the air. "I got it," said Dutch. "Me too," said the other three simultaneously.

"I smell machinery, gas, oil, and such," said Buster. "It smells sort of like the neighbor's tractor but different."

"I got a whiff of that too," said Dutch, "but mixed with something else."

"It's fish," said Cookie. "We went fishing and I know it's fish. I know it isn't hogs—I would know that for sure. It has got some kind of smell like a lawnmower too—machinery, like Buster said."

"It's mean men," said Dutch. "They smell like sweat and stuff. I smell human poop too."

"I can add something," Rocky said. "I smell food and a fire like when our neighbors had a cookout way up on the mountain. I got most of the other stuff too including dirty men."

"OK," said Buster. He ran his purple tongue over his white teeth. "We have a problem. Would these men help Leader or hurt him? We have to think about it for a spell. If we can't sniff it out, we will need to send a scout. The scout I choose should go when it is dark tonight. Are there any volunteers for the mission?"

Igor and Frankie stepped forward and Buster nodded his approval.

Dutch sat quietly for a long while sniffing the air. Finally he spoke.

"I can answer part of your question, Buster. I am pretty sure one of the smells is the bad man's boat and a faint smell is the bad man himself—the one who shot Leader."

All of the dogs bared their teeth and gave low growls at the news that Leader's shooter was near.

Buster moved so that he was sitting in front of the other three dogs.

"This is getting serious," he said, as he sniffed the air. "I think there are one or more boats, a cooking fire, and one or more men. Let's try again real hard and see if we can sort it out."

"It's three men and two boats," said Rocky, a few minutes later.

"It's three men and two boats like Rocky says," announced Twinkles in a small voice from the bushes. "Mom agrees with us too."

"Three basset hounds agreeing is proof enough for me," said Buster.

"I think we will go with that. Now we have to decide what to do with the information."

CHAPTER 14-I

Dog Breath and Bugles

I smelled dog breath. In fact, I tasted dog breath. Then the smell and the taste faded away. My hand went to my lips, for some reason expecting them to be hard and chapped. They were soft and moist. Somewhere I heard the sound of a bugle sounding assembly.

It was late afternoon and the wind was cold and cutting. Thankfully, they had blown the bugle call for overcoats. The sound of marching calls echoed around the quadrangle as the white-belted "rats" were marched into company formations. "Rats" were freshmen and were easily identified by their white web belts with large shiny brass buckles. You could also tell they were "rats" by their nice fresh and well-fitting uniforms. When they wore their great coats with the crimson cape thrown back, you only knew they were "rats" by the knife-edge crease of their new wool trousers.

Besides, I knew they were "rats" because they were being marched to formation. The sophomores, juniors, and seniors wandered to the company assembly point and were not eager to be formed up and held at attention during the roll call. It was not an optional formation. If you wanted to avoid demerits and hours marching with your M-1 rifle on the penalty ramp you better be in formation. This was Virginia Tech, Blacksburg Virginia, in 1952. I was a sophomore, having survived my "rat" year.

I had left a very liberal progressive school filled with piano practice, classical music, and operettas and three months later was carrying a rifle and being "abused" by upper classmen. We never thought of it as abuse, just something very difficult and painful to handle. Nobody hit us but would us stand at attention for hours while being shouted at nose to nose, most of the words having to do with your mother's sex life, etc. Quite honestly, it has helped me all of my life.

The cadet company commander nodded to the squad leaders and they began to form us up as they marched the "rats" into place. We counted off and everyone was accounted for. The squad leaders made sure the ranks were square and neat and then fell into position as the distant calls of the squadron leaders went through their formality, calling from rank to rank.

"Companies report," came the call from the center of the quadrangle.

Company A commander stepped forward and saluted. "Company A present and accounted for, sir." The sound of his voice echoed off the buildings. Then my company B commander sounded off.

On it went around the quadrangle from company to company. The word was passed up the line of officers and finally the flag was lowered accompanied by the appropriate bugle call. I really liked these formations as the various calls echoed against the stone buildings surrounding the drill field. Our great coats stopped the wind and the sight of the scarlet capes thrown back over the shoulders off the deep blue fabric of the coat was exciting in a military sort of way.

Finally the welcome word "dismissed" made its way through the chain of command and we headed toward the mess hall. Naturally, we cut the line in front of anyone of a lower academic class. When I was a "rat," dinner was the toughest time of the day. We sat at attention, four on each side of the table with an upper classman at each end. We were forbidden to look at our food and had to eat making square gestures with our fork hand while looking straight ahead. It was called a "square meal."

You had to memorize your position at the table in relation to both ends. The upper classman would shout "first gentleman on my right, attention." That required you to drop your fork and clamp your arms to the side to your already stiff back. You had three answers: "Yes sir, no sir, and no excuse sir." You could also ask "permission to speak sir" if you needed more words to answer his question. About the time you were given permission to eat again, the other guy would shout "fourth gentlemen on my left" and you dropped your fork again and snapped your arms to your side. So it went while indigestion cramped your belly.

As an upper classman, you had some immunity to harassment in the dining hall but any class above you could hassle you if they took the notion. A guy named Hundley gave me hell all of my freshman year and tried to keep it up when I became a sophomore and junior. I lay in bed nights trying to figure out a way to slowly murder him but never got the opportunity. Luckily for me he found a short fat boy to harass and that took the pressure off me. I think what made him so rough on me was that he was a shrimp and I was nearly six foot four. When he found someone shorter than he was he could really dominate. Thanks to Hundley, I probably spent at least half of my freshman weekends walking off demerits on the penalty ramp carrying my M-1 rifle.

I touched my lips and they felt moist and smooth, and the faint scents of flowers seemed to be around my head. Did I see brown eyes or a field of flowers and trees? My brain seemed to be changing pictures.

One early morning about 2:00 a.m. the trumpet blew "class A uniform." The call went out to assemble on the walk below our barracks.

We had three minutes to put on our dress uniform and be in formation.

Most of us made it and the late ones got "gigged" a few demerits. They marched us out in total darkness and formed up with the rest of the cadet corps. Then a torchlit procession approached with the slow beat of a drum echoing off the stone building.

The story was that some guy had been caught cheating and found guilty by an officer jury. He was marched to the center of the field, the charges were read, and all insignias were ripped from his uniform, and he was expelled from Virginia Tech. He was turned around and marched away to the slow beat of the drum and the flickering torches. Whether sham or real it sure made and impression on me. Then the various levels of command were shouted in the darkness.

We marched to our barracks and were dismissed for the remaining two hours of sleep time. I have often wondered why a young man would allow himself to be treated this way. Supposedly it was a badge of honor to endure a "drumming out" and live with it the rest of your life. It sure did impress the rest of us and we made sure that the Honor Code was never violated. The Honor Code included being expelled if you saw someone else violate the code and did not turn him in.

Things changed. I could hear the drums and the marching band echoing off the downtown buildings of Richmond. Then other bands and other marchers joined the parade. You felt like you wanted to march to battle, right into the enemy guns. The drums do something to the mind and the cadence of the march blends with the sound—it seems like there is nothing else.

Then I smelled the peanut butter.

CHAPTER 15

Shell Mound

Kate was lying on the floor of the cabin with a large jar of peanut butter between her paws. She had gnawed off part of the cover and it smelled really good. Her tongue was bleeding a little, but she seriously wanted to worm it into the opening and have a lick, but she knew that Leader really needed it. While she worked on the peanut butter jar, the other dogs were having a meeting.

Igor stepped forward with Frankie at his side. "Look, guys, me and Frankie are making the patrol. I'm quick and he's quick. We are both small and streetwise. The snakes shouldn't be crawling at night, and if we stay quiet and on the high ground we should be able to get by the gators. They get slower at night anyhow, according to Penny who knows gators."

"It's really dangerous for you little guys to go at night, so be careful," Buster said. "And when you put yourself first it lessens the value of the other guy."

"Got it, sir," Igor said. "It's just that I owe Leader and am excited to be able to help. Let me tell you something." Igor went on with a rush of words. "Leader went down on a rope about forty feet to explore a sinkhole up on a mountain. My brothers and sisters had gotten too close to the edge and fell in. Mother tried to stop them and fell in too. I was last and landed on mother. All of them were dead except mother, and she couldn't move. She still had milk and nursed me for several days while she was dying.

"When I was about dead, Leader came down to check out the sinkhole for a cave, found me, tied me in a bundle made of his shirt, and had his buddy hauled me out. He came out too and gave me his sandwich which was mighty strange but I was ready to eat anything, and it filled me up but made my stomach hurt. I ate the whole thing in about three bites. He gave me water and held me. When he put me down I ran into the bushes and hid like mother had taught us to.

"He started to go, so I followed but kept hidden and almost changed my mind and really wanted to run to him. He got into an old car and began to leave. Then I finally changed my mind and ran after him. His old car made lots of smoke so after he was out of sight I followed the smell. It took me all that day and the next to follow that smell through a town and all. I was about done in when the smell got stronger and I found the car behind a big building.

"There was lots of food smells coming from the big building, so I snuck up to the back door and hid under the steps. A real nice, black man came out carrying a big can that smelled good. I ran out, and he saw me and reached into that can and tossed me the best food I could hope for.

It was a pile of steak bones and scraps. I got another bellyache. Later, he came out with a pan of milk just for me. I could smell Leader and hear his voice once in a while, but he didn't come out for two days. When he did I ran to him. He recognized me and I went to live with him.

"So you see, I owe him my life and want to go on the scouting mission for Him, no matter how dangerous it is. Frankie just wants to go because it's his kind of thing. He's a pint-sized macho energy bar."

"OK, guys," Buster said, "I understand love and I understand exuberance.

It's dangerous out there so be careful. Leader's, Him will help you, so get a few hours' sleep and then takeoff. We don't know how far it will be to where the men are, so reserve your strength."

"I saw a little river coming out of the mangrove about two miles north before the bad man shot Leader," Dutch said. "After the man broke his boat, he headed that way. I don't know how far it will be in the swamps but probably a lot longer."

"It's about noon, Pack," Buster said. "Let's lie low for a while and get some sleep. We can't do much today except to tend to Leader."

A large, white pure breed Collie with a long aristocratic nose walked over to Buster and sat down beside him. "Hi, Buster, I am glad that the big, Him put you in charge. I like quiet strength and this is no come-on, but you have a magnificent black coat. You must be Chow/Lab mix. Looks like you have the best of both breeds. I'm Lady." She touched her nose to his and then gracefully stood up and walked toward the shade of the bushes, her long-feathered tail held high and gently swishing back and forth. Buster looked confused.

"Buster, sir," Sheila said, as she approached and sat down in front of him with her gray ears cocked toward the sky. "I hear an airplane off in the distance. I heard it some time ago and waited to see if it was just passing by out in the big water. It has begun going in circles. You know, I was a lead dog on a sled team and I had to be aware of everything."

Buster listened for a moment. "Excellent, Sheila, thanks. This calls for work, and right now."

"Everyone, listen up," Buster growled to the pack. "An airplane is circling in the gulf and may come this way. I have watched search patterns over the mountains when they were looking for pot. We have several minutes, but we need to camouflage the boat. It's under this big oak tree but we need to disguise the lines of the hull."

"Sir," called a big, red dog. "My name is Red Rider. He named me after a good guy gunfighter. How do we know it's bad guys and not good guys?"

"No way," growled a large, black dog with a white neck. "My name is Chinook, as Sheila said. We were friends. If the bad man is a drug dealer, he probably has a radio and a friend with an airplane. Besides, Dutch says that Leader was on a long trip so why would anyone be looking for Him so soon?"

"Good logic," said Buster. He stood and gazed into the eyes of every dog in the pack. His heavy hair and the rolls of extra skin around his neck made him look massive and strong. He had the poise of a strong leader.

"Here is what we do," he growled. "We find brush and drag it up on the boat to hide its shape. The boat is white and the water is black but you may have noticed that we are standing on a mound. Cookie and I talked about it. Her family lived in this part of Florida for generations. She says this is a shell mound made by the oysters and clam shells harvested by the Indians. They harvested, camped, and ate shellfish here for hundreds of years. This whole mound is full of white shells and white sand."

"You short guys," Buster continued, "Camper, Twinkles, Flash, start digging and turn up the sand and shells and get rid of the leaves and such, so that the mound will be white. The rest of you find branches, dead reeds, and such and spread them over the boat."

"Just for your encouragement," Buster said, "Dutch and Harry are on the boat with Him, and He is moving and groaning and sometimes opening his eyes and taking a drink. Leader is getting a little better so let's get busy. Kate, worry some sail over Leader to hide him, then everyone on the boat take cover in the cabin."

The sound of the aircraft was coming closer on each cycle as it circled around the area. Soon it passed directly over the *Pelican* and the pack of dogs. The shadows cast by the big live oak mottled the ground, breaking the white of the mound and white of the boat with dark lines and shadows.

A patch of tangled branches clustered against the white mound. The pack had found cover so all was quiet and unmoving.

As the small yellow plane passed overhead, the pilot and passenger looked down at the maze of waterways and hammocks of trees. They could see the bottom of the shallow bays and the arching roots of the mangrove holding up the green canopy of leaves.

"Not a thing," the pilot said. "I sure don't see any boat. Anyhow, a sailboat could never get into the swamp this deep. You sure can't sail in the Everglades."

"If it was here, it would stick out like a sore thumb," said the passenger.

"Wait, what was that white spot we just passed over?"

"It's a shell mound," replied the pilot. "A place the Seminole Indians camped and ate shellfish. They're all along the coast. Well, I'm heading home before the afternoon storms build up."

"I'm with you," the passenger said. "King is overreacting and the sailboat is bound to be a hundred miles down the coast by now. How could anybody suspect King anyhow, when this is nearly two hundred miles from St. Pete?"

"Roger that. I'll radio King and tell him that we are out of here."

CHAPTER 16

Reconnaissance

The night patrol returned several hours before dawn. They both flopped down on their paws in front of Buster, panting. They were wet, covered with mud and plastered with slime. Both wanted to talk at the same time, but Buster chose Igor.

"There are three men and two boats, the bad guy was working on his black boat when we got there and talking to two men on another boat.

They were all drinking strong liquor and acting drunk. By the time we left, they had all passed out or gone to sleep on the bigger boat that has a small house on it where they sleep and cook and a canvas top over the back part where they sit in chairs.

"They also had a campfire with meat bones around it. We didn't bother any of them, but they smelled tempting. They were talking about looking for the sailboat and burying the body if they found it. The two men were laughing about Leader being shot—they wanted to go see his brains on the boat. The bad man wanted to get the body out of sight and into the ground or a gator."

"Slow down, Igor, I can hardly keep up."

"When did they say they were going to search?" asked Dutch who had joined the debriefing.

"Let me tell," Frankie said quickly, as he bounced a foot into the air. "They said tomorrow, which is today because it's today and not last night, but they stopped talking real late and they were about out cold so they probably won't start till noon and then it will be too late to get here because it is far and real wet and bad running."

"I think I got that," said Buster. "You even talk faster than Igor. I take it that there is some swamp and not much high ground between them and us."

"About half and half, maybe more water," replied Frankie.

"Not that bad," said Igor. "Frankie is so short he thinks dew is deep. We didn't look for a good way. We just went straight once we smelled them. We came back straight too. Men may find a better way but it will be longer."

"Good job, boys," Buster said.

Red Rider stepped forward and spoke. "I've seen men looking for enemy men and they go slow and poke into everything. These guys don't know where the sailboat is. It came from the gulf and that's a long way from here. They will be looking in the mangrove bushes near the water."

"Excellent observation," said Buster. "We need someone quiet and smart to go back and keep watch and to follow those guys. Two dogs should go, so one can come back and report if the men come this way."

"Us, us," said Frankie, bounding up into the air with each word.

"Not this time," said Buster. "We need noses to follow your trail back to the camp and to stay back out of sight following the men."

"That calls for bassets," said Rocky who had joined the group. "I'll go with Twinkles."

"No!" said Dutch, with his teeth showing and his lips quivering. "You are the nurse and you stay here. Leader has to have water and you can do it. Right, Buster?"

"I agree," said Buster, "but Rocky is just trying to wear too many hats.

I agree that for now he should spend his time nursing Leader. Twinkles is fine and Penny can go with her. Both are fairly short, have good noses, and are not likely to act macho and do something stupid like a boy dog. They blend in too with their spots and colors. Red, go get them started and then send Chinook a hundred yards behind in case of trouble. Nobody would want to mess with that guy. Tell him to be cool and keep under cover."

Flash stepped into the council of war. His head and tail were held low and he spoke in his growling voice. "That Penny is a nice dog, but she has twisted front feet. I'm going to go in her place."

"No, sir," growled Buster with authority. "She got her feet bit by a gator when she was a pup and they grew pigeon-toed, but have you ever seen her run after a rabbit? She goes and you stay. When we need a street fighter, you will be the one I call."

Flash trotted away with a drooping tail, glancing back with an angry look on his face.

It was still dark under the trees, but a smudge of light was on the horizon. Buster marched into the center of the clearing and spoke to Red.

"Have your night guards sack out and then you and I will too. Dutch will take over for a few hours. Rocky, as soon as it is light try to get some more water into Leader."

Dutch was hungry. It took lots of calories to run 125 pounds of dog flesh. He and Kate were on the boat alone, except for Leader who was quiet under his blanket. Dutch would call Rocky soon, but first he nudged Kate awake and used his nose to lift the lid on a locker in the cabin. The top of a forty-pound bag of dog food was open. As a hulking macho purebred, he would ordinarily have his fill while Kate looked on. Under the circumstances, he invited her to join him with his head in the bag.

They ate their fill together.

Rocky awakened Bart with his tongue on His lips and helped him lift the water jug and drink. This time he stayed awake several minutes and smiled at the three dogs looking down at him. He groaned, turned a little on his side, and passed back into unconsciousness. The dogs sniffed his hands, his wound, and his face and smiled at one another. The smells were all good and they were glad.

Red Rider bounded on board, rocking the boat with his weight, and joined the others beside Bart. He sniffed and agreed that things were going well. He pulled the blanket up on Bart's shoulder.

Buster gathered all of the dogs together for a meeting. It was nearly noon and the shade of the giant oak was welcome. A token breeze filtered in from the gulf.

"Listen up," Buster said. "You know we have a big problem here.

Leader is unconscious most of the time and needs a hospital. We can't move him except by all of us dragging him and that's not a good solution.

Besides, we don't know which way to go. On top of that, we have three guys looking for us who want to bury him. If they find him alive, they will try to kill him for sure. So who has a solution?"

All of the dogs went down on their bellies with paws outstretched in front and muzzles flat on the ground. Several low whines came from the circle. All eyes were on Buster.

After a minute of silence, Buster continued. "We are dogs. We like being dogs. Leader is our Him. But we all know that Leader has a Him too. We can't talk to Leader, so let's try to talk to His Him. I know that we all recognize that we have awareness that there is someone in charge of everything, a pack leader of pack leaders or even of people and cows and such. Let's think about that even if it is really hard to understand.

Maybe the big Him will help us out."

"One last thing," he said, while looking around at the pack solemnly, "we may be in for a fight to save Leader. We are fearless, but we must use prudence and brains. Only if that fails do we turn to bravery and brawn."

Buster was exhausted by what he had just said. It was like there was a cloud that he was trying to see through. He just said what he felt, but didn't understand.

Chinook was having a hard time concentrating. He needed some action to start and then let his instincts click into gear. Anyone taking a quick look at him would think that he was staring with huge white eyes.

Actually, he had a white spot about the size of a quarter set into the black fur just above his eyes. He looked like he had a black mask on, with white erect ears and a white snout. His chest and legs were white as was the underside of his tail. The rest of him was coal black.

He and the other dogs were quiet and doing what Buster had said but found it very difficult to think of a Him of their Him. But they all tried.

CHAPTER 17-I

Higher Ground

First I heard the whistling off in the distance and drawing closer. I propped myself up on my elbows so that I could see over the deep clover around me. It was still a clear and idyllic day. I felt as if I had been sleeping for hours. Then a head appeared, and as the man approached more and more of his body became visible. Whoever it was continued to whistle with exquisite notes: as pure as the scent of trailing arbutus that wafted around me. A grin spread on my face as I recognized my favorite hymn, Higher Ground by Johnson Oatman Jr. I began singing the words in a voice surprisingly good for me:

I'm pressing on the up-ward way
New heights I'm gaining every day
Still praying as I'm onward bound
Lord, plant my feet on higher ground

Lord, lift me up and let me stand
By faith on heavens table land
A higher plane than I have found
Lord, plant my feet on higher ground

My heart has no desire to stay
Where doubts arise and fears dismay
Tho' some may dwell where these abound
My prayer, my aim is higher ground

Lord, lift me up and let me stand
By faith on heavens table land
A higher plane than I have found
Lord, plant my feet on higher ground

I want to live above the world
Tho' Satan's darts at me are hurled
For faith has caught the joy-full sound
The song of saints on higher ground

Lord, lift me up and let me stand
By faith on heavens table land
A higher plane than I have found
Lord, plant my feet on higher ground

I want to scale the utmost height
And catch a gleam of glory bright
But still I pray till Heaven found
Lord, lead me on to higher ground

Lord, lift me up and let me stand
By faith on heavens table land
A higher plane than I have found
Lord, plant my feet on higher ground

Hearing me singing, the stranger stopped whistling and joined me in singing the words. He made a big deal of the last words, flinging his arms wide and grinning like an idiot. We both laughed.

"May I join you, Bart? You are surely welcome here. I understand you are the guy who got shot on the sailboat. I'm sorry, but trust that you are comfortable now."

"Fine," I said, patting the ground beside me. "Sit down, but please don't crush the flowers. That trailing arbutus put me to sleep and now I feel great.

"However, I have another problem besides you sitting on my favorite flowers. You seem to know my name and you have some story about a guy getting shot. My name is Bart, but I don't know anything about being shot."

"Thanks, I will sit with you, and I certainly won't crush the flowers."

"Who are you?" I asked. "And what are you doing here? I certainly don't feel shot, so where do you get your faulty news?"

"Oh, I'm working. Just call me Shepherd, or Gardener, Keeper, or Watchman or about any other nice name. I agree you don't look shot and my sources are confidential."

"OK, then. If you are the Gardener or the Keeper or whatever, you must know where here is. I sure don't. You said that I was welcome here."

"That's very simple. Here is where you are, and where you are is here."

"That's a rather circular answer isn't it?"

"Well, seeing that you are sleeping in my field, I think I should be asking the questions. Agreed? First, where did you come from?"

"I don't have a clue. You know my name so you must know where I came from. You mentioned both 'shot' and 'sailboat' a while ago."

"You don't remember anything?"

"No, there was a bright light and then everything started. I don't know anything that happened before that. What would you like to know?

Somehow, you already know my name, and I can tell you everything else I know in about two minutes, or even much less time than that."

"Well, I am sort of a Traveling Preacher too, and it is of great interest to me to find out about a person's spiritual walk. I guess it is a hobby of mine. I just can't keep myself from asking a lot of questions."

"Hey," I said, "if you have the time, I have the time. I'm sure you know the Willie Nelson song with the line, 'If you have the money, honey, I have the time.' That may have been a bar scene and not really applicable.

However, for some reason, I feel the inclination to answer your questions building up in me. That sounds crazy, doesn't it? No matter, but you have some answering to do also."

"Great, just take another whiff of that arbutus, lie back, and pour out the whole story on me."

I sniffed again, inhaling the delicate fragrance. I could see the bed of flowers where I first found the arbutus, near an old vacant house unused for many years and standing on a small rise in the middle of nowhere in New Hampshire. It was 1940 and I was seven years old, walking the two miles home from school. I found lots of things to do on the way. I remember searching through the leaves of fall to find the tiny flowers. Mother had shown me this patch and I became nearly addicted to their fragrance. That was a long time ago in another place.

I stretched out in the Preacher's field and began to tell the Whistler, Shepherd, or whatever, what I was suddenly seeing.

"I sat on the seawall in St. Petersburg, Florida, wearing my shorts and light pullover shirt. My feet were bare and dirty. The smell of low tide was in the air. My bike was lying in the grass behind me and my gig was in my hand. The handle was large and long, the head fashioned with five sharp metal tines. It was a killer gig and I was taking fish home tonight.

It didn't work that way. The one fish I saw got away.

"I was supposed to be recovering. I had only been out of the hospital a week or so, and they wouldn't let me go to school. It sounded so good when I first heard the sentence, but now it was a drag and the Snook gigging was not working out like I dreamed it would. I thought it would be like gigging suckers in Black Brook in New Hampshire. I had done that often enough.

"One night I came home with so many suckers in a burlap bag that I could hardly carry it. That was when the bobcats followed me, screaming."

"Excuse the interruption, Bart, but who was screaming, the bobcats or you?"

"The bobcats were screaming like insane women do in the movies. I was too afraid to even open my mouth. Anyhow, this wasn't Black Brook, in New Hampshire. It was St. Petersburg, Florida, in 1943 and I was about ten years old recovering from a ruptured appendix. The folks had left New Hampshire for the winter, trying to find work after 'Tall Timbers' had burned down and before Steel Hill Inn hired Dad.

"I had a terrible bellyache one day and it lasted three days with me screaming and mother dosing me with castor oil. Suddenly the pain stopped and I felt better, but really terrible. Dad was working as a guard for the Merchant Marine base in St. Petersburg. He took me to the doctor on base but I had to walk in from the guard shack. when I got to the doctor he took one look at me and called for a stretcher and an ambulance, and I was soon in Children's Hospital.

"My fever went to 105 degrees and was edging up. They didn't think I was stable enough for surgery so they gave me a blood transfusion, a tube from my uncle Jim to me. He was on one gurney and I was on another. Then they advised Dad to call the family because I wasn't responding. My belly was full of infection and I was a sick pup. I can still remember how hot I was from the fever. This was before air-conditioning and before they packed people in ice. Just another degree or two and I would be a goner.

"We had been going to a Unity church so those sweet people called a special prayer meeting and the Pastor, Leader, Reader, or whatever visited and taught me a little prayer:

God is my help in every need
God does my every hunger feed
God walks beside me and guides my way
Through every moment of the day
I now am wise
I now am true
Patient kind and loving too
All things I am
Can do and be
Through Christ the Truth
That lives in me

"I had been to the congregational church in New Hampshire many times. We lived two miles of dirt road away but used car, buggy, or sleigh and managed to get there nearly every Sunday. However, I didn't have a clue what it was all about. I had just a glimmer of what this poem was saying but I repeated it hundreds of times.

"I liked the fat, jolly red-headed Preacher at the New Hampshire church. Every Sunday, he did an impassioned altar call but no one responded. Those country Yankees didn't respond to much passion, although as I learned later in life they all had large families. Anyhow, I felt that my belly was cut open each time he called on us to accept God, or Christ, or something I didn't understand. I was super timid and hid behind the chimney at the back of the church when called on to recite John 7-14 that mother had drilled into me.

"Well, one day, I just bolted out of the pew and ran forward. I don't recall what happened there, but the next Sunday the elders called me to a private meeting in chairs set out in front of the 'meeting house,' actually the Grange Building. They asked me a few questions I couldn't answer and somehow decided I was a candidate for baptism and was subsequently taken to the lake and submerged. I was eight at the time.

You know, I have questioned that prayer the Unity lady gave me because it talks about the Christ dwelling in me. Now I think the theology is a little warped and that you have to ask him in. I don't think it happens automatically. I bet that happened when I went forward even if I didn't know it at the time or maybe when I was down at the bottom of Lake Winnisquam being baptized."

The Gardener, Shepherd, Keeper, Preacher, etc., chuckled. "Well," he said, "you ran to accept him. Don't you think he honored that?"

"Yes, I can see it now for the first time. But wait, there is more. Years later, I was in a Christian group that was quite sure they had everything figured out. They thought that the Unity church was a cult with no connection to God—or even worse. If that was so, how come their prayers had a lot to do with my healing? I have never doubted my healing for a minute.

That issue softened up my theology in many areas as I thought about it later in life.

"I ended up at boarding school at the insistence of my dad's boss who didn't like kids, especially me. For some reason the sudden dislike followed immediately after I set off a cherry bomb among the propane gas tanks on the back porch of his exclusive Inn. He turned to my father and said, 'Harry, if you will send the kid away to school I will pay the tuition.' Four of his five children were spread across New England in the best of private schools. The oldest was in the horse cavalry with the elite of Boston. Early in World War II he died in a military plane crash, and not much later his new wife died in a commercial plane crash. The rich have their sorrows too. They are really just people like the rest of us but a bit more privaliged.

Anyhow, I spent the next seven years in a coeducational boarding school. "We had a chapel service every Sunday evening where they recited poetry, talked about great composers, and such. It was a progressive school so chapel was a bit different than the word chapel usually implies.

They believe in God but seem to wish that he would keep his nose out of their business.

"However, they had a songbook with the great hymns of the church. I loved the sound of them and always made a request or two. Those hymns got into my spirit. I still didn't know a thing about the Bible, Christ, salvation, and such. The progressive folks thought of God as a sort of a fist-sized cloud up in the rafters, the attic, or maybe a closet somewhere.

They were of the opinion that the elites like them were a bit higher than God, selected to take care of the little people with less money and education. Luckily, I only got a little bit infected because my folks didn't have any money so we were a part of the rabble. I was treated well and really enjoyed my years on their mountain top.

"In college, I tried to become a Christian Scientist, but try as I may I could never figure out how Mary Baker Eddy came up with the stuff she did compared to the scripture she used. In my unlearned opinion, Mary and the Bible never got on the same page.

"I gave that up after about six months of honest effort. In the meantime, I started three-quarters of comparative religion at VPI. I got A's because I was at least searching. Most of the kids took the course because it was 'easy credits' but they got fooled. My final papers must have been a convoluted contrivance of some kind—nothing even slightly Christian or spiritual but using many of my artist mother's thoughts on the subject which were definitely not 'main line. I was given an A.

"Well, going forward for baptism, and that little prayer that I repeated hundreds of times in my feverish fight for life must have touched God.

Three days after the prayer meeting, and my expected demise, I walked out of the hospital without an operation or drainage tubes. Later I came down with a terrible case of boils as the infection was carried to the surface. I knew in my heart that something spiritual had occurred."

"I would say that God was in there somewhere," the Keeper, Shepherd, Watcher, Pastor, Whistler said. "That simple act of going forward to accept Christ may have been the anchor that kept you steady through your searching."

"Yes, kind of like a lifeline that keeps you from falling off a boat in rough seas. Well, life went on. My appointment to the aviation cadet program came through and I was off to Texas. I had previously been through a week of testing, physical, psychological, IQ, and several others including a battery of coordination tests. I qualified for navigator, multiengine pilot, and fighter pilot. In Texas, they were giving a final physical exam and I passed everything except the eye test which was just a bit off. I was sitting at the eye machine that you looked through at the usual spread of letters. The technician running the machine gave me several chances. Finally he said that he was going for coffee and left the machine running right in front of me."

"Say hello to the old deceiver. I bet he came to call," said the Traveling Preacher.

"In spades, I would have had about fifteen minutes to memorize the bottom line but would not let myself cheat. A bunch of tiny voices in my head were saying—go ahead, take just a quick look.

'The guy came back, I flunked again, and he called me a jerk, and sent me on my way. That disqualified me for pilot training and off to navigator school I went.

"I have thought of that episode hundreds of times and wondered how my life would have changed if I had cheated by taking that offered look."

"Well," said the Philosopher and my Personal Prophet, "you could have died that year."

"Well, several of my classmates in preflight went to pilot school and three of them crashed and died that summer. Would I have become an ace aviator, a dead aviator, or a dishonorable aviator?"

"You won't get me to answer that," my New Friend said, "even if I could."

"However, in my opinion you made a very difficult and probably very correct decision," he added with a sparkle in his eye.

"Well, I have actually felt proud of myself for that decision, but still wishing I could have gone to flight school. Do you still want me to keep talking after that confession?"

"Sure," he said. "It's interesting to see how a person gains wisdom."

"Later I was working as an insurance adjuster in Florida spending every noon listening to half an hour each of Herbert Armstrong and J. Vernon McGee. I soon recognized that Armstrong was not teaching the same Bible that McGee was teaching. You don't even have a radio so how would you know those guys? Anyhow, that's what happened."

"Now you have added a bit of discernment to your thimble full of wisdom. About not having a radio—I do have ears to hear."

"Well, both Armstrong and his son got into some kind of trouble and to me that signaled the end of their teachings for me. I stuck with McGee for the next twenty or more years. I bought his Bible commentary and actually read my Bible a bit. I still had no personal knowledge of Jesus Christ. I am sure McGee taught it but I didn't hear."

"That's finding wisdom," the Preacher said with a smile.

"Then the bottom fell out of my life. I was sinking."

My Pastor, Watcher, New Friend, etc. gave me a broad grin as I opened my eyes to glance at him. The way the light was hitting him it looked like he was glowing.

"I've heard that one before," he said. "Most just say they had hit bottom. But you being nautical and an old salty and crusty and such have *to have the bottom fall out—like with a boat. Oh, well, you know what I mean. So what did you do now that you are shipwrecked?"*

"You seem to know more than I'm telling you. Where did you get that 'salty' and 'crusty,' stuff?"

"I guess it is in the wind or something, Bart. It's easy to smell bay bottom at low tide. You were shipwrecked and about to tell me where you went."

"I went to the beach! That's where shipwrecks usually end up. 'It was a dark and stormy night and the wind was blowing a gale . . .'"

"Spare me the ancient mariner stuff, skipper. Get to the point."

"Aye, aye, sir! It was a wild night with wind, high surf, and spume flying through the air and knee deep on the sand. I waded into the surf with the backwash cutting the sand from under my feet. I raised both arms to the dark sky and shouted at God. I said, 'If you are real, if you are there, if you care about me—I give up! I give up! You take over!'

"Well, he must have both heard and cared because a bolt of something shot through me and all I could see was a pillar of light surrounding me.

"No kidding. I have shared this before and most folks think I am either exaggerating or lying. Honest, it was a real jolt of something. I began to dance and laugh and cry and run through the waves and spume. I eventually ran to my car wet, with my feet hardly touching the ground.

"That night I prayed and said: 'If I am going to be one of your people I need to believe the Bible. Please help me.' Six months later, I had no doubts. That experience was so vivid and dramatic that to my dying day I could never deny it. The Lord knew that I needed big proof and he gave me enough to last until my dying day—bad choice of words considering . . ."

My Preacher, Pastor, Gardener, Keeper, Watcher, Shepherd, or whatever else, New Friend just gave a silly grin. *"I thought that all you cared about was boats and dogs. Now I see that you run pretty deep in other areas. Well done, son,"* he said gently. He waved his hand across my eyes and they closed as I sagged back into my clover bed. Just before my going to sleep, the smell of peanut butter and dog breath was in the air.

"Wait, wait, I need to ask you a question," I said. *"How come a Shepherd, Keeper, etc., doesn't have a dog? This is the perfect place for dogs!"*

"Oh, we have dogs, very good dogs. I guess they are just out taking care of dog business somewhere else right now. We all have our duties, you know. Right now I have mine, so lie down and take a nap."

"I still smell dog breath and peanut butter," I said, as I lay back in the clover and drifted off to sleep.

CHAPTER 18

Bad Guys Advance

Two miles north of the *Pelican,* three men waded through knee-deep water just inside the mangrove line along the gulf. With the shallow water going so far offshore there was no beach, just a transition of mud to mangrove and still more water under the mangrove. There was no real way to know where the gulf ended and the Everglades began.

Twinkles and Penny lay in the brush on a bit of dry stuff where rafts of seaweed had caught on the mangrove and dried. Unknown to even them, Chinook was well back and downwind of the trackers. He had seen the pistol that King kept waving around and understood what it was. He wasn't worried. He had his orders to keep well back and out of sight. The two basset hounds were doing a good job of tracking, and he was glad that they were part of the pack.

Twinkles nudged Penny with her nose. "Penny," she said quietly, "don't you think Rocky is really cute?"

"Sure," she replied, "but he only has eyes for you."

"I have a million brown spots on my white nose, or is it a million white spots on a brown nose. Anyhow, it's freckled."

"So what? He still really likes you. Now stop dreaming about Rocky and get back to watching those men."

"Hey, King," the fat man shouted, "the tides too high for us to walk inside the mangrove line anymore, and I'm all skun up from crawling through these mangrove roots. These little coon oysters on the roots are tearing me up. I'm for getting drunk. Ain't nobody finding that guy in this swamp!"

"No way," said King, "you guys owe me big time for all the wages I have been paying you, so head inland to where there is some dry land

and then go south. I'll be right behind you all the way. That boat has got to be there somewhere. If someone else finds it with a gun-shot body in it, there is going to be trouble. We don't want that."

"OK, let's go find it, and tomorrow we can come back to burn the boat and bury the guy," said the heavy man, with the huge belly sagging over his belt. His shirt was soaking with sweat and it had rings of dried salt. His red, puffy face was streaked with sweat. He was well past his prime and damaged by drugs and alcohol.

"What a jerk you are, lazy as a clam!" King replied harshly.

"If we find the body, we bury it today and maybe burn the boat," King said. "I don't give a rat's tail how tired you are. Now get moving and you go first, gators love lard."

"Let's hope we find it fast. I aren't fond of this swamp walking," said the fat man's buddy.

"Cut the talk and keep moving," King growled. "We'll head east a half mile or so until the ground firms up so we can get out of the water.

Then we head south. Remember that I have the gun and yours are on the boat because you didn't want to carry the weight. I recommend that you keep your eyes open because as the water gets less salty there will be more gators and snakes. I hear there are pythons in here that are twenty feet long. They live under the water hyacinths or other floating stuff. One of them gets hold of you, they'll crush you into a bag of bones and then you get swallowed, dead or alive."

"Now why did you tell us that?" the fat man asked. "I don't want to be gator's meal, but the thought of a twenty-foot snake scares me a lot worse.

Getting eaten all at one time is one thing but being slowly swallowed is something. I don't even want think about."

"Me too," said the thin man. "I seen on TV how they swallow really big animals and you just see a huge lump in their belly. Then they go hide somewhere and digest the meal for a couple of weeks. It ain't pretty, and I heard that they can stalk you for miles if you look like a good dinner."

"If I was you," King said, "I'd talk less and look more."

Chinook lay belly tight to the ground and heard it all. He stood so the bassets could see him and then hid himself again. The bassets slinked carefully over to him.

"Girls, you have done a good job. Now I want you to split up. Twinkles, follow the men, and Penny, you go around them and back to the pack and tell Buster that the men are headed their way. Tell him everything you heard, even about the snake. Talk fast 'cause he needs time to get the dogs ready to slow the bad guys down. And Penny, ask him to send two big dogs to meet me at the bad man's camp. Maybe we can cause some kind of racket in the camp that will make these guys turn around. You just heard about the snakes, so be real careful. This is a mighty dangerous part of the world. I would rather have to worry about avalanches and bears. They don't lurk underwater ready to lunge out and eat you."

Without even asking questions or making comments, as female dogs often do, they nodded and wormed their way through the brush, tall grass, and water. They were off to do as told.

"Most miraculous behavior," Chinook said to himself, as he turned toward the bad man's camp.

CHAPTER 19

The Drug Lord's Camp

Two operations unfolded at about the same time. Chinook walked stiff-legged around the camp and finally relaxed when nothing seemed to be there. He was ready to fight and didn't much care what might have come out to challenge him. He looked over the situation and sniffed around to identify objects, all the time trying to think things out. Less than an hour after he arrived, Moose and Cookie showed up. Both dogs were mud splattered and panting. Their legs were coated with slime nearly to their belly. Chinook looked them over.

"OK, Chinook," said Moose, "we may be muddy but we are ready.

We had to take a circle around the bad men. Cookie wanted to stop and eat all three of them but Buster had said you wanted us right away."

"So here we are," said Cookie. "Let's do something before I bust. I need some action to keep my blood moving."

"First," said Chinook, "we put some wood on the hot coals of their fire. Then we move the ends of those planks from the boat to the fire ring. Then we tip over that barrel of gasoline that has the fill cap off. That should do the trick."

"Then we run!" said Moose.

"Roger, over and out," said Cookie. "Action I asked for and action I get."

The fireball was magnificent as it reached up through the trees and palms. The dried skirt of long dead fronds on a palms and the shroud of flames billowed into the sky as the old fronds burned with a fury.

The flames reached up into a group of palm trees and set them on fire.

Then the planks caught fire and the flames marched up the gangplank, while flaming fronds from the palm caught in the oak and fiery shards rained down on the fishing boat. In minutes, the fishing boat was shrouded in flames and the fuel tank lines had burned through and turned to blowtorches. The flames reached into the sky. King's black boat crackled with the heat and as the fiberglass out-gassed, it suddenly erupted in a ball of flames.

Burning palm fronds rained down on the rusted metal roof of the drug storage shed. Old dried fronds and dead moss ignited with a vengeance. A large branch fell from a pine, puncturing the shed roof and letting burning material fall into the building. It was soon a pyre of flames.

"Not bad," said Chinook.

"Awesome," said Cookie.

"We sure did it," said Moose.

"Let's move," said Chinook, "before we all get high from the drug smoke."

Halfway back to the pack, Cookie stopped. "It's men ahead. Dogs are around them in the bushes."

"It's an ambush," said Chinook.

"Let me at them." said Moose.

"Fade back, guys," said Chinook. "They are starting to run this way. We'll give them a fright when they come by. They have guns so we can't give them a target."

As the men passed, the dogs growled and rattled the bushes. The men sprinted as the pack of growling dogs followed.

"It's wolves," one screamed, as Dutch lunged through an area of palmettos, nailed a leg deep to the bone, and retreated quickly.

The fat man fell, screaming "it's wolves, it's wolves" and then shouted again to his retreating buddies, "I'm bit bad, help me!" No one responded so he got to his feet and limped toward the camp.

Soon they saw the glow of fire. King shot at a shadow in the swamp. He was the first one to run, and the fat man was last, limping with a bloody leg.

"Let them go," Buster commanded. "Back to the boat and we will make plans to take care of them one by one if they try to get to Leader again."

The pack was jubilant when Chinook told the pack what Cookie, Moose, and he had done. They were already congratulating Dutch on his attack on the fat man. The pack had struck on two fronts and done a lot of damage to the bad men.

Igor and Frankie scouted the camp and returned with news that both boats were smoking wrecks, supplies burned, and the bad men exhausted.

They had found some unexploded bottles of liquor and all three were drunk and laying in the ashes of their camp.

Igor finished his report with a crooked smile and said, "They smelled like they had all peed in their pants."

Frankie jumped straight up, his tail like a helicopter rotor, and with each bounce shouted, "Yes, yes, yes."

Rocky stepped forward proudly, with head held high and tail erect.

"I have good news too. Leader sat up today, drank water, and ate some peanut butter that Kate had retrieved and gnawed open and put a spoon in. He looked around for a few minutes, then pulled a shirt under his head for a pillow, and went back to sleep. Kate and I have him covered up now. His wound looks good and his fever is gone. Our official medic, Red Rider, says the crisis has passed, but He still needs help. The gash in his head is still gaping open but clean. We keep the bugs off."

Buster sat near the bow of the sailboat and the pack sat in a semicircle in front of him on the shell mound. All were on their haunches with ears cupped forward.

"We need to talk about getting help for Leader," Buster said. "There is only one of two possible things to do. We have to get him out of this swamp and to people who can help, or get help to come here. I doubt that we can do the latter, so it seems to me we have to work on getting Him out."

"Buster," said Harry, "I was named after His dad, 'Harry.' You were named after His dad too because his nickname was 'Buster,' so we both have a good reason to want to do all we can for Leader. My problem is that those bad guys probably won't quit looking for Him and we really can't do much until we deal with them. I'm Bonne's mate and father of Twinkles. We have been talking and think we should attack those guys.

It's not basset nature to be mean but we could sure make an exception in this case."

"I agree," said Cookie. "My instincts are different. Boar hounds go for the throat and hang on like a bulldog. I know you have some Chow in you, Buster, judging by your purple tongue and extra skin, and Chows are mighty protective and can work up a mean pretty fast if need be.

Dutch, Chinook, Moose, and Red Rider are all over a hundred pounds. Heck, even five-pound Frankie could hold his own against most threats. With the whole bunch of us attacking at once, those men wouldn't have a chance."

A murmur of agreement came from the pack accompanied by ears laid back and bared teeth.

"Let's remember our mandate. I would sure like to inflict a lot of damage myself," Buster said. "The problem is that we were sent to help Leader and to see that he stays alive until aid is available. I don't feel that our orders would allow us to be directly responsible for killing the bad guys.

"I don't think we should turn into man killers. I'm not afraid of man or bear but we were raised as 'good dogs,' and He would be upset if He knew we had turned into killers."

"What about Dutch nailing that guy on the ankle?" asked Bonnie.

"That was a bad bite judging by the blood and the scream. Why can't we all do the same?"

"Different rules of engagement," answered Buster. "Dutch was in the boat with Kate. His instinct is to guard his Leader and attack when necessary. We were in the pack and have specific orders."

Penny stepped forward and then sat down before she spoke. Her long, light brown hair was as fine as silk and fluttered in the breeze. "You all see my twisted front legs. I was near a pond and a gator came out like a flash and grabbed me by my front legs and began to pull me toward the pond. I screamed, bucked, snarled, and pulled my feet loose and ran like lightning, howling and hurting. Anyhow, I hate gators and saw several on the spy mission. I was wondering if maybe we could get gators to do our work, and that way we wouldn't be bad dogs." Penny stepped back into the circle.

There was quiet for a minute. Everyone was trying to think it through.

Deciding to chase a cat was easy, like heading for the food bowl when called. You didn't even have to think. But this was hard to ponder.

"I got it!" said Frankie, jumping straight up with excitement. "We find where some gators are lying, and then we get the men to follow us and we lead them to the gators and the gators get them and take them to the gator hole, and that takes care of the bad men and we are good dogs."

He took a gulp of air.

Dog grins and silent chuckles came from the pack. Frankie continued.

"I saw several of those big, round snakes with white mouths—think they are water moccasins—they were in the edge of the water. We could push the men in—well, not me maybe, but Moose could."

Flash was a muddy brown with dark areas, a big body, and very basset like with short legs. He stepped forward and spoke. "I saw a rattlesnake near the trail, so I growled and snarled my best snarl but it just curled up in a heap, looked at me, and then jumped at me. I jumped at the same time and left the area immediately at my best basset speed. Maybe we could make that snake part of our plan too."

"I like that idea, but I have one too," said Chinook in his deep gravely voice. "When we went up to the bad men's camp I was following Moose and he leaped across a wet spot, but I decided to run through it to cool off a bit. The mud gave way under me. My legs began to sink, and as I struggled it got worse and I sank more. Moose didn't want me to tell you, but he turned back and got hold of me, and with me clawing and digging and him pulling I got out. It was quicksand. It's easy to get into but hard to get out of without help. We could use that in our arsenal."

Buster thought a minute and then stood up. "I guess what you all are saying is that we don't need to kill those men ourselves. All we have to do is to introduce them to something that will. I could go for that. Our mandate was to save Leader but we were not to kill the men.

It didn't say we had to keep them from being killed by their own anger and stupidity."

"OK," Buster continued, "let's think about our options and discuss them later. One last thing, the bad men think we are a pack of wolves and I have been thinking that we should keep it that way. We are going to appear to be a pack of wolves. Chinook, your ancestors were wolves and probably know how to howl, so I put you in charge of the wolf chorus."

Buster stretched out in his sphinxlike position with eyes open, still thinking. The meeting was over.

CHAPTER 20-I

Happy Hunting Ground

Bart sat up in the grass and sniffed the air. Immediately his New Friend strolled up and sat down beside him.

"New Friend, I smell smoke. It smells a little like burning fiberglass.

I know that I have smelled that smell a bunch of times before now, but I don't know when or where. It's a real distinctive smell."

"No fiberglass here, Bart. If we had boats they would be made of wood or reeds, not fiberglass. All I smell is fresh air and the scent of flowers and grass."

"Before I went to sleep, I smelled peanut butter and dog breath. It's all very strange and fractured. Don't you smell it?"

"Like I said, I just smell fresh air. I don't go around on a beautiful morning and try to smell anything but wet grass, flowers, and sunshine."

"Now that's strange. I never heard anyone say that they smelled sunshine."

"I know that things are different around here, but that's because we think blue sky and sunshine thoughts, not burning boats and gasoline."

"There you go. I didn't say a word about gasoline but now that you mention it, I smell that too. I'm getting worried about this place. Are we caught in some science fiction place between two worlds, dimensions, or such? It's real nice around here but kind of spooky."

"I wouldn't worry, Bart. Remember I told you that I wouldn't leave you. I know you feel like you have parachuted into a strange world but I assure you it is all real. Maybe it's like when you dream too much after eating a whole pizza by yourself and have a stomach ache."

"No, I feel fine and I bet you can't even order a pizza here, or even a hamburger and fries. Heck, even a milkshake would be appreciated."

"I bet you don't even feel hungry and are just giving me a hard time," said the Friend. *"If what you mentioned were delivered by a raven you would probably be too persnickety to even eat them, afraid of a little raven spit."*

"So now you are a Prophet, telling me what I would do in the future.

Maybe you can see other places too. I seem to have lost my two dogs that I am sure I had before this place appeared."

The Prophet Friend chuckled. "What I know for sure is that you can't seem to get fully connected here. If this was the happy hunting grounds, as you seem to think it is, wouldn't there be dogs here?"

"I liked you better as a Gardener, Shepherd than as a Prophet Philosopher. Actually, I liked the Shepherd, Teacher, Leader thing. Our walks and talks have been really great."

"Then, are you are going to forget dogs, burning boats, and such and concentrate on being here?"

"Burning boats? I said fiberglass, not boats."

"So I made a connection and assumed something. Anything wrong with that? You're behaving a bit contentiously."

"It's not contending when you are straightening out someone."

"It's the manner and the attitude of your correction. And who says that nitpicking stuff needs to be corrected at all."

"OK, Literary Professor and Philosopher, let's move on. I'm not sure which hat to address but I do have a very profound question to ask," Bart said with a grin.

"OK, since you are lightening up, I will do all I can to answer your profound question. Ask it."

"OK, where is here?"

"Bart, you seem to be much stronger than when you arrived and your rather abrasive personality is awakening."

"That's a new one. I have been called a lot of names but never accused of having an abrasive personality. I am Mr. Good Guy—Mr. Cooperative."

"Didn't I tell you before your nap that you were to head to the tunnel and take a walk in it?"

"You did, but I liked it here and decided to stay with you."

"*That sounds a bit like rebellion. You decided to do your own thing?*"

"*Hello, everything here is your thing—how can I do anything else but your thing?*"

"*You should be a lawyer—that thinking is called obfuscation. OK, you can stay a while. Let's go take a walk around that pond we saw. It will be hard going but worth it in the end. Maybe you will start telling me some personal stuff—you know, how you feel about things.*"

"*What do you mean, feel? Feel is female thing. I don't feel, I either know or don't know. Feel is a marshmallow word for airhead people.*

When I say we should do such and such I am just being polite. What it really means is that my way is the only logical way."

"*Macho! The big guy knows everything and has no feelings.*"

"*Come on, you know what I mean. To me how I feel is kind of a psychological thing—lying on a couch, or a girl crying over something she thinks might happen someday.*"

"*Real men don't feel—is that it? Well, I think life is like a nut: the good stuff is inside but you have to crack the nut first. No insult implied, of course.*"

"*You are implying. You are saying that I have a hard shell and maybe it's getting cracked.*"

"*Wow, you have sudden insight. Let's hope that it doesn't take a sledgehammer because that leaves just squish and shards.*"

"*So OK, I do have some feelings when I hit my thumb with a hammer, and maybe just a little inside, but have never found anyone I dared to share them with. When you share personal stuff, it usually comes home to bite you—right out of the mouth of your wife, friend, kid, etc. I have noticed that guys raised with just a mother or a mother and three sisters are big feelers. They talk all this soft stuff repeated about twelve times, and when it's over everyone goes away smiling and thinking the same stuff they had when they started. It seems to me that when you share feelings something good should happen.*"

"*I agree that sharing important stuff should make both people grow, but nobody cares how you fold your chewing gum wrapper.*"

Bart shook his head. "*Once or twice I have shared feely stuff and the other person's eyes either glazed over with boredom or sprang open like I was an axe murder. Every time I shared it came back to bite me on the butt.*"

"You just need a friend who talks straight, understands your heart, and will never hurt you!"

"If you find one," Bart said, as he lay back in the grass, "I hope you will introduce me."

"I'm working on it even as we talk," the Rustic Psychologist responded.

"Now, let's take that walk around the lake. You need to get that smell of burning boats out of your nose. You can hold on to the peanut butter and dog breath smell. They are acceptable."

CHAPTER 21

The Dogs Attack

In the burned-out drug camp, King grunted and forced his body into a sitting position. His face and hands were black with soot and ashes. His head pounded, he felt sick, and his stomach churned. He was filthy, hungry, and mosquito-bitten. The other two men were in a similar condition as they began to awake amid the charred remains of their boats and camp. The dog-bitten man moaned and fondled his ankle. It was swollen with black puncture wounds and red-inflamed flesh.

"What I can't figure out is how that barrel of gasoline got tipped over," said King. "I remember we were going to transfer the gas to my fuel tanks but how did the bung get unscrewed and why did it tip over?"

"It was them wolves that did it," said the skinny man. "Them is smart animals and I have heard stories about them doing stuff to get to stock and such. They work together to get things done."

"Yeah," said King, "but why knock over a barrel of gas? It doesn't make sense."

"Could be they was curious and just jumped up to check and their weight pushed it over," said the thin guy. "It wasn't full and not too hard to tip."

"And I know why the bung was unscrewed," the fat man said with a groan. "We was going to siphon the gas out into five-gallon cans to take to your boat but then we were off hunting that Casey guy with you and forgot to put the bung back in." The fat man groaned again and lay back with his head in the sand.

"That's stupid incompetence," King said. "That's what I get for working with dumb druggies like you two."

"I guess you get what you pay for, Mr. King," said the skinny guy.

"OK, forget it for now. I'll settle with you weed heads later. We need to find that body and that boat. If a helicopter comes looking for him, they will spot his sail and the white decks. When they see him dead in the cockpit, where I saw him fall, this place will be crawling with cops of all kinds.

"There is enough left of our boats to identify them and then everybody will be looking for us. We've got to bury that body and burn that sailboat real quick, and then hope one of our guys comes by and we can get a ride home."

"Not to cause any trouble," the thin man said, "but your buddy in the plane didn't find Casey or his boat. He probably thinks that Casey is on the way to Marathon."

"He's here. I can feel him," said King as he struggled to his feet and began brushing leaves and sand from his clothes. "Even dead he's after me."

The fat man rose up on an elbow, eyed King, and then spoke. "My daddy was a preacher, and once after I had stolen a melon from a neighbor's field and was hiding in the shed he told me a scripture. I've thought about it for years. The Bible says that the evil people run away and hide even when nobody is after them."

"Enough Bible crap out of you, fat man. It sure hasn't gotten you very far."

"That's because I turned my back on it," the fat man said. "My brother listened and now he is a businessman and I'm a bum."

"Well," said King, "I turned my back too and I am doing just great."

"It don't look that way to me," said the fat man.

King pulled his pistol, aimed at the fat man, and thumbed back the hammer. The fat man just stared back at him. King grunted, released the hammer, and put the revolver in his pocket.

"OK," King said, with a grimace on his face, "we're going after Casey right now."

"You're the boss," the thin man said. "But as for me, I am thinking we should be headed east to find a road."

"We can just walk out to the east just like my buddy says," the fat guy agreed. "I doubt it's more than ten, or twenty, miles to a road or something. The Tamiami Trail should be east of us, but as you go south it cuts inland toward Miami. We could wait here a week for someone to come by and we've no food or decent water."

"You wouldn't make it two miles before something bit you or ate you,"

King said, "probably both. Besides, like you say, US 41 turns inland and if we are too far south we could walk for seventy-five miles and would surely be dead and eaten before we could make it. Anyhow, by the look at that leg you won't be walking much of anywhere by tomorrow."

"I've been thinking," said King, "Casey should have arrived in Marathon about tomorrow. What if he was supposed to call home or something? When he is overdue, everyone on VHF radio will know about it. He has surveyed half the boats out there and they will be on the lookout for him. We haven't much time before the word gets out, and that grouper digger that messed me up a few days ago will set everybody looking for me and they will know about where we are."

"There you go," said the fat man, "just like my daddy told me. You think everyone is after you when probably no one is, and won't be for some time yet."

"Your daddy can take a long walk off a short dock, just like I wish all those Bible thumpers would. I use brains, not religion."

"Well," said the thin man called Dingo, "I ain't much, and I know it. I think Cotton's daddy may have had it right.

Well," continued Dingo, "I think Cotton here is more right than you.

Him and me has kept this place a secret for a year or more and when you show up it all comes unglued. It's like you brought the trouble down on us."

"Shut your mouth, Dingo. It was a wolf that bit fat boy, not me, and besides I don't like talk like that. I'm still the 'King,' and don't forget it."

"I'm seeing things a bit different now," said Dingo. "I'm like Cotton. I don't amount too much and never have, but at least we admit it. You don't seem to know what you really are. You are just a cheap thug who thinks he is something special."

"Keep talking, Dingo, and you won't live long."

"I think you may be right, and that's why I'm telling you like it is. I won't never get out of this swamp, and something tells me that you won't either. I'm doing some deep thinking about stuff. I've been hearing my daddy talking, things I remember him saying. He weren't much but he was honest."

"I've been hearing things too," said King, "and it's telling me I'll win this game and go home to enjoy my money and sell more drugs."

CHAPTER 22

The Wolves

King led the way with the thin man behind and the fat man hobbling with a stick that he was using as a cane, trying to keep up. He was a hundred feet behind but King pushed on.

Several of the dogs ghosted through the underbrush, watching carefully. The fat man felt their presence, but King refused to slacken his pace. King had his gun, a short-nosed revolver stuffed into one of his pockets. The fire had destroyed their automatic rifles.

King and the thin man were skirting a swampy area, jumping from one clump of grass to another. The fat man remained on the higher ground, unable to jump to cross the watery areas.

Penny and Igor had remained ahead of the men. "OK," said Igor, "Penny, you need to tell Buster that the men are approaching and will probably find our camp, and our Leader, in about an hour. Make it swift girl."

Penny turned and flashed away, her two twisted feet a blur of speed.

She skidded into Buster, burying her nose in his deep black fur. "Sorry, sir," she said. "The men are less than an hour from here." She gasped for breath. "Igor sent me to report."

Buster touched her nose with his and then raised his head as he spoke, "Gather in a circle quickly. Chinook, do your thing."

Chinook lifted his nose toward the sky. "OK," he said, "all together, a pack howl, as wolf-like as possible."

Hearing the first notes of the howl, Igor let out a growl and thrashed against some bushes. King was in mid leap across a swampy area as he heard the sound of the howl, the growl, and the rattle of bushes nearby. He froze for a moment, and missed his footfall on solid ground and plunged into the swamp. He thrashed and tried to stand, but the mud gave way under his feet and he sank thigh deep into the slime. On the trail the thin man came to a stop to listen.

"Oh god," he said. "It's a renegade pack of wolves. I've seen in the papers that something has been killing stock. Must be them."

"Help me," screamed King.

Cotton recognized what had happened, picked up a heavy stick, and rushed to King. He held it out and King grasped it.

"Help me," Cotton screamed to Dingo, who stood staring into the woods as the howl continued. "We got to get King out of this mud and get out of here."

"I'm sinking," screamed King. He was up to his ribs in mud and had let go of the stick, and was flailing his arms. His eyes were large with terror.

"Get me out of here you scum," he shouted as he grasped the stick again.

The two men stopped pulling and looked at one another.

"I'm sorry, I'm sorry—just help me and I will make it up to you," King whined.

The two of them began pulling and managed to work King near the higher ground and dragged him out of the mire.

King was caked with mud from head to toe. He wiped the mud from his face with a muddy shirt sleeve, and then stood listening to the howling.

"It can't be," said King. Wolves are only up north, or in Alaska, or the Klondike, or some such. We're going on! We're going to find that boat and take care of Casey."

"I'm not going any farther," said Dingo. "You got the gun and six shells, so go and see how well you do against a pack of ten, or twenty, or more animals."

"OK," said King as he grimaced and swore. "We go back and when those animals move on we try again. I got a feeling that we are getting close. It would be nice if they were eating Casey right now—save us some digging."

Igor trailed the men back to their camp. King charged past the fat man, who was sweating and white faced. It smelled to Igor that the man's wound was infected, and the man was sick with a fever.

The thin man helped his buddy back to camp and laid him in the shadow of a palm tree. Cotton groaned with pain. Pulling King from the mire had sapped his energy. His infected leg throbbed with pain. He had sobbed as he limped his way back to their burned-out camp. King didn't thank either man for saving him.

"Keep listening," King commanded as he washed the mud from his clothes and body with the water of the swamp. "When the howling stops, we head back that way."

Igor reported the near death of King, the condition of the fat man, and the conversation about resuming the hunt to the council. Buster seemed to smile, as did most of the hounds at the description of their enemy in the quicksand. Most were disappointed that he had been pulled out.

Chinook stepped forward. "I'm glad it wasn't me in that quicksand again. That's scary stuff. Anyhow, as you know I have had a little experience with wolves, and we sounded really good. My suggestion is that we make some scattered sounds every hour or so, and then when the moon comes up we go about halfway to their camp and give them a full choir serenade. That should keep them awake all night. We can have a spy up there to see how they respond."

"I second the motion," Red Rider added as he sat on his haunches tall and straight. "I know we don't vote but just want you all to know that I think, Chinook has a good idea. Those guys must be mighty uncomfortable, skeeter bit, chigger bit, dirty, hungry, and drinking swamp water. A little sleep deprivation should finish them off."

"That's a fact," said Bonnie. "When I had my puppies, I didn't sleep for a week, and it was terrible." She looked over at Twinkles in time to see Rocky swipe her nose with his long wet tongue. She got up off her haunches, shouldered Rocky aside, and sat down between him and Twinkles.

Buster noticed protective instinct toward her daughter, Twinkles, and grinned. He glanced at Dutch, sprawled in the sand with eyes closed. Just then the bushes rattled and a golden blur rushed out, grabbed Dutch by the throat, and did a flip over his body. His huge mouth found the other dog's throat, so that they were mutually locked together with their jaws.

The golden dog made herself into a ball with both feet gouging at Dutch's face. Suddenly she broke loose, jumped to her feet, and streaked back into the bushes. Dutch was still on his side, unperturbed. He raised his head to look at Buster, and then flopped it back down onto the still-warm sand.

There were chuckles around the area. All the dogs knew the explosive exuberance of Kate and loved her for it. Buster glanced at her stretched out under a palmetto bush, not panting at all. Then he nodded to the dogs, and went down into his sphinx position. It was the signal that the plan was accepted and that the day was over. Packs don't vote; they follow.

CHAPTER 23-I

The Arboretumist

When Bart awoke in the field that he had been in before his New Friend was off some distance near a young tree. Bart got up and walked over to the tree and patted his friend on the shoulder.

"I see you are doing some afternoon gardening. I guess this is serious work, and that you have changed hats again."

"Good afternoon, sleeping friend."

"Actually, I am an Arboretumist—far more lofty title than Gardener. Are you feeling well, my field-dwelling friend?"

"Yes, but I was sound asleep when I thought I heard a pack of wolves howling. Do you have killer wolves here?"

The Master Gardener smiled and fingered the sharp blade of his saw.

"No bad wolves, maybe some good wolves doing some good things. I'm sorry they woke you but I am sure they didn't do it to disturb you. They are very good wolves."

"I can accept that, but I also smelled peanut butter, and that made me hungry. I'm reluctant to say it in this lovely place but I also smelled dog breath."

"Tell me," my friendly Master Gardener, Pruner, Arboretumist asked, "why do you seem to like dogs so much?"

"Well," I said, "for one thing they are usually happy, always happy when they see you come home, and very happy when you feed them."

"I don't want to disillusion you, Bart, but maybe it is just all about food."

"No, sir! They want to please, they always forgive, and they are never vindictive. Oh, and you never get judged, never have to explain, and never have to dress up to please them."

The Gardener, Shepherd, Wildlife Expert, Marriage Counselor looked at me with a grin on his weathered face. "You sound like you've been married."

"Let's just say that I am observant. But don't read anything into what I said—I'm talking about dogs."

"You're a strange man, Casey, hearing wolves and smelling peanut butter and dog breath and talking about women on a day like this. Anyhow, I am busy pruning this tree and don't happen to have any peanut butter, or dog breath in my pocket."

"Yuck," said Bart at the thought of a pocket full of peanut butter and dog breath. "Anyhow, I like the dog smell, and I wasn't talking about women. But how come you are attacking this poor tree with a saw?"

"Pruning is not attacking. Pruning only hurts for a little while and then you grow better. If a limb is heading in the wrong direction, it has to be cut off to allow the other limbs to grow properly. If the connection of the limb to the tree is weak, it needs to be cut off before it breaks and tears the skin of the trunk. If the limb is growing downward instead of upward, it needs to come off. One theory is that you prune trees kind of open, so a bird can fly through them. Do you want me to keep on giving you reasons to prune?"

"I noticed that you said 'you grow better.' You slipped that in like a poke in the ribs. I guess it is the same with people," Bart said. "Like kids, you sometimes have to cut off unhealthy things in their life or they may go bad. I know it's the truth but it's hard. I had two friends. One protected and coddled her kids—let them do and say anything they desired—and they seldom obeyed and were always in trouble. She never made them go to church, because she said everyone had to make their own decisions. I never did find out where they were going to get information for decision making. Between school, TV, friends, and such they got plenty of input, but nothing remotely spiritual.

"The other mother was hard on her kids in a quiet way, requiring that they be mannerly, and to obey. She and her husband took them to Sunday school, had deep discussions with them, and they turned out to be really fine kids. I guess that is pruning or the lack of it."

"Wow," said the Listener, "you are in a really loquacious mood this morning. I thought you were the strong silent type."

"And gardeners usually don't know the meaning of five-dollar words like loquacious and arbor—whatever."

"OK, truce," the Pruning Man said. *"You have something wise and profound you want to tell me?"*

"So how do you know that? Well, one time I had a garden and put the seeds in real close. The little seed bag said to put in a seed every two inches, and then when they sprouted to pull out every other one. Well, I couldn't do that, and left them all to grow. As they grew everything got crowded, tangled, and stunted for lack of enough room and food. No matter what I did I couldn't get a good crop."

"You learned pruning the hard way," said the Agricultural Expert, Arborist, and Forester. *"You learned from the lack of it. I plan to clean out all the unnecessary and improper branches from this tree, and when it grows up it will be straight, well formed, and fruitful. The way your garden didn't grow."*

"You keep glancing at me out of the corner of your eye every time you cut off a branch. Are you hinting that maybe I need some pruning too?"

"You need pruning?" asked the Gardener sarcastically as he tossed his saw on the ground. *"I thought you were perfect."*

"I am, or was, a pretty good guy. I learned a few lessons the hard way but was basically self-sufficient, independent, kind of a perfectionist, and prideful of my work. I really liked to talk about all the stuff I knew, and all the stuff that I had done—to help others, of course. Is that a bad thing?"

"You know, Bart, a knife can be sharp, but it takes an expert to make it razor sharp. If you have serious cutting to do, just sharp isn't sharp enough. OK? Did you ever hear of the sword that was so sharp that it could cut between soul and spirit?" asked the Philosopher Theologian.

"That's for serious pruning. Enough talk. Let's go find a spring I know of that gives really life changing water."

"Is this the Preacher talking now? If it is, I have a question. If I smell peanut butter and my stomach growls, and, noticing that you never seem to eat, I'm confused. If I am dead I shouldn't be hungry, and if I am in heaven I shouldn't smell peanut butter or dog breath. So where are we?"

"Cut it out, Casey! All these questions make my head hurt. Come on! After a drink at the spring I'll take you to a tree that has the best plums you have eaten. Some say that's because of the chicken manure we use for fertilizer."

CHAPTER 24

Fat Man Down

When the moon rose over the palm trees the howling started. The sound was much nearer to King's camp than the night before.

"It's them," said the thin man. "They've come to get us."

"God, my leg hurts," said the fat man. "I just as soon get eaten by a wolf as live with this leg."

"Coward," King said. "You two are big guys with a gun in your hand, but turn to mush with a little howling."

"Well," said Cotton, the fat man, "you didn't sound so brave yourself when you were sinking into the quicksand."

King pointed the pistol at Cotton. "Let's march you over to that same place, and see how brave you are when you start to sink deeper and deeper into that slime. There ain't no bottom."

Cotton looked right at the gun and then raised his eyes to King. "I also didn't recall you thanking Dingo and me for pulling you out. We could just as well left you there to sink, and we would have been rid of you and everybody would be better off."

King scowled. "Mister, you must have gotten religion all of a sudden or figure you are dying anyhow to talk to me like that."

"I don't figure on getting out of this swamp alive," said Cotton, "so for once in my life, I plan to speak my peace even if it gets me killed.

Doesn't much matter how you die."

"Mr. King," Dingo said, "Cotton has been a buddy for several years, both in jail and out, but right now he ain't speaking for me. I like this job here in the swamp, and plan to get out and come back to work here for you. You are sure enough bad clear through, but you know how to make a lot of money and pay me more than I can earn elsewhere. Besides, I'm not bothered by religious thoughts."

Just then Sheila streaked across the clearing in the edge of the fire light. Her thin gray form appeared and disappeared in seconds followed by a long guttural growl.

"Oh god," screamed King as he fired his pistol into the darkness. He was on his knees, holding the pistol in both hands—staring wide eyed into the gloom beyond the firelight.

"That's three shots gone and three left," said the fat man with a groan. "When the guns empty we're all dead."

There may be no such thing as a red wolf, but Red Rider made it look real as he leaped across a corner of the flickering firelight with a howl that turned their blood to ice. The pack responded with a circle of howls around the campfire. There were another pants wetting, or worse, and a whimper from King as he shot into the darkness again.

"Two more shots wasted and I'm dead," said the fat man.

"How about me?" asked King. "I'm rich, I've got a huge house, sports car, fast boats, women, and anything I want, and I'm going to die with you scum. It isn't fair. I deserve to live."

"Sure," said the thin man, Dingo. "Just like the people you killed with your boat and with your drugs. You even killed kids. You deserve to die just like us. Me and Cotton has talked about it and we wanted out at first, but know we are in too deep. Moving a little grass was one thing but this herion and stuff, and killing people, isn't for Cotton but I am still in."

"If Cotton is ready to die, I can sure oblige him."

"No, we plan to live this thing out just like it is written down somewhere. Cotton says his daddy believed that every life was planned out. I ain't saying that, but we got ourselves into this mess and I for one and Cotton too, don't really mind the consequences. It just sounds kind of fair to us."

The dogs faded away on signal and the night was quiet except in the minds of the three men, each contemplating the situation. When the gray of dawn finally came, King rolled to his knees and slowly stood to his feet. He flipped out the cylinder of his revolver and extracted the four spent shells. Only two live shells remained.

He kicked the fat man in the ribs until he slowly sat up. His face was soaked with sweat and even his shirt wet. He pulled up his pants leg and moaned. The ankle had putrefied and burst open. Maggots wiggled in and out of his flesh. The physical pain was obviously harsh, but the emotional anguish of seeing the maggots in his flesh reduced the man to tearful whimpers. Lying on his back and looking up his eyes followed several buzzards as they circled overhead. Then he screamed and writhed until he passed out.

His thin buddy sat with his hands around his knees and rocked as he moaned. King put his pistol to the fat man's head.

"Only two bullets left," said Dingo.

King spit near his shoe, and then stuffed the revolver into his soggy and mud-caked pocket.

"Me and you are going for a walk," King said. "We need to find that boat and that meddling insurance jerk. I never heard of a wolf attacking in broad daylight. I never even heard of a wolf in the everglades, so I'm not afraid to try for the boat again."

"You looked mighty afraid last night, and even you talked about wolves," Dingo said with a defiant tone in his voice.

It came to me last night that I don't have a thing to fear. There are things bigger than Cotton's imaginary God, and it's telling me to go for it. You ain't getting out of here alive, so I will tell you something. I was half asleep on my bunk in an old derelict boat after working all day long for a boat repair guy. I seen the pirate Gasparilla just as plain as day. He told me about an old lady, who lived on an old Trumpy yacht and had a stash of money in the bilge of her boat. All I had to do was, kill her, take the cash, and use it to get rich. I did, and financed my first load of weed.

From there on it was easy. The pirate said that I could pay him back.

"All I have to do now is to walk through the swamp till we find that boat, and take care of Casey and his dogs. There's nothing to it. I got the confidence now. If you think that getting religion is going to save your butt you are wrong. I'm the only one that can save you now, so get on your feet."

"What about my buddy here? We can't leave him or them birds up there will peck out his eyes."

"He got himself hurt; it wasn't my fault, so he can take care of himself. I have more important things to do than nursemaid that pile of fat."

"By the way, Mr. King, his name is Cotton and my name is Dingo. At least you can use our names. We've both worked for you for the last two years tending this camp, and that shack full of drugs that's now just a pile of ashes. I feel that you owe us some respect."

"I couldn't care less about your name, how you feel, or anything else.

You were born scum and you will die scum. Me, I have made something of myself, I'm rich, I'm the 'King' and I intend to stay that way. Now get to your feet and start walking or I will have only one bullet left."

"Mr. King," I'm not too confident about your pirate friend, even if he is Gasparilla in person. More like a ghost than anything else. Cotton would say that his daddy would call it a demon. I don't know about them but it doesn't stoke my confidence much to have you talking to spirits.

Are you sure, Mr. King, of jest who was talking to you last night?

CHAPTER 25

The Snake

In contrast, it was quiet back at the shell mound. Dutch and Rocky listened to the story after bringing the pack up-to-date and telling about Bart's improved condition. He was awake long enough to drink some more water and eat a spoonful of peanut butter. At nightfall they covered Him up and He had slipped into a quiet sleep.

"That was a great wolf impersonation," Bonnie said to Sheila. "For a shy girl you sure put on a good show." They all chuckled silently.

"What about that ten-foot leap that Red Rider made?" asked Penny. "I didn't know a dog could jump so far and howl so loud."

"It's easy when someone is shooting at you," Red replied. "I learned that on the battlefield."

"I thought the chorus was good too," said Buster. "It's been a good night but let's get some sleep, and in the morning we need to figure out how to end this standoff. Somehow we need to help Leader get out of here."

"One thing is sure," said Bonnie. "The fat man is real sick and his ankle is putrid. Something may smell him and drag him away for dinner.

Everything knows that he is too sick to fight back."

"Something else we learned too," said Chinook. "Only the bad man has a gun, and it's a pistol. They must have lost their other guns in the fire."

"It's a lot to think about," said Buster. "Now let's bed down for a few hours' sleep. I think that Leader's Him, is helping us so let's all ask for more help to get Leader out of this swamp."

The late-night moon shined down on a pack of sleeping dogs. Dutch sat in the boat with Kate beside him, on guard in case of trouble.

Dawn came early with King crawling on his belly toward the shell mound. The thin man was behind. They had left the fat man at their camp, wrapped in his blanket moaning. Mist rose from the warm waters of the swamp and the palm heads were an island above the mist. The giant live oaks formed a misty presence in the fog. A gator looked at King and slid back into the black water. All was quiet.

A cormorant was drying its wings after a night of fishing. It squawked as King moved. A chorus of birds replied. Buster awoke amid the squawking.

"Frankie," he called, "check the perimeter and watch for gators." The response was quick with Frankie spinning and jumping.

"Bad men and gators," Frankie reported.

"Battle stations!" Buster growled. "Howl as you go!"

The thin man heard the nearby howling, jumped up, and ran up the trail toward the burned-out camp. Rocky, the gentle nurse, circled through the underbrush and confronted him on the trail. He snarled viciously out of frustration. The thin man backed toward the swamp. Rocky barked and a huge gator looking for a dog breakfast surfaced near the edge of the swamp, looked around, and then submerged.

The surface of the water moved slightly as the gator passed beneath it.

The water became still near the bank as two eyes slowly broke the surface.

Suddenly the gator emerged in a great leap of water and slime, grabbing the thin man as he backed toward the edge with Rocky snarling in front of him. He screamed repeatedly as he was dragged to the water. No one heard his last scream as it bubbled from the bottom of the marsh.

King retreated on hearing the screams and splashing of the thin man.

He swore a spew of filth and rushed through the darkness of the swamp, wallowing in mud, sinking knee deep in the slime. His face and arms sprouted streams of blood from thorns and branches, but he crashed onward.

He stumbled into camp and kicked the fat man awake.

"Get your fat tail into motion or die where you lay," said King. "A gator, or the wolves, or something have eaten you buddy. You go first and I cover you. If I die, so do you." He kicked the fat man again as he tried to get up but only got to his knees, swayed a moment with a drooping head, and then fell face first into the dirt.

"That's how you reward me for all I have done for you," King screamed as he swore and kicked the man's ribs time after time. King hurled pieces of wood and hands full of dirt into the swamp while screaming in fury.

"Casey, you are going to pay. This is all your fault. I'm going to find you and feed you to the gators, dead or alive." He screamed and then he spewed a vomit of profanity, sat down in the ashes of his camp, and sobbed with his filthy hands covering his filthy face.

Kate was in the bushes on spy duty. She had shadowed King and his unfortunate buddy, as they crawled toward Leader's boat, and had passed the word on to Frankie to report. She had seen Rocky panic the thin man into the jaws of a gator, and then she followed King in his frantic dash to return to his own burned-out camp. She felt compassion for the dying fat man, but she had a grin on her face as King sat in the ashes sobbing.

She had told Igor and Flash to remain hidden down the trail until she got the lay of the land.

King finally heaved himself up, pulled out his gun, and aimed at the fat man's head. He changed his mind again, shoved the pistol under his belt, and turned toward the south. "Here I come, Casey," he muttered.

The dark form of a rattlesnake appeared in the shadow of a palmetto thicket. Igor made a valiant jump but the snake nearly caught him in the belly. The fangs squirted venom into the air as the open mouth struck a branch. It began to coil again. Flash rushed in, clamping the neck of the snake in his teeth. The snake was too strong. Flash let go of his hold on the neck of the snake, and jumped back before the snake could gather himself into a coil to strike.

The dogs heard the sound of a man crashing through the underbrush and retreated into the bushes as King appeared. The snake sensed the new enemy and tightened its coil, with head raised and beady eyes scanning the situation. Its heat sensors targeted King.

The snake lunged just as King heaved himself backward, just out of the reach of the fangs. He stumbled back as the snake was recoiling, pulled his pistol and shot twice. Both rounds missed. King turned and ran as the snake slithered the other way into the underbrush.

Kate followed King back to his camp, and lay in the bushes watching as he searched the rubble of his boats and camp looking for water, food, or ammunition. He found another bottle of whiskey in the flooded bilge of the burned boat. The boat was in only a few feet of water with the charred remains on the bottom, the sides, and some of the deck was only partly burned. He stumbled into the shade and gulped down the liquor.

In minutes he was passed out or asleep.

Kate met up with Igor and Flash, and asked them to take over spy duty until Buster sent them a relief. She was cautious and watchful as she trotted south toward the boat. She was exhausted but was formulating her report for Buster. She whispered with Cookie and then trotted to Buster.

The dogs sat in a semicircle with Buster in front of them as Kate finished her detailed report.

"That's about it," she said. "The thin man is dead, the fat man is about dead, and right now King is drunk and hasn't had food or water for a long time. He shot all of his ammunition and it sounds like he is going nuts." That big oak tree near the camp has about twenty huge ugly birds crouching on the limbs. Cookie just told me that they are called turkey buzzards, because they look like turkeys. They only eat dead stuff.

The dogs responded with grins and happy growls.

Buster said, "Well done, Kate. You have been a faithful friend of Leader, and now you need to take some time off to rest. Go to the boat and sack out on one of the bunks."

CHAPTER 26

I, Me, My, Mine

IS, IS

When Bart awoke, it was early and the grass around him was wet with dew but he seemed to be dry. He stroked his clothing, finding it dry and crisp. As a matter of fact, his khakis seemed fresh and his shirt clean. Raking his fingers through his hair found it well combed and the slick greasy feel was gone. Even his deck shoes were clean and polished.

Perplexity showed clearly on his face.

"Hi, Bart," the lanky Steward standing beside him said as he folded a towel, tossed it carefully beside Bart, and sat down on it. "The dew waters things, you know. We don't allow rain this time of year."

"How can you keep it from raining?" Bart asked, looking at the man's sharp profile. "By the way, no offense, but you look like that stone profile in New Hampshire, called the Old Man of the Mountain."

"No longer, it fell off the mountain some years ago—or so I heard. Besides, speaking of rain I didn't say that I wouldn't let it rain. I said we."

"Big deal, I, Me, My, Mine, Us, We. Who cares?" said Bart.

"The other guy may care. You used Us and We, one time each. You used all the I stuff four times, and put them all before Us and We. Never once did you say, You."

"OK, forget the rain and the I, stuff. We, You to be exact were talking about where IS, is, and You said it was where I was. So now I have some facts that may cause You, to give me, an explanation for Your, circular logic."

"OK, You do the talking and I will listen," the English Master said.

"Here we go! I saw a cypress tree growing on yonder hill and near it was a tamarack."

"So what?" the Listener replied.

Well, the cypress trees grow in semi-tropical swamps in the South.

The tamarack grows in northern swamps. Both are growing in this land of IS, and both are growing on a hill. A Jacaranda and a Giant Poinsettia are growing near a clump of Black Spruce. The two flowering trees are tropical and the Black Spruce is found in boreal forests, or high on a mountain in the Smokes, or in New England, or Alaska. I see a White Oak standing beside a Live Oak. The Live Oak belongs to the south, and the White Oak belongs in mountains or the North.

"Whoa! Are you jousting my title as an Arborist, sailor boy?"

"I'm just getting my lance ready. Try this. There is a Lilac blooming over there beside that wall, which is covered with ten shades of Bougainville.

And to top it off, I saw an apple tree growing fruit right beside an orange tree. That just isn't correct biology."

"Well, I certainly can't tell trees what to bear, but I hear that they all give fruit in their season. As a matter of fact, I am seeing a few green nubbins of fruit in your life. You need to speak to the fruit inspector if you have any more questions."

"I suppose you wear the Fruit Inspector hat too. Oh, well, never mind. I have a few more observations. I saw an armadillo sitting next to a porcupine and a giant iguana sunning on a rock next to a polar bear. Then there was a moose and a gray wolf talking to a parrot and eating papayas off a tree.

"It is all very confusing. I like things in their place. This land of IS, is a strange place, but I do have a very profound thought to share with you. I have thought it out and decided that no matter where I go I am an American, even if I visited China. I could even go hiking in the desert and still be a sailor. I could go to India and still be a Christian. It all goes with me to wherever I am, so, that is the land of IS." Bart grinned and slapped his chest.

"I hope the man with the big net doesn't hear your philosophizing or he will toss it over you and carry you off on the elevator to a warmer, lower level."

"Now you are scaring me," Bart replied with a serious note in his voice. "As long as the net man isn't listening let me tell you something else that is profound and personality shattering. I have discovered that the land of IS does not fit in a lot of little boxes to open one at a time. IS, is all the time. I have always put things in compartments and opened

them up as the situation dictated. Now I see that if IS, is everywhere, and all the time, I better clean up my act and enjoy being a citizen of IS, continually."

"Bart, it looks like you are stealing my philosophers' hat too. Let me just make one observation, and then you and I are going for a hike.

I believe you have found the kingdom of IS within yourself, so you don't have to worry about all of the externals. You just need to have a good relationship with the King and everything else will work out. Citizenship is a question of mutual choosing."

"Wait, wait," Bart said a little too loud for good decorum, "in feudal times a King who had the most knights took over your village and changed its name to his name. Suddenly the land of Nod became the land of Lash.

So what happened to IS?"

"That's just it," said the Historian. "It might be Lash on the outside but still, IS, on the inside. After all, life can be short and then you are back in IS."

"That really is comforting to know. I finally found IS, and if I lose it and someone kills me, Bingo, I am back in IS. What a great deal. By the way, I may have a bridge to sell you."

"Look, numbskull, the land of IS, is Love, Joy, Peace, Patience, etc., and Hope. Not the hope like 'I hope it doesn't rain,' but the Hope that means it is an assured fact. That's what the word really means. My Hope, my assurance is that the land of IS, is within me forever and no one can take it from me."

"Dear Preacher, Theologian, Christian Philosopher, etc., you know that I am a Christian and that I have asked him into my life, along with the Holy Spirit. So why all this talk about IS?"

"Sorry, I called you knucklehead, Bart. No, it is not the same. Most people 'have God in their lives,' but that is only a part of it. IS, is all reality within you. It is much broader and deeper. Of course, some argue over what reality is but it is the totality of your life, beliefs, fears, loves, and doubts. It is a total commitment that you are a resident of IS and a subject of the King."

"Oh my gosh! This is deep stuff," Bart said. "You mentioned a walk.

I will go with you on one condition, that you won't say another spiritual thing. Shift back to Sheep herder, or something."

CHAPTER 27

The Aeroplane Returns

Late in the afternoon the sound of thunder sounded inland. A few minutes later the bright blue sky darkened and the thunder increased in volume. Kate awoke on the bunk and yawned. She heard the thunder and a commotion in the cockpit. She sprang up the companionway ladder, and saw Red Rider and Rocky tugging at the sail which had hung in a great fold of canvas on the boom, held in place by the small lines that caged it. She understood the art of retrieving things and soon had the folds pulled out while the other two dogs pulled the canvas over Bart's recumbent frame.

They had just finished when the rains came. It flowed off the sail in streams into the cockpit. The scuppers drained it away. Katie lapped at the faintly salty water and called to Dutch, who was faithfully guarding the boat. He bounded into the cockpit and lapped at the pooling water.

Satiated, Katie found the nearly empty milk jug of water. She nudged it under a stream of water and watched it fill with great satisfaction. She was growing in knowledge, proud of herself, and no longer afraid.

Her three years in a cage had left her deprived of understanding a lot of things. She exulted in her new freedom when Bart's son rescued her, but was foolish. Now, all the recent experiences had matured her, and she felt adequate for the first time in her life and knew in her heart that she was doing her duty to her Leader and to the pack.

Red Rider and Rocky seemed indifferent to the rain as they tended Bart. Dutch was wet and beginning to shake from lack of food, which was very important to him. He knew that he was too fat, but also knew that the last couple of days had slimmed him down. Responsibility, alertness, and awareness had burned a lot of calories. He was accustomed to being taken care of with hours to sleep and lots of food to eat. This was a new experience.

He nudged open the bunk that held the sack of food, and he and Kate filled their bellies.

The storm passed. The pack emerged from the underbrush and sat on the damp ground of the Indian mound. They engaged in a group howl, just in case King was listening. The "pack of wolves" was still in the area.

Brilliant orange clouds, deepening to red at the horizon testified of the scattering storm clouds and the ending of the day. Bart had awakened after the storm, been supplied with water and several gnawed open sticks of jerky. A bit was missing and Kate was smiling. Later she covered Leader as he slept soundly. He did not hear the intermittent howling of the pack during the night.

All of the pack awoke at the same time. The sun had not yet risen, but the sound of an airplane was droning near.

"Everybody take cover," Buster ordered. "Rocky, cover Leader with the sail and hide in the cabin. The sound is like the other plane that belonged to the bad guys."

The plane did not bother with their area except to circle north of them, around the burned-out camp. It was the same yellow plane that had come the last time, circling several times as the occupants looked down.

"Look down there," said the observer, holding binoculars. "The boats appear to have all burned, and so has the storage shack and everything else."

"How about that thing near the fire ring?" asked the pilot.

"My god! It looks like Cotton, the fat guy that worked for the thin dude, Dingo, that ran the camp," replied the observer.

"They must have been attacked by one of our competitors, the DEA, ATF, or someone," the pilot muttered.

"Look," said the observer, "that's King waving his arms. What the heck is going on down there? It couldn't have been the Feds or he would have been captured. If it had been the competitors, King and Ding would be dead."

"No wonder he didn't answer the radio," the pilot said. "He was burned out. Probably one of the flunkies did something stupid."

"We need to get King some help."

"Well," said the pilot, "we can't land or talk to him. I'll wag the wings of this old aero plane to let him know that we see him, then head back to St. Pete and send one of his men back in a boat."

"The word is airplane—one word," said the observer.

"My daddy said 'aero plane' so that's what it is," the pilot said with a laugh. He flew them in World War II, and then for thirty years as a duster.

"He ought know what they are," the pilot said as he laughed.

As the airplane droned away north, Buster called the pack into the center of the mound. Kate, Dutch, and Red Rider joined them while Rocky attended to Bart.

"Listen up," said Buster, "I think we may get company and it won't be good. Red says that when men wiggle the wings of an airplane it is a signal that they understand what is happening. They know King needs help and will probably send a boat as that is the only way into here. Our efforts to save Leader have worked so far but a new bunch of killers will make it hard. Dutch, how long will it take for new men to get here?"

"Depends on the boat they have," Dutch replied. "If it is fast it will arrive before nightfall."

"OK, let me hear some suggestions," said Buster.

"Let's fight them off," said Frankie with another jump. "I want to see Rocky push another one into the mouth of a gator."

"We would all like to see that, Frankie," said Red Rider. "When new men arrive they will be heavily armed, and probably won't be as cowardly as the thin man and the fat man. On the battlefield, when guys go in to help their buddies they go hard and fast. I don't think we can hold the line."

Rocky jumped off the boat and trotted into the ring and sat before Buster.

"Leader just sat up and moved around a bit. I don't think He knows what's going on but I think he could walk some with help."

"I'm the tallest dog here," said Moose. "I could be a guide dog and he could hold on to me."

"I haven't said much," said Harry, "but I am tall too and could walk on the other side of Leader."

"I'm so white he could surely see me," said Lady. "I can walk ahead to show him the way."

"It looks like we are breaking camp by mutual agreement. Is that right, pack? I know you will follow if I say so, but it is important that we all agree and work together."

Every dog nodded. "OK," he continued. "Try not to trample down stuff or leave tracks. Sheila, you're the smartest. Follow us and try to clean up our trail."

Bart was stiff and his head still throbbed, but the pain wasn't bad.

Kate had managed to find a bottle of aspirin that she had seen him take many times. She gnawed the plastic top off and pushed it into his hand with her butting motions that she used when retrieving socks and shoes.

He took some pills and dropped the bottle in his shirt pocket. He seemed to be on automatic, not really aware of what was going on.

Moose and the white Collie, Lady, helped him off the boat, and within minutes he stood in the center of the clearing, gazing at the ring of dogs around him. He grinned and swayed on his feet.

Moose leaned against him and he reached down and grasped the hair at the huge dog's shoulders. Chinook took point, Lady followed him, and Moose and Harry walked by Leader. Rocky followed on Bart's heels, watching him carefully.

The smaller dogs had all volunteered as scouts. All had fanned out in an easterly direction, looking for high ground and a safe path. The larger dogs walked ahead, picking the path as reports filtered back from the scouts. In an hour they had moved a mile inland to a high hammock of palm trees. A tall pine stood in the center, Spanish moss draped from its sparse limbs, waving a welcome.

Bart was obviously exhausted, and appeared totally disorientated.

A halt was called and a place made for Bart to lie down. Rocky was ministering to him and placing the milk jug near his lips. Kate had faithfully carried the partially filled jug and lay panting and content in the shade of a young live oak tree.

"OK, pack," Buster said. "I have talked with some of the older dogs and we feel that we have moved about a mile, and should be far enough away that the bad guys won't know what to do for a while. I sent back Frankie to help Sheila check where we walked and to get rid of any of Leader's footprints, straighten up bent branches, and such. As you know, we took a crooked way around ponds, gator holes, and such. It will take some doing to find us."

"Buster, Leader is really exhausted," said Nurse Rocky. "He needs at least two hours to rest up, and then may be able to go another hour or so."

"Rocky, just let me know when we need to stop," Buster replied.

"My family hunted hogs, as you know," said Cookie. "Hogs don't go in a straight line. They make lots of jigs and jags and are hard to follow, because they walk in the water where you can't track them. I suggest we do the same."

"Good plan," said Buster. "You scouts take a break and then get back into the swamp and find us a way east. Make it hard to follow. I want two dogs to take the flanks and make sure that no one can surprise us from either side. The cleanup dogs behind us will alert us to anyone following."

"Where is the Saluki?" 'Buster asked. "The beautiful, skinny dog with the long nose?"

"She's shy," said Lady. "She usually hides in the bushes. I'll go find her."

Lady returned with the stately Attira walking behind her. Anyone familiar with Egyptian art would recognize her distinct look. She was tall, with a deep chest and narrow waist, long legs, long ears, and a beautiful feathery tail. Her nose was long and pointed and her eyes large and brown.

"Attira," Buster said, "you are fast and like to keep hidden. We need that. Your kin were hunters, so you know how to handle yourself around snakes and gators. I want you to backtrack to the bad men, spy, and return to us as soon as you have news."

"Thank you for letting me do something important. I'm up to your trust and I'm on my way." She turned and flashed through the swamp in long bounds, leaping up into the air occasionally to visually plan her way.

The dogs had been on the trail for an hour after the rest stop. Bart was walking better but obviously tiring fast. Much of the going was in thin water with rough coral and coquina rock below the clear surface.

Bart stumbled often, but stumbled on, a testament to his character, even if he didn't know what was happening.

Lady was taller than Harry, so she dropped back and took one of Bart's pockets in her mouth to steady him while Moose did the same on the other side. Rocky still followed behind. He watched Bart carefully, ready to do whatever was needed.

Buster moved to the back of the line and gazed at the trail behind.

There was no trail, just the reflection of sky on water.

A scout reported to Harry, who found Buster, and reported to him.

A large dry oak hammock with a sandy clearing in the center was off to the south about a mile. Buster gave orders to turn toward it and to have big dogs precede them and clear the area of dangerous animals.

So it was that forty-five minutes later Bart was led to the clearing and allowed to collapse on the warm sand. The habitual grouch, Flash, had faithfully carried Bart's blanket, and deposited it, somewhat wet, on the sand. Faithful Kate straightened it out to dry. She had watched Leader drying his clothes on the deck railing off their home, and had a glimmer of understanding as to the mechanics.

To everyone's surprise, Bonnie Lass showed up with the peanut butter jar, somewhat diluted with basset drool. Twinkles held a mouthful of jerky sticks, wet, but still in their wrappers. Bart was in for a feast for dinner.

Cookie showed up with the water jug.

Attira found the pack by moonlight, wet, muddy, and tired. "The new men have come by boat, three of them. One has a big tan looking hat, and one with tape on his nose. The fat man has died and something ate part of him. The bad man was making the two new men walk with him toward our old camp and the boat. I howled like a wolf and rattled the bushes. One new man shot a gun with many fast bullets but I was not in the same place. They went to the boat but found no brains, because the rain had washed away the blood and everything."

"The bad man wanted to put fire on the boat but they talked him out of it because it might draw attention. They are going to search the swamp tomorrow." She added a lot of detail about smells, sounds, and important dog information to her report as Buster listened.

"An excellent report," Buster said. "Are you up to going back about dawn to watch what they do?"

"Yes sir," Attira replied. "It would be my pleasure. I'm really excited about doing something positive and exciting. I never really contributed anything in life before now. I can't believe how good it feels just to serve."

CHAPTER 28-I

The Plum Tree and Politics

They both ate several plums and drank water from the spring in the meadow. They were lying on a grassy spot in the sun, surrounded by daisies.

"Let me say something positive before I go to asking question," said Bart. "Those plums were as good or better than the ones in a hen run somewhere, and sometime." Now, let me ask another profound question inasmuch as you probably won't answer anyhow. "Does heaven have Spicy Jerky sticks?"

"Is this another attempt to try and find out where you are? If so, why ask about Spicy Jerky sticks?" The Plum Farmer grinned as he didn't answer, and then asked his own question.

"You know something, for a while there I thought that you might be God. Now I know you aren't"

"Why don't you think that I am God?"

"Because you don't know that I taste Spicy Jerky sticks, and because I bet there are no Spicy Jerky sticks in heaven"

"Wherever this is, we have the best plums, the best apples, the best flowers, spring water, and trees. Why do we need spiced jerky?"

"But you still have no answer, my evasive friend."

"Some things are difficult to define, Bart. And by the way, just for your edification, I did notice the fragrance of Spicy Jerky on your breath.

Now sniff an arbutus or something and let me do my work."

"I would really rather talk," Bart said. "Now that's kind of unusual for me, wanting to talk. I mostly want quiet and really resent too much talk.

Most talk is nonsense and I have better things to think about. But let me ask a question, have you ever felt like someone was walking beside you?

I keep looking around while we were walking toward the spring but there was just the two of us, yet I felt someone on each side of me."

"Maybe it was a spirit guide," said the Plum Tree man.

"You must be kidding! You don't believe in spirit guides anymore than I do. That's New Age, Shirley McClain's 'Out on a Limb,' Edgar Casey—no kin of mine—or Moon or something else weird."

"Well then, how about angels, or cherubs, or maybe even the guy who said he would never leave you or forsake you: could be it was him."

"If it was him," said Bart sarcastically, "then I must be dead, because he is in heaven and this place doesn't have streets of gold."

"You know, Bart, I am a real nice guy, letting you lay down on my flowers, drink my water, and eat my plums, but all the thanks I get are more questions. Why not keep it simple and just be satisfied."

"Well," said Bart, "I know that someone once said to be content wherever you found yourself, but my brain just keeps making suggestions and asking questions."

"You must think that you are God, and are running the universe. You ask a million questions, mull them over and then decide if God has it right. Quite honestly, Bart, if you don't like it here there is nothing that you can do about it, until the next elevator headed down."

"Wow, the plums must have given you a stomach ache—you are a grouch all of a sudden."

"Why am I a grouch when it is you who wants to question everything? I think you better cool the questions and be glad for all that you have."

"I'm truly sorry that I am being a pain in the grass. I'm being like a secretary I once had. She always had problems and asked my advice over and over, and each time I told her the same thing. She invariably went away ringing her hands, still asking the same questions of everyone else."

"Bart, a lot of people don't really want a solution to anything. They just want you to hear their 'very unique' problem that 'you can't possibly understand'—not recognizing that the problem is familiar to everyone.

So many people strive for attention by thinking that they are unique and need special understanding. Of course, they are unique creations in one way, but they have similar emotions and similar problems like millions of others."

"Now you are a psychologist in a land with only one person," said Bart. "So what makes you an expert?"

"I believe you were thinking of me as a 'Rustic' some time ago," said the Farmer. "In a way what you say may be true if you mean plain and simple, but not uninformed about the real things."

"I will definitely concede that you are very informed about a lot of things, including my thought life. Now let me expound on my pet peeve.

I am sure you have met people who think themselves as elite. They think they have a better education, a better alma mater, better family, smarter, understanding the needs of the 'little people'. Well, I'm not one of them, but I do know a bit about human nature. That's missing with the elites.

They think they are so special that they don't recognize the good aspects of human nature in others, they only recognize the base characteristics of human nature, and of course, they are exempt from them. They only have the good stuff."

"They usually don't have a God, and if they do it's subrogated to themselves. They think that laws are for others and not for them. They have no absolutes—everything is pragmatic—changing to meet the situation."

Bart took a big gulp of air.

"Wow that was a 'proffessoritorial' pronouncement. I take it you don't like people who are different."

"Oh, I like peculiar people—peculiar because they actually believe in something real. As a matter of fact, you seem a bit peculiar using all those huge words," said Bart.

"So being real is the basis?" asked the Master Debater, kicking some dirt off his boots.

"No, you can be real bad," Bart, the lecturing professor said with a laugh. "What I am saying is that you have to find what bed-rock real is, and then stand on that. Bed rock is truth. One guy said that he was the truth, and I believe that. Wow," said Bart, "this is worse than calculus, or finding square roots. My head hurts."

"It's time for you to roll over in the grass, and smell the arbutus, and give me a chance to do some other work. There's other stuff going on besides just you lying in my field that's the truth."

"Wait," said Bart. "I went to a school that billed itself as Progressive and they thought that people educated their way were the 'elite' set apart to rule the masses who really didn't understand much. Why didn't I come out believing that junk after seven years of being spoon-fed?"

"Did you ever fit their mold?"

"Not really, most of the kids were really nice and the teachers too, but I came from a family short on cash. My dad managed a very upscale Inn but his pay was pathetic by today's standards. His boss paid my tuition just to get rid of me. Plus, I had spent eight years on the farm feeding pigs and chickens, herding cows, working hay, and that sort of thing. Plus I was good with an axe, and that set me apart from the Boston and New York boys."

"OK, but what do you think is wrong with Progressives'? They are just smart people who find their way into political leadership."

"Well, they think that the constitution is a living and changing contract.

Which it certainly isn't or if it was it would be worthless. They think that they know what we little folk need, that the rule of law is nonsense, except of course the ones they make. They believe that government needs to be big enough to care for the masses. It all sounds great if you want to live in a nest, and have mama government stuff things down your throat."

"It sounds like utopia to me," said the rustic with a smirk on his face.

And I bet they wish that Christians would fall off of the earth."

"Yes, they think that absolutes are for the narrow minded, and I guess they are correct. It sure doesn't sound like a democratic republic where the States have a big input to the laws of the nation. I grew up with the words of the founding fathers, got chill bumps when the National Anthem was sung and felt goose bumps when we recited the Pledge of Allegiance.

I memorized the whole Gettysburg Address. This new stuff is foreign to me.

Being politically correct is like a whitewash job—just one big lie. I like being called a WASP—white Anglo-Saxon Protestant. That's what I am. My black friend is my black friend, and the Jew down the street is a Jew, or just Joel. The neighbor friend Martin, with a herd of cows is a farmer. Mr. Messer, who drives dump trucks, is a truck driver. I just like it simple and understandable.

Being called what you are sure doesn't denigrate anyone. Do you really think that a garbage collector wants to be called a 'sanitary engineer'?"

"Well, Bart. I hate to be the one to break this to you but society has moved on from the practical to the ridiculous. Everything has to be blurred and indistinct. That way you don't have to make an explanation or to take

a stand, and right and wrong are just like cornmeal mush—which nobody knows anything about these days."

"We ate a lot of cornmeal mush when I was a kid."

"I'm sure you did and it seems to have planted your feet on solid ground. It's not being Poor, Rich, Republican, Democrat, Conservative, Progressive, Fascist, Socialist, Communist, etc. There is only one test and that is believing in the truth—and by the way, there is only one truth."

CHAPTER 29

The Wolves Close In

Shortly after the noon break as Bart and the pack were slogging through water-covered mud, Attira returned to report that the bad men were headed their way. They had no trail to follow but were basically headed east. Red Rider spoke with her briefly, and then she turned and dashed back through the swamp to resume her surveillance.

Red Rider reported to Buster. "Buster, it looks like these guys are trying to humor King. They think a gator pulled Leader's body off the boat and into the swamp. One guy has a pack with some food and water but not much. They have automatic weapons from what Attira experienced, and they are a mile or so west and north of us. They are slogging through grass and coral rocks, according to Attira. It's shallower there but is really littered with coral heads. Attira has had to stay in the water and below the level of the grass to keep from being seen."

"They won't find us anytime soon," Buster said. "Let's watch them till they camp or turn back, and then give them the wolf treatment after dark. We can send Frankie to entice some gators near their camp and see what happens. Maybe we can cause a bit of trouble for them. Get Flash, the grouch, to steal their supplies once they stop for the night."

"Buster," said Red, "Flash is, or wants to be, a good guy. He just doesn't know how to do it. He had a bad life before Leader and is just a bit warped.

He really wants to help and will be glad to accept the assignment."

"I'm not into therapy, Red, but I had it rough too, before Leader. I took two rides to the pound and my master wouldn't bail me out. I used the word 'master' because he was a tyrant and not a Leader. OK, I'll work with Flash. Look at Attira how she steps up to danger and responsibility when we all thought of her as just a gorgeous wimp."

"Bed, everybody down to get some rest," growled Buster. "We may be busy tonight."

Buster lay down in the sun and the discussion was over. Red walked away a few paces, growled Buster's orders and then lay down in a bit of shade.

"Leader ate two sticks of jerky," said Rocky excitedly as he trotted up to Buster. "He almost seems to know what is going on but really doesn't. If you know what I mean, but I can't really explain. He is cool, his wound is clean, he drinks water, and he expels it. It is his brain that is not functioning very well. He can walk better but can't talk. His eyes look like he is trying to get out—if you know what I mean. Not sure I know myself but I feel our Leader is in there."

"It's all kind of heavy, Rocky," said Buster. "I'm not into philosophy or religion but I know two things. First is that duty is a grave responsibility, and second is that religion is simply believing in Leader's Him. I can handle simple things like that. I don't want to muddle up things like asking why, to either thing. I just know because it's so obvious. You do things because you must, and you believe because you're not stupid. It takes real stupid not to believe. Simple is real."

"You run deep Buster," replied Rocky. "For me most of life is getting pets, and eats, and fun, and rabbit chases. I don't do much thinking. This nursing Leader is really bending my frame. Helping is a lot harder than getting helped."

Shortly after sundown Penny rushed into camp to report. She was wet, her coat full of twigs and mud but she was smiling. "We found the camp," she reported to Buster. "Frankie walked all around the edge and gators from everywhere have come to visit. They smell dog and we have about ten dogs in the bushes to give them lots to smell. We plan to send dogs out all around the camp and at a signal everyone starts to howl. Then the ones close in will howl a few minutes later. By the way, they don't know it but a Florida Panther is on the hammock with them. When the dogs begin to howl who knows what the panther will do."

As the moon rose in the east, the howling began. The men grabbed their weapons and shot into the night. The howling stopped.

"I guess we showed those buggers," King said.

"No problem, boss," the older one said. "Them animals is afraid of us."

Then the inner ring of dogs began to howl and the panther went into a panic, leaped from cover directly into the camp. She was on her way out of the hammock and nothing was going to stop her. But when she saw the dogs, she turned and leaped back across the camp, uttering a demonic sounding cry of fear and anger.

The men scattered and fired shots into the brush. The dogs howled again and the Panther screamed again. One man rushed to the edge of the hammock, stopped, and fired into the trees as two gators claimed their prize, one holding each leg. As the gators rolled and thrashed in the shallow water the man was torn apart. Others joined for a piece and soon there was quiet.

The dogs quietly made their way back to the hammock where Leader slept. They sat with Buster and gazed at the fire on the other hammock, where the three remaining men had made a huge blaze to drive back the darkness and the "wolves," and the panther.

"One down and three to go," said Buster. "That leaves King, and that new young guy, and the big one in the tan cowboy hat. Let's give them an occasional howl to keep them awake and make them afraid to come this way."

The men were in no shape to explore the darkness as they huddled next to the fire. Each time they dozed off a howl would jerk them awake.

When dawn came they were more tired than the night before and silently held their tin cups of coffee in their grimy hands. The dogs had silently returned to the hammock to report to Buster. One had remained.

"Boss," said one of the new men, "I'm heading back to our boat.

Gators got Fred and with all the thrashing there were many of them, and they may have a taste for us."

"If you head back you better move quick," said King, "because I plan to put a bullet into your back. You go with me and Cowboy or you're gator bait, too."

"It don't seem like a very smart move to me to keep looking for that insurance guy. You got no idea he came this way. Me and my buddy thought that a gator got him too."

"It's a feeling. I can feel him, and he's here somewhere. We keep going east. He would go east," said King.

As the men put out their fire Kate slid back into the brush to spy and listen.

King suddenly began swearing a vile spew of profanity mixed with the Leader's name. She couldn't take it and launched from the bush into the face of king, grabbing his nose as she passed. She landed in a lump, rolling head over heels. She tasted King's blood and was glad.

The new man fired a burst from his long gun. A round cut a furrow across Kate's side, the impact tossing her into the swamp. She sank into the water, too stunned to move. With an effort she found the surface with her nose and took a deep breath. It hurt really bad and blood was coming out of her. She began to sink into the mud.

The pack heard the shots. Dutch leapt into the swamp. Buster was calling him back. He wasn't listening and floundered on with only one thing in mind, to find Kate. Then Chinook was beside him, and beside him was Buster.

When they came in sight of King's camp a spray of bullets plowed the swamp around them. The new man was standing in the water, eyes searching for movement. He sighted Chinook and fired. The big dog dove for cover, and Buster dove down beside him. Dutch bounded on, splashing water and mud. The man took aim in the center of Dutch's huge chest.

"Snake!" shouted King.

The man glanced down into the yawning white mouth of a cottonmouth moccasin. He lunged backward, off balance as Dutch lunged his 125 pounds directly at his chest, the giant mouth closing on his throat. Dutch lost his grip on the man's neck, but the impact had sent the man sprawling.

His rifle spiraled out of his hands and sank in the mire. The snake had found its mark, as the man would soon realize as he began to die.

King ran back into camp to retrieve his rifle but was thrown from his feet by the hurtling form of Moose, 150 pounds of fury. The breath was knocked out of him, and he rolled in the dirt trying to breathe. His arm blazed with pain, useless at his side.

"To me," called Buster.

Moose bounded into the swamp.

"We have Kate," Dutch shouted.

"Keep down low, help us with her," growled Buster as Moose sloshed up to them.

Sharp teeth sunk into the loose skin of her neck as she was dragged forward. Three of her legs began to work as they pulled her into tall marsh grass and brush. She wanted to quit, she hurt, but they pulled her along until they climbed the sides of the palm hammock where their camp was.

She lay inert, eyes closed, and blood drenching her golden fur.

CHAPTER 30

The Awakening

Rocky was waiting and went to Kate immediately as she lay panting and colored with blood red mud. He cleaned the wound of debris. She whimpered with fear and pain until Bonnie, the only natural mother around, sat beside her and licked Kate's face to calm her.

While the medics did their thing, Buster circled the troops and issued instructions.

"We have a problem as you can observe. The bad men know exactly where we are now. Flash, I want you to sneak over to their camp and observe what's going on. You may have to fight your way over as every hungry animal within a mile knows about men torn apart, and dogs, especially a bloody dog, so be careful. This is your time. Maybe you were born for this hour, Flash."

"The rest of us need to make plans to move," continued Buster. "I want scouts out to find us a new place. I want the rest of you hidden in the bushes and watching in the direction of the bad men's camp. Let me know as soon as you see any movement."

"Red, move Kate in near Leader, and you and Rocky tend her. I want a report from you two on her condition. Dutch, you, Moose, and Chinook come over here by me."

The four big dogs sat side by side, looking through brush at King's camp. "I am of the opinion that we need to examine our mission," said Buster. "I think a surprise attack would take care of those guys. But our mandate did not include our killing the men. To be honest, I'm a bit confused."

"You know Leader's character," said Chinook. "He is really easygoing but has definite principles that he won't compromise. I doubt that he would shoot King if he had any chance to avoid it."

"So," said Moose, "you are saying that we need to keep fighting Leader's way. What we have been doing has worked really well so far.

Like we agreed a while back, we need to fight prudently first and bravely last. I think we are about up to bravery now."

"You are helping me think properly," said Buster. "My instincts are to act now and ask questions later. Leader wouldn't do that. He would think it out."

"Buster," said Chinook, "no one in our pack is ever going to question your authority. You say the word and we all attack to the last dog. It's your call, but by the same token, not one of us will question you if you have another plan. I personally like the idea of doing what we think Leader would do."

"So do I," said Buster. "He would look things over and weigh the options. As I see it, we have done well so far. Three men have died because of the swamp, we burned their camp and their boats, and Leader is alive and doing better. We only have one dog hurt in the process. We are winning by following our mandate from Him, so let's stick to it. We head east tomorrow and if King or his buddy get in the way we will deal with them as the situation dictates, prudence first and violence if necessary."

"You know, guys," Buster continued, "this is hard. A pack leader is usually only concerned with killing stuff to feed the pack. That's survival.

We don't worry about mandates, morality, and saving someone except by killing the enemy. I shouldn't even be talking to you guys or even making eye contact with you, just deciding, and killing you if you disagree.

"Being domesticated has made it real hard," continued Buster, "because it goes against the innermost dictates of the ages. When He is with us it is easy because we slip into His way because He is the Leader.

But now, on our own it pulls me in the opposite direction. I want to be like him but my paradigm is the pack, and not goodness and mercy."

"I know," said Chinook. "I am a wheel dog, all I know is working and eating. I pull my guts out and it's my whole world. Sheila is like me but smarter and faster. It's just the sled and the team—nothing else matters.

Now this takes a lot of thinking and it's so hard to do. There is something else in life that we are up against that we don't really understand. It's so hard to be changed."

"I'm stupid," said Moose. "My IQ is about room temperature but I know there is more. I want the window shade to go up and the light to come in. I see glimpses of it when we do good things and I know that Leader walks in some of the light. I understand, Buster. What we are doing is a new thing. We are awakening to something."

"You make my head hurt," said Buster, "but I know you are right. I was so safe with Him but that safety was Him and now I need my own, from somewhere else."

"Too much theology," said Chinook. "I like being a wheel dog, I like being part of the pack—being more is very difficult."

"Let's talk to Him and ask Him to show us more," Buster said with a sigh. His purple tongue protruded and wiped over his ivory teeth.

"We still have much to do and not much understanding to do it by. Now you guys go sleep. I'll wait for the report on Kate from our vets"

The report was good. The bullet sliced across her side but did little more than open up a twelve-inch gash. Rocky had cleaned it and the bleeding had stopped. She would be sore and limp but she could walk, and would heal if they could keep the wound clean. Buster went to her and without apparent compassion assigned her as constant attendant to Leader. He smiled to himself when she received the order gratefully, not realizing that he was trying to make her life easier while hurt. Even badly hurt she wanted to serve.

Before the gray of dawn had given in to the pink of a new day, Flash emerged from the swamp dripping water and slime. He shook himself.

He approached the sphinx-like shape of Buster and sat down a foot from his nose.

"Give me your report," Buster said sternly.

"Yes, sir. I spied all night and kept awake because the men were mostly awake too. They talked mean, said swear words, and slapped at mosquitoes. It was a bad night. I think King got his arm broke when hit by the flying leap of Moose. He is moaning and trying to hold the arm still. He won't even let the other two help him. Then the young one got sick and began to shake. When I left he was propped against a tree and I don't know anymore about him.

"They let the fire burn down to just coals. They were too afraid to go looking for wood. They were afraid of another attack and just sat with their backs to a palm tree. This morning King and Cowboy were itching themselves and I bet the jiggers were in their pants. They look dirty and mean, like their words. I know bad words and they said them all."

"Did they make any plans to find Leader?"

"I don't think they are in any shape to make plans. They are just living on hate. They didn't have any food to eat, because I dragged their pack away and something got it during the night. They are hungry for food but also for hate and revenge. King thinks Leader is responsible for all his troubles. He just eats hate and gets more hungry."

"How long can they live on hate?" Buster asked. "Does it fill their belly?"

"I've been thinking," said Flash. "I have been a grouch all my life.

I thought mother was mean just because I bit her a little while nursing.

My siblings were mean for grabbing all my food. My master really was mean when he hit me, because I growled when he was cutting my toenails.

Then I bit him. Now I see that it was mostly in me and in what I did and thought. I think I understand that King is blind to what is real. I think that will make him very weak."

"Flash, it sounds like you are awakening to yourself. Him is truth and we all begin to see ourselves in a pure light. Like me, I ran away, disobeyed, dumped garbage, ran from the dog catchers, and was mad when I got caught and no one came to get me. They were going to execute me if no one came. Then a lady came, fell in love with my big brown eyes and took me to Leader. The experience in the pound opened my eyes to me and my rebellious exterior. Just receiving her love and taking me to fields and creeks, and the freedom I had yearned for but that I no longer needed. It bent the kinks out of me and made me see what I had been and what I could be.

"The strength and loyalty of the ancient line of Chow in me, mixed with the quiet goodness of my loyal Labrador ancestors rose to the surface, and I was no longer just a scavenger, runaway mutt. When I recognized all that Him wished for me, it changed me inside. When Leader appeared I knew I belonged and had a mission to watch over him. I became what I was supposed to be."

"Thank you, sir for telling me, Buster. I've been redeemed in a swamp and you in a pound about to be executed. It is too hard to understand, but I like it." Flash smiled for the first time in years and lay down.

"We are going to move eastward as soon as Leader is up." Buster said.

"You hide somewhere and get some sleep, then be our rear guard. Come to me if the bad men start this way."

CHAPTER 31-I

To the River

My head hurts! I've been here thinking about God, life, business, and such. I've been thinking about bravery, prudence, evil people, and sacrifice, and my head hurts! Where did this muddle of thoughts come from? I had felt a terrible hurt on my head but the pain is just a dull ache now.

I rolled to my knees and gradually stood up. The field looked familiar.

Then I remembered the man who had talked with me, and who sat near me on the grass as we discussed so many things. I looked down but the grass was matted only where I had slept. I smelled the arbutus and looking down saw a small bouquet tucked into my shirt pocket: the tender flowers were wilting.

Suddenly the world began to fade and darkness was falling. I felt dizzy and sat down. Then there was total darkness. I felt around me. Something was different. The grassy field was gone. It was cold sand!

Something moved beside me and then a terrified scream echoed around the cavern. There was shuffling and scraping, and the screams continued.

Then there was a muffled thump. Then there was only silence.

I was in a cave. It came to me suddenly. Bill had been lying in the sand just a few feet away. We were exhausted, wet, cold, and lost. Our carbide lights had gone out and we had no refill chemical. Our flashlights faded to a tiny pinprick of light then extinguished. The darkness was complete.

The silence was broken only by occasional drips of water.

Memory flooded back. I was about twenty-four years old. This was supposed to be just a short outing to show Bill, my young preacher friend, what it was like to be in a cave. We were deep in the side of a Virginia mountain, in a mind-bending confusion of passageways and rock. Others had been there before us and used their carbide lamps to write with soot on the wall: "To the River."

We had traversed several hundred yards of the main entrance tunnels and through huge debris-filled rooms. We came to a clear spot and slipped out of our backpacks to rest and have a snack.

"To the River." To Bill who had never been in a cave it was a siren call to lure him on the rocks, but he wasn't as seasoned as Ulysses and he let the words sink into his soul. He had to see the river. How, he asked, could there be a river in a mountain? I had been to the river several years before but knew that it was a long way—many levels and passages below us.

I partially relented and agreed to go a short way, but not all the way to the river. I had recently had a knee operation and needed to take it easy. I suggested we leave the packs and the ropes and extra supplies behind, because we were only going a short way and then return and head home.

We descended a steep rubble slide for several hundred feet until we spotted another smoked message with an arrow pointing to a small hole:

"To the River." We skinned through the hole on hands and knees and sometimes on our bellies. It finally opened up to a small room and then another sooty message and a hole.

"No farther, Bill," I said firmly but he was already in the hole and only feet remained. We kept following the siren song of "To the River."

We could now hear the distant sound of rushing water. It acted like a personal challenge to Bill, who climbed and squirmed and twisted until the river flowed below us in a crack in the rock with vertical sides. The crack narrowed as we looked upward to where it disappeared into darkness.

Below us it widened out and the solid rock had been smoothed by many years of rushing water.

"Take a look and then we are going back," I said. "We shouldn't have come this far."

A smoked message on the wall said: "To the Falls."

"How could they get there to know there's a falls? The water looks dozens of feet deep and moving fast." Bill asked.

"They chimney walk," I replied. "You put your feet on one vertical wall and your back against the other, and just scoot along above the water. If you slip, you drown."

Before I could say more he leaned across the chasm and planted his hands on the far wall, and then walked his feet up on the other side, managed to turn himself right side up and with shoulders against the wall crab walked toward the falls. I followed like a sheep to the slaughter.

After that followed two hours of brutal challenge—a waterfall fifty feet high, a slide down a muddy ramp, and being catapulted through space into a deep pool of water. Our helmets went flying off, soaking the carbide, and making the lights useless. We were in total darkness in swiftly moving water, but my flashlight was still in my pocket and we found his shining in the water and retrieved it. We were soaked, cold, and exhausted, but guess what Bill said next.

"Let's follow the river."

Luckily the river ended in about a hundred feet. There was a large cavern about fifty feet across where the river ended as it swirled like a whirlpool and was sucked down through the floor of the cave to some lower level. We stood in the swiftly moving water near the entrance to the room. The water tried to pull us forward toward the circling whirlpool.

Bill was finally satisfied and we headed back toward the waterfall with our dimming flashlights. I had him shut his off and walk in front of me, and then climb the slippery ramp to the spout high above where the river became a waterfall. He made it but I didn't.

I got stuck ten feet from the top, because our traffic had slicked up the mud and there no handholds. I flopped on my belly as I began to slide toward the edge. Forty feet below was a pile of jagged rocks beside the waterfall pool. Slowly I was sliding toward the edge. I dug in my fingernails and tried to burrow my chin into the mud for a brake. My feet were in space.

Needless to say, I prayed. All I knew was the word, God, and I knew very little about Him. Bill was wide eyed and silent. There was no way he could reach me. My body was skidding slowly toward the edge. Rescue had to happen in minutes or I was a goner. I resolved that on the count of three I was going to make a valiant scramble away from the abyss or I was going to die on the rocks below.

"One, Two, Three," and I scrambled with fingers digging, nails breaking, and elbows flailing and just out of my reach was the tip of a stalagmite that neither of us had seen before. By now my knees were over the mud and I pounded them into the goop and lunged. My hand closed on the stalagmite and I pulled myself forward. I got my foot behind the stalagmite and by reaching up could just barely grasp Bill's outreached hand. Exhausted, I flopped on my belly on the ledge at the top of the falls.

I had lost my flashlight in the struggle so Bill followed as we chimneyed back, found the passageway upward, and climbed with an ever dimming light. We reached a sandy beach like a place that I recognized, I turned off the barely visible light from the flashlight, and sprawled on the sand in the darkness.

My knee hurt, I was wet, filthy, and cold. Bill was exhausted, wet, cold but excited—hardly believing what he had seen.

In fifteen minutes I tried the light but it gave only a feeble glow. I knew where we were and knew there was a small hole that led to the rubble slide and up to our equipment. We went together but couldn't find the hole. The light failed again and we crawled back to the sand in total darkness.

The light regenerated slightly. We kept if off and crawled to where we thought the exit hole was, turned on the light but it failed again. By feel we were back on the sand pile again. After a few minutes of silence, Bill let out a scream and bolted into the darkness.

There were holes in the floor of that room so deep that you could drop a stone and never hear it strike bottom. I hoped that Bill wasn't in one of them. I crawled on hands and knees, stopping to listen. Finally I heard a groan, found him in a hole about six feet deep and pulled him out with his help. For several minutes I had been calling without answer, so he had been knocked unconscious for a while. I guided him back to the sand pile in total darkness and we both stretched out.

In a few minutes Bill began to preach in a strong, resounding voice.

He prayed, called on God, spoke to Jesus, and preached a moving sermon about Jesus as the light in the darkness. It was so good that it made the hair stand up on the back of my neck.

Awhile later, I crawled in the direction where I thought the exit was, and after searching in vain, I put my head down on the rock to rest. A small trickle of air touched my cheeks. I crawled forward but touched only blackness.

The movement of air was stronger. I reached around and felt stone on all sides except forward. I was in the exit hole. Bill followed my voice as we crawled through the hole and climbed the rubble hill in total darkness. We found our gear and flopped exhausted next to our packs and supplies.

With fresh batteries, the bright light revealed that one of Bill's legs was drenched in blood, and he had a dark bruise and a lump on his head. We made it out with him having more and more trouble walking. I helped him down the mountain side and drove him to the hospital to be sewn up.

For weeks Bill preached on aspects of our fiasco. The congregation agreed that he had improved considerably as a preacher.

"So what did you learn from that experience, Bart?"

I opened my eyes and there stood my variously named New Friend.

With gratitude I surveyed the field, the tree, the birds, the animals, and even the bugs. The cave had been as real as on the day we were lost.

"The light in the darkness," I answered. "Without the light the world is a dangerous and scary place. But how do you know what I dreamed?"

He ignored my question but deep down I knew the answer.

"Well spoken. Anything else, Bart?" my Inquisitor asked.

"Yes," I replied, "I should have died three times and Bill should have died at least twice except for the grace of God."

"What do you think about Bill going crazy and rushing off into the darkness, and falling into a hole and being hurt?"

"He found out that he wasn't a prudent man and that his actions could hurt both him and others. He learned that his own desires could lead him astray. He found that at some point he could break and be stupid. He also found out that when he turned his eyes on the Lord, things began to get better and a way of escape opened for us."

"So you are saying that bad things can be used for good?"

"Well," I answered, "that experience changed both of us. But you know what, the main reason it worked was because we both knew God.

Well, at least I knew him a little bit, enough to see his hand revealed in the darkness. Someone who didn't know God would either take credit himself, or say it was just good luck, karma, or anything other than God."

"So how did you like that stalagmite that gave you a handhold?"

"There you go again knowing stuff you haven't been told. But I will say this, it wasn't there when we slid down that mud bank. I've given that a lot of thought."

"So tell me this," my tall Friend with boots and calloused hands asked. "If something very dangerous was happening to you without your knowledge, how do you think it would affect you?"

"Well, Preacher, Gardener, Watcher, New Friend, I know the answer.

Try Romans 8:28, 'All things work together for good to those who love God and are called according to his purpose.' After my experience on the beach I know that God—Jesus—has a purpose for me so everything will be for my good, even if it looks bad."

"Well spoken, Bart. Let's take another walk around the field together.

The ground is very rough and wet here but we need to keep going to get to a smoother area. Just stick with me and keep on trucking."

Bart looked down as he got up. "I think my feet are wet already!"

CHAPTER 32

Metamorphosis

Just as the sun was in the center of the sky Flash reported to Buster.

"King and his buddy came to our last camp about three hours ago. They found one footprint of Him, and tried to track you guys. They went straight when you turned south and are in water up to their knees. King is blaming everything on his buddy and Leader."

"Thanks," said Buster. "Go and tell Sheila to come to me. You get some sleep while we take a few hours to let Leader rest."

Sheila cautiously approached Buster and sat down. Her sleek gray coat was somewhat tangled but she was still sleek, slim, and graceful.

Her eyes were alive and ever vigilant.

"Sheila, we need you to follow the bad men. Flash will tell you where he last saw their trail. Stay back and try to find solid ground if you can.

They are wading now and headed east. If you need help give your wolf howl and I will send dogs to work with you. Keep out of sight because they have guns."

Sheila nodded, turned, found Flash, and then was away with her body stretched to match her flying feet.

Frankie bounded over and skidded into Buster. Harry was sitting beside Buster, his mate Bonnie Lass beside him. Their daughter, Twinkle's sat in the shade of a palm several yards away.

"I need to go with Sheila," he said jumping up and down on stiff legs.

"I just can't stand walking along in line like a camel. I need action."

"A small camel," said Harry.

"An energetic camel," said Buster.

"I'm sure, glad he wasn't my puppy," said Bonnie Lass. "Can you imagine a whelp of jumping jacks all wanting to nurse? It would drive me crazy. Basset puppies are docile by caparison."

"Please, please, let me go," Frankie begged while doing his spring-loaded jumps.

"I guess you missed those twenty or more gators we passed this morning," said Red who had walked over and stood by Buster. "Luckily they were still cold from the night. If you went out in that saw grass and water by yourself you would be swallowed whole in minutes."

"Look," said Frankie. "I wasn't nice to Leader. I lived in his house and ate his food, but bit him on the ankle every once in a while. It seemed right at the time, but now I see him hurt I feel really bad. I have been full of myself and usually don't think of anything but me and my mouth that keeps barking. Walking with you guys and keeping quiet has done something strange to me. I see you guys doing stuff so quietly, and thinking about stuff. I never thought about anything. Thinking hurts and makes you change. I thought I was the top dog, as big as an elephant, ready to prove it. Now I'm just a little dog with a lot of limitations and it bends me.

Being in a pack is hard unless you submit and that is really hard. I think I'm learning but I still want to do what I want to do—understand?"

"Frank," said Buster," you are about to become a dog. You just never learned to be a dog. You thought you were a human and I bet you always tried to warp them to do what you wanted to do. When you understand the pack you find freedom in being what you were designed to be."

"Hey," replied Frankie, "I want to be me. I like me most of the time and don't want to be something I don't want to be or do anything I don't want to do."

Buster lay down with his legs stretched out fore and aft, one front foot curled over the other and his chin resting on them. He gazed intensely at Frankie. "There is just one problem with your theory of independence, Frankie. First, you are a dog, and second, you are in my pack. Both of those realities limit your options. Not even mentioning that you have a big ego and a small body."

Chinook slowly got to his feet and then sat down on his haunches, "We all have to learn to live with a few limitations, Frank. A team is even tighter than a pack, so I have had my share of experience. As I see it, like Buster said, you have four things to consider when you are thinking that you are an elephant. First, you are a dog—more than that, a dog in a pack. Then there is your big ego and the small body. You can be anything you want to be just as long as you work within those four realities. We all have realities to work with, not fight against, or rebel from, but to work with."

Chinook lay down with crossed feet like Buster. He was exhausted and a bit surprised by his philosophical rant.

"I guess it is easier for bassets," said Bonnie Lass."You know we sleep in a pile and can't tell whose tail is in your ear. You could put about six of us in the backseat of a car and we would just lie on top of each other and sleep, and no one gets upset about anything. We are kind of like just one instead of many, but we each still have our own personality. It is kind of a mystery."

"Oh my gosh," said Red. "Here's more philosophy to make my head ache. You guys are really stretching me. I was happy just being courageous and strong. This deep thinking stuff is new. I never even worried about getting killed in action. I just did what I knew to do and then had dinner."

"Frank," said Buster. "No one wants to take away your individual initiative, your gifts, abilities dreams, etc. We just want you to work within the framework of where you find yourself. You are free to walk away and be whatever you want, and do it on your own. Possibly you will do something wonderful. However, even the broad term of being an American has restrictions and beliefs to live by. If you don't like it you can move and call yourself anything you want to. But if you want to be an American, you need to follow the basic precepts of a Constitutional Republic. You need to understand the founding Constitution. You don't have the right to change my system in my land. If you are in the pack you follow the rules of the pack. It's not slavery, it's liberty!"

"I think I'm beginning to get it, but it is way too big a bite to swallow all at one time. I plan to think about it a lot," said Frankie. "For starters, let me be the lookout and watch and listen for Attira. That way the pack can get some decent sleep and be ready for action."

"I believe he's getting it," said Buster as he rolled to his side and stretched out.

CHAPTER 33

Where Does It Come From

Bart was exhausted by the walk and his head pounded. His New Friend took his elbow and helped him up to some higher ground. They sat down on a dry rock.

"Bart, you haven't said much about yourself or anyone else except the preacher and your experience in the cave. Just for the fun of it, let's pretend that you have a farm on the side of a mountain. I come along and ask you if you have a brook and you say sure, and take me to the edge of it. How much do I know about that brook after looking at it for a few minutes?"

"You know it is small, fairly shallow, full of stones, and must be on a slope because the water babbles as it goes—and it's wet."

"Where did it come from? By just looking at it can I tell where it came from or where it is going?"

"No, not unless I tell you that it came from up on the mountain to the north of us. I think it starts with some small seeps from the mountain and they gather together little by little and make a stream."

"Does it just wander around up there in a field just meandering around without direction?"

"No, it's all steep ground, so it digs in and makes a gully to follow. It follows the low spots. You can see here that it has cut a really wide and deep gulley."

"Where does it go from here?"

"The one you're talking about is Murray Creek, and down a little ways on my property it is joined by Fines Creek which was joined by another creek that comes out of the Roger's property, and it had been joined by who knows how many creeks and seeps as you follow it down the mountain."

"Then what happens?"

"It goes down about ten miles, joining other creeks and then dumps into the Pigeon River that flows down the gorge to Tennessee."

"Where did the Pigeon River come from?" he asked.

"It has two starts. One starts up high on the west side of Cold Mountain and one on the east side, the East Fork, and the West Fork.

They meet all kinds of creeks and go for thirty miles or more before the Fines Creek joins in"

"From where did all that information come? I didn't think you knew much except for flowers and peanut butter."

"And dog breath. Don't forget the dog breath. I don't know. Kind of like all this other stuff I have seen, it is all sort of familiar and just leaking out."

"OK, so let's say that you are just a seep up on the side of the mountain. How did you get big enough to be Fines Creek, and how did it get big enough to be Pigeon River?"

"Everything just added together. But listen, if you are trying to tell me that we all flow together and become one body of water—I'm not buying it. That sounds New Age, you know, everyone becoming part of the continuum—whatever that is."

"I agree, Bart. I think it's like homogenized milk—everything just the same. Let me put it this way, you are born stupid and hopefully you die smart. Getting from dumb to intelligent was like a seep to a river. There is a lot of input along the way. Jerks think they are smart, and flip off everything around them, and remain stunted all their lives. What is most important is that you get a dose of wisdom along the way. Being smart without wisdom just makes you a useless intellectual."

"Why this lecture? Do you think that I am messed up?"

"No, Bart, not at all. You have done very well in the character department and have developed a rudimental body of wisdom. I just think you need to put a little more effort into the wisdom areas. It's not that you don't have all the parts that make wisdom, it is just that you don't seem to recognize it." Wisdom isn't easy to obtain. It is built on knowledge, experience, and intelligence, but you have to take the time to mull over that stuff and find sense in it.

The wise man continued. Two guys were riding in a car when they ran into a storm. When they arrived at their destination a friend asked one man if they had been in a storm. He replied that they had some rain for a while. When asked the same question the other guy said that it had been a heavy electrical storm. He said that the wind was strong from one direction and suddenly changed, and came from the opposite direction just as a heavy cloud blotted out the sun. Lightning bolts were striking around us even before the rain came. Then there was a deluge and heavy gusts of wind blowing the small branches out of the trees. Streams of muddy water flowed onto the road. We had to slowdown to a crawl, because the wipers couldn't clear the water fast enough for us to see the road. We finally pulled off and stopped like hundreds of other people had done.

Finally, it was over and the sun came out.

"Now," Mr. Wisdom continued," which man gained some weather wisdom, the guy that just shrugged it off or the guy that experienced all of the details? "

"I would say that that is a no-brainer," Bart replied. The one guy just let all the facts roll off his back like a duck, and the other guy absorbed them."

"Yes," said the Philosopher, "but there is more to it. Lots of well-educated people are very short on wisdom. The trick is that you have to consciously seek for wisdom. You have to learn to connect knowledge, and then manipulate it to answer questions that the knowledge alone can't answer."

"OK," said Bart. "I get it. It's the old adage that the whole is greater than the sum of the parts."

"That's it," said the professor." Wisdom makes more understanding than the facts you know. Wisdom doesn't intend to offend, but sometimes it does. It's taking what you know, and making it usable. Wisdom makes things work. Wisdom is something to seek after, and its foundation is The Truth. How's that for a rant? "

"I appreciate your intense concern, but why do I need wisdom in a field of flowers and animals and one very intrusive Gardener."

"You know a lot of stuff and are reasonable bright but you don't go very deep. You haven't given me one clue about what you feel about things, and you don't talk about anybody. You probably have friends and family, planning your funeral right now and you haven't said a word."

"Now we are back to feelings again. I hope a woman gets off the elevator at the wrong stop one day, and you can talk feelings with her.

My dad left a bookcase full of journals when he died. My mother took an afternoon thumbing through them and never found herself mentioned even once and found no feelings. She put the books on the shelf to collected dust.

"You seem to have some feelings about that."

"Well, at least he mentioned me once. 'Bart came home from school in a heavy rain.'" "I knew Dad had feelings and could tell his reaction to things. I loved him but maybe I shouldn't imitate that closed part of him. How do you recommend developing feelings?"

"It's that nut we talked about that needs cracking. You can't get to the meat without cracking the shell and being vulnerable."

"OK, Mr. Psychiatrist, you may be right but I resent your intrusion.

Speaking of intrusion, how did you know about a brook in back of my house?"

"Look, Bart, I don't want to insult you but you have been lying around in my field for a long time and you don't really belong, and your ears don't hear. Possibly you got off the elevator at the wrong level. I am just trying to give you something to think about on your ride to wherever level you are assigned." The Philosopher chuckled.

CHAPTER 34

It's Hard to Trust

Attack!

King and his man had circled wide and began to close in on the procession of dogs. There was no sign of Casey but he had to be there somewhere. The gators were thick and seven buzzards sat in a dead oak, surveying the swamp below them. King was watching from a small hammock with only one big oak and several palmettos, surrounded by cabbage palms and mangrove.

"Buster, sir," said a wet Flash. "Frankie and Igor have spotted King and his buddy closing in on us. Lady has taken Leader south to some higher ground. Attira is with them as guard and runner if they need help.

You should see her smile. Rocky is nursing both Leader and Kate."

"King has one man with guns," Flash continued. "This is a big guy with a cowboy hat and real pretty boots that are covered with slime and squish when he walks. What we need to do is stop him because he looks strong and mean. Right now they are on a small island near here."

Moose and Chinook stepped forward. "We are ready, sir. Just say the word and we attack."

"No," said Buster. "It is not right that we should attack King now. If we really trust Him, Him, we need to be patient and see what he does, or what he tells us to do."

"How do we know his voice?" Chinook asked. "My mind hears only one voice and that is to kill these men who want to hurt Leader."

"Following is hard," said Buster. "Waiting is hard. But if you trust, you have to wait. We are not allowed to kill these men so either Him, Him must kill them or somehow deliver them to something that will. It's very confusing, but when you need to hear His voice, you will hear it."

"I am a follower," said Chinook. "I trust my Leader but a leader you can't see is hard to trust."

Harry stepped forward, his white and black spots gleaming in the sun.

"You need some history to really trust." He sat for a moment. "I know Buster and Moose and my own family, but how can I trust Him, Him when I don't really know him as a leader?"

"Leader knows him," said Buster. "I have heard him talk to Him when the apples are ripe, 'the sky is blue and the smell of grapes and blueberries are on the air.'"

"It's more than that," said Red Rider. "Soldiers pray and believe, when they know they will probably get killed."

"Him, Him isn't logical," said Bonnie. "You think He will save you and then you die. Why? It's because He is different than us, or humans. It is his world and He does things differently because he has another plan."

"Then why follow Him?" Igor asked. "Why follow when you don't understand?"

"Do you follow me?" asked Buster.

"Sure," said Igor. "I can see you and know that you are my pack leader."

"Do you have to see me? What if I ask Red to tell you what to do?"

"Yes," replied Igor, "because I know your authority."

"Do you know His, His, authority?"

"Yes," answered Igor. "I know in my heart that He is real, because I am beginning to feel Him. Let me tell you something else I just remembered. When Leader left me on that mountainside when I had hidden myself, I knew I was to follow even though I didn't really know him. I just knew I was to follow. It's the same with Him, Him."

Dutch stepped forward. "I have known Him most of my life but I don't think as deep as you guys. Is something wrong with me?"

Buster replied, "Dutch, you have been busy with life, getting loved, running cows, challenging other dogs, swimming in creeks, and walking with Leader. You have been so full of life that you haven't taken time to think about anything. Dogs need to get lost, or hurt, or hungry, to begin to think."

"Well," Dutch said, "I'm thinking now. Seeing Leader hurt and the bad men trying to kill him makes me think. I see evidence of another leader, of Him, Him. No disrespect, Buster."

"None taken," said Buster. "I am just an interim Leader and am just learning to hear His, His, voice too."

"It's more than just doing the right thing," said Twinkles. "The vet said my leg would never heal. I was a cripple as a pup. They prayed for me even though the vet wanted to put me down. Leader's Him gave me a new leg joint and I am healed. I didn't do anything right, I didn't know what right was."

"He just honored you with a healing," said Bonnie. "It isn't about you, it's about Him."

"That's hard," said Igor. "I see your point but my life is me, me, my, my. I'm the center. I'm what it is all about. Now that I am fighting for Leader things are cracking and I am getting smaller. It is hard."

"Enough, enough," said Chinook. "My head is exploding. I got my foot stuck in a foxtrap. It had iron that dug into my leg and wouldn't let go. I did not bark but I did howl, I was way down in the woods and master walked near me, but didn't see me because I was excited but quiet. His dad came the next day and found me, and opened the trap. My leg was hurt badly, but why didn't Leader find me? Why did I have to stay in the trap another day? It wasn't Him's fault, and it was me who stepped in the trap and me that didn't tell Leader. Now I know that Leader loved me, his dad loved me and Him, loved me. It was me that caused all the trouble. I wouldn't call out."

Everything was quiet.

"This is hard," said Red Rider. "When men got shot on the battle field they all called for God. I guess that is the name of Leader's Him. Not one asked why. They got changed because most had never gone so deep."

"I know the feeling," said Buster. "None of us will be the same after this. This is our first experience of asking why, and who."

"I am the biggest one here," said Moose. "I should feel Him more but it is so hard. Leader let a neighbor girl take care of me for a week and she didn't know my chain was tangled and couldn't let me get to the water dish. After a day or so I howled and neighbors swore at me and threw sticks at me. It was terrible but Leader's Him, came to me and let me sleep. It changed me, but I don't see clearly yet."

"They're coming! They're coming," shouted Flash. He ran with head and tail erect for nearly the first time in his life. He sat in the circle with head held high, giving his report to Buster.

"The bad men are only a hundred yards from us and headed this way.

The new guy wants to quit, but King is charging on and even the snakes and gators get out of his way, but I won't," said Flash with a growl.

"We have had a time for thinking, but now is the time for fighting," said Buster. "Get low and get under cover. When I begin to howl you all join in. Then we rush them. Dutch, you lead the attack."

King sloshed out of the everglades swamp and onto the dry ground of the hammock. The new man was a hundred feet behind, holding his rifle across his chest.

The howl came suddenly as the dogs leaped from hiding and rushed toward King. Dutch led the pack, Buster, and Chinook a step behind on either side. Three hundred pounds of dog struck King simultaneously and he was catapulted back into the swamp. The huge Lab had a death grip on King's throat. Something also struck King's shoulder a blow. King somehow got his feet under him and in spite of the hot pain in his shoulder pried open the great jaws of Dutch and clubbed him with the rifle butt. He reversed his rifle, aiming at the Lab who snarled with lips pulled back with gleaming teeth coated with blood.

The new man had watched as three balls of fur hurtled toward King.

Another came in low and mean. He fired at the dogs, missed and hit King.

King pivoted with the impact of the bullet and the impact of the dogs.

The new man took aim again at the black dog that appeared ready to launch at the wounded King. The Husky was circling behind King and ready to spring, teeth bared in a terrible snarl of passion.

As Cowboy sighted on Dutch, a Python swung a wrap of its body around Cowboy, deflecting his shot and pulling him screaming into the swamp. There was a thrashing and writhing of man and snake as the huge mouth opened and began to swallow Cowboy, head first. In a moment all was quiet and Cowboy's hat floated on the water.

"Fall back." Signaled Buster. "Everyone circle south and meet up with Leader."

No dog wanted to give up the battle but all obeyed except for Dutch.

He stood over King with his huge jaws just inches from King's face.

King's neck was bleeding profusely as he lay in the swamp, his rifle well out of reach. King's shoulder was bleeding too and his face grimaced with the pain of the gunshot wound. The deflected rifle shot by Cowboy that was meant for Dutch, had struck him in the shoulder. One arm lay at an unnatural angle, broken the night that the panther leaped through his camp.

With stiff legs Dutch backed away from the ruined man. The carnage of war was sobering after the adrenalin of attack. He turned, and joined the pack.

King dragged himself from the swamp and up on to a sandy mound.

He had retrieved his rifle and used it as a crutch to lower himself to the sand. He lay back only semiconscious from the brutal pain, blood leaking from his shoulder and from his crushed throat.

A hawk flew circles overhead, attracting a coven of huge, ugly turkey vultures looking for a warm dinner. When King sat up they lifted off ponderously, looking for a dead dinner.

CHAPTER 35

Truth and Contention

Bart was sitting beside the Game Warden as they finished an inspection of the wildlife. The rock they were sitting on was warm and seemed soft—a bit strange for a rock, but Bart was getting used to such things.

"Tell me, Mr. Game Warden, why are things so comfortable around here? This rock I am sitting on seems soft and kind of warm. I noticed your rock seemed to squish a bit as you sat down. Really strange, even for Is.

"I was sometime, someplace, in the Bahamas, or somewhere in the Caribbean, a few times for some unknown reason. It was a steady eighty-five degrees day and night, and the breeze was always blowing.

At first, I thought it was heaven, but soon tired of the sameness and the constant press of wind. This is a different kind of paradise."

"You don't seem to be too positive about exactly when or where you were, so I really can't comment. We have rules here, Bart. There is a legal limit to the snow—winter is forbidden before December and must depart by March the second. By 8:00 a.m., the fog must disappear, and by 9:00 p.m. the moon must appear. Surely, there is not a more convenient spot for happy ever-afters than here . . ."

"Oh, oh, you have just plagiarized some lines from Camelot. Don't you have copyright laws here?" Bart acted dismayed.

"Here we go again, you liked my rendition of Higher Ground, and didn't complain at all. Now, I challenge you to find Camelot on a map.

If it doesn't exist, then I can't be breaking any laws, right?"

"So now you are a Cartographer," said Bart. "I don't know if there is a real Camelot or not, but I bet your map won't show one."

"Whatever my map shows it will be the truth, whether you like it or not. The guy that said 'what is truth?' wasn't me."

"To try and answer that logic would take all day, so let's forget it.

Besides, I see no evidence of snow to measure and no evidence of winter at all. I was trying to compliment the weather here and all I get in return is obscurantism. So how do you like that word my Rustic Friend?"

"I am not opposed to the spread of knowledge, Bart. How do you like that answer?"

"Truce! I have the very sure feeling that you have swallowed all twenty volumes of an encyclopedia and probably the thirty pound, 1950 unabridged Webster's Dictionary. It is fun trying to cross foils with you, but I now know that I have no hope of prevailing. Actually, it is kind of neat to relax, have a good time, and not have to worry about competition with you. I have some friends and acquaintances that contend with everything, thinking that what they believe is reality. I never got into that because my father was a Connecticut Yankee, firmly grounded in reality I prefer to yield to irrefutable evidence, whether I like it or not."

"Thanks, Bart. Contentious people who always contradict you and demand the last word are at heart, rebels, whether they know it or not. No one can work with a rebellious heart. Contentious people are usually very opinionated, and when you disagree with them they brand you as making hate speech or are lying. They just can't stand a disagreement based on truth and logic. It's just a futile effort for them to retain their own identity, as faulty as their view may be. It's a fact that contentious people don't have many friends and usually don't have a good job, or marriage. In a way we need to contend for what we believe, but not contentiously. You and I understand who truth is and that we know the way, but we need to use wisdom about who we share it with."

Bart thought a moment and then replied. "I guess you know that in my heart I don't want to contend with anyone about anything. I would just like to live here in this field. I wasn't too sure about you in the beginning but have come to really appreciate your presence. Unfortunately, I feel like I am about to be pushed out of the nest."

"Not yet, Bart. I have really enjoyed our time together. You haven't lost your reputation as a nice guy but I think the wider view has given you a little more backbone. Pragmatism may get a job done but if you think about it, it's not really the truth. There is no way you can get from A to Z, the Alpha to Omega, without straight line truth. In pragmatism you

determine the end result, and then do anything you need to do to get there. The idea being that you can lie and cheat, because your end goal is the best for the little people. By their definition they are right, and you are wrong, by virtue of their education, family, organization, ideology, etc."

"You know about the 'unbroken chain of evidence' that a court of law requires? Your life requires an unbroken chain too. The claims you handle can't be settled with pragmatism, Life can't be lived with pragmatism, the end does not justify the means. No one can prosper who believes that. It sounds good but in reality it can't work. You can't depart from the truth to gain a truth. Every link of the chain has to be true."

"This is deep, Counselor. In my heart I know that it is true, please know that the saying we had in my office about letting the chips fall as they may, implied truthful reporting, no matter the consequences. However, letting the men do whatever was necessary was a cop out. You can't do what is necessary if it isn't truthful. Our intent was to be completely truthful.

Gosh this is hard to explain."

"How about 'the truth and nothing but the truth' like one TV show repeated every episode?" the Moralist expounded.

"That sound like a good philosophy but why are you talking to me about this stuff?" Bart asked. "I don't even understand some of my answers. Things just come out of the fog and then duck back in. I came out of the tunnel and don't have a clue of what was before that except for the bright light. I don't know why this whole place smells like spiced jerky, peanut butter, and basset drool."

CHAPTER 36

Rest Stop

The dogs guided Bart to a small hammock and let him rest on the warm sand. The heavy marsh grass to the north of their path had given way to a lake of black open water. They deviated to the south, to keep in the shallower and reed-filled water: then climbed up onto the small hammock. The ground was two feet above the swamp, punctured by hundreds of cypress knees on the edges and into the water. The cypress trees towered two hundred feet into the air with a few Spanish moss-draped limbs moving in the breeze. One monster had its top broken out but the trunk supported small limbs that fed life to the tree. Their base was fourteen feet or more around with supporting roots formed into the tree and burrowing into the ground, pushing up knees by the hundreds. The trees were huge at the base, ribbed with buttresses, and tapering to a round trunk that carried high into the tree.

Huge golden spiders clung to their webs that spanned between the trees. Where a tree had fallen into the water a row of turtles sunned themselves, while an eagle soared high above looking for a meal.

Around the giant cypress, cabbage palms seemed short by comparison sporting heads of frowns. Palmettos, pepper berry bushes, and mangrove struggled for a hold on the island. The white droppings of seabirds whitened the scrub growth, and rank grass with protruding runners matted the ground with sandspurs. A few bleached animal bones attested to the reality of life and death in the everglades.

Dutch stood beside Buster as they surveyed the swamp for any evidence of King. To the north was a wide expanse of black water with thousands of coots, flamingos, and cormorants. Each of them was busy, paddling around, ducking for food, and apparently enjoying life. A dog splashed into their world. The birds roiled the water with their takeoff and climbed into the air, and circled. Satisfied with the threat they one by one descended to the water, ignoring the splashing dog.

"Dutch," said Buster. "See that tree over there with the big green things growing under the frowns. That's a coconut tree. If we knew how to open the green things, we could feed Leader some good food. We are low on peanut butter and jerky. All we can do is feed him some raw crawdads. I don't think he would like uncooked frog legs, but I have seen a million frogs. Honestly, I wouldn't eat one myself."

Cookie arrived amid a splash of water, setting the cattails waving as she ploughed through them. She shook off the water and slime before she approached the other dogs.

"I saw you guys looking at the coconuts. No way we can get one down or get one open if we did. You mountain dogs don't know it, but a man could stay alive just eating the 'hearts' out of those cabbage palms but it would take an axe. That's out too. One thing we could do is pull some of the hearts out of the palmettos. You can eat the white tip off and get a little nourishment. Let me give it a try and show the doctor dogs how to do it too."

As the dogs talked, a flock of noisy green parakeets swarmed through the trees, sounding like the aviary at a zoo. One or two parakeets are just fine but a thousand of them are just a cacophony of sound. The dogs looked up and barked simultaneously. The flight of birds flew off to another hammock.

Buster looked over at Bart, who was lying on his back, eyes open, and a smile on his face. Buster looked up in the direction that Bart was looking and saw the expanse of blue sky, and the puffy summer clouds drifting by. For a moment he thought he saw a face smiling down at them.

Then the cloud changed and moved on. He was sure that he recognized the face.

Attira bounded toward them and sat beside Buster with water dripping off her body. She wasn't breathing hard and seemed to be smiling.

"Buster, the bad guy is lying on a hammock about a mile back. He looks exhausted from wading, slipping on coral, and watching for gators and snakes. Another big Python is slipping through the saw grass toward him. His body is very bloody and one arm doesn't work. He tries to talk but just squawks like a duck."

One by one all of the dogs gathered on the small island, wet and panting.

"OK, pack, King is hurt bad and lying on a cypress hammock about a mile away. You probably heard that the man called Cowboy got swallowed by a python.

It looks like we are winning with all the bad guys dead except for King.

We can't afford to let down our vigilance, so I want you all to take two hours off and then we will move on to widen the distance from King just to be on the safe side. Attira says that a python is stalking King, so we don't want to distract him. It must be the mate or buddy of the one that swallowed Cowboy. I'm sure that that one will be digesting those boots and the rest of him for a long time.

This hammock is too small to defend. It's a real nice place but too exposed and too small. After two hours I want the scouts out ahead of us and Attira to the rear to watch for King. She can take Penny with her. Flash, you go as guard. Now, everyone take a nap, you deserve one."

CHAPTER 37

It Depends on the Mission

Flash had found a mission in life as a spy. He rushed into the camp reporting that King was writhing on the ground and still swearing. Bugs were crawling on his wounds. "And the biggest snake in the world is submerged just a few feet from them. He has been following them, and I am pretty sure he wants to eat King. It leaped at king but he shot it with his rifle, and there was blood. Then it went back into the swamp. Attira told me to come with the news, because they didn't need a rear guard because it looks like King has passed out. They will keep watch. Flash showed particular relish in giving the gory details."

"Don't fall in love with revenge and death, Flash," said Buster. "When it comes to you personally it is not so welcome. It is not a time of rejoicing unless it is in Him, Him's plan for his own. These men are not His. Their master is very cruel. I know this because I am supposed to tell you, not because I know it. There is a bad master out there, driving his people."

"It was still a great fight the other day. I keep thinking about it," said Frankie. He spun around in a circle with excitement.

"Sure," said Chinook. "I noticed how you little guys all piled on after we had blasted King back into the swamp." He chuckled. "Seriously, you guys did fine, we big guys need some follow-up help to keep us honest."

"Enough," said Buster briskly. "Igor, you go back with Flash and Harry, and keep watch on King. Tell the girls to come back to us. That guy King is energized with hate and will be after us again, unless he dies, which I doubt. I think he is getting orders from his master and is afraid to quit. I don't think he even knows that his will has been taken captive and that he is doing the will of his evil master."

Flash looked confused. "How can an evil master that you can't see cause you to do stuff? I had a bad twelve-year-old kid in charge of me, and he tormented me all the time, but I could see him and sometimes get away."

"I don't fully understand myself," Buster said. "It's a thing called spiritual. You can't see it but is still real—kind of like the wind. It does things but you can't see it. There is a bad thing that you can't see and there is a good thing you can't see, like Leader's Him. I don't know the name of the bad one, but do know that he is walking about to see who he can trouble."

"I have a good report," said Rocky. "I missed the meeting, but it was even better to see how Leader is healing. He is still in another world but his body is working just fine. The trouble is he has eaten all the peanut butter and all the jerky that Kate, and others, managed to carry from the boat. Red caught some crawdads in the mud and Leader ate them raw and spit out the shells. He is drinking some of the swamp water, but it is clear and fresh so should be just fine for him. Kate is stiff but healing and her wound is clean but she needs a real vet and lots of stitches."

"You do good work, Rocky. The nurse business seems to be your thing," said Buster.

"I get jealous of you guys fighting the enemy while attending the sick. But a still little voice tells me that what I am doing is just the right thing for me. It's kind of hard to understand."

Buster looked sternly from one to another and then spoke to Rocky.

"All of us wanted to tear those men to shreds back there on the hammock. I stopped the pack because it wasn't our mission. Dutch did the real damage to King because it was his mission. You do your thing by feeding Leader.

It's all very simple, but very hard to understand."

The pack moved on for two more days. It was difficult going but Leader was stronger and able to follow Lady without too much difficulty.

He ate lots of raw crawdads but seemed to like them. Rocky, Red, and Moose stayed close. The other dogs fanned out on guard duty or took turns as scouts. Attira ran from point to flank to rear. She was tireless, reporting information in minutes. Buster stayed in the middle of things, quietly issuing orders and taking reports.

On the following day Sheila flashed into camp with the news that King was on his feet and following. King was sick, feverish, and obviously in pain. He was alone, hungry, tattered, infected, and furious. He had nothing left but rifle, bullets, and hate.

As the dogs talked a huge flock of pink flamingos circled and landed in the everglades swamp near them. The dogs stopped talking and watched the magnificent birds.

"Why am I a grouchy dog when I could have been a beautiful bird?" asked Flash to no one in particular as he watched the pink birds catch a glint of sun. It was the first time he had ever noticed anything truly beautiful. He was confused.

"It's called faith, Flash. It opens your eyes to lots of things," said Bonnie from the shade of a palmetto bush.

CHAPTER 38-I

Tombstone

We sauntered through the fields side by side, laughing and talking.

I was continually remarking about the brightness of the flower colors, their fragrance, the size of the huge trees, and vistas into the distance.

We topped a hill, and below us was a small lake populated with geese and other water birds.

"You know," I said, "except for the lake I have seen a place just like this. It was on a high hill of uncut, flowering weeds, and hay. There was an enclosure made of large gray and moss-covered granite rocks. In it were a scattering of grave stones, most leaning, and a few on the ground and covered with creeping vines. I was alone and just a kid and it really spooked me. They were old stones with dates like 1729 and 1779. Some had visible writing, some were so weathered it was hard to make out anything. One really bothered me."

"Tell me about it," said my Hiking, Watching, Gardening, Caring Friend. "Let's sit down."

"Remember, I was just a kid, about ten or eleven. I had prickles up my spine just being in a cemetery. As I read the words they burned into my memory:

> *Behold me as you pass by*
> *For as you are so once was I*
> *So as I am*
> *So must you be*
> *So prepare to die*
> *And follow me.*

"That little word 'So' repeated three times was like hammer blows to my mind. They sounded so cold and so definite—almost like they were accusations from someone lost and angry."

"Well," said my Friend seriously, "maybe he was driving three spikes."

We were both quiet for several minutes. Finally, breaking the silence, the Philosopher, Teacher, and Preacher Friend of mine asked a question.

"What would you write for your headstone?"

I thought for a minute or two and then looking at the pond that wasn't on the hillside near the graveyard, I smiled. I would write:

<blockquote>

He led me
Beside the still waters
My cup overflows.

</blockquote>

"Or," I said, "how about this one that just popped into my mind?"

<blockquote>

Yea though I walk
Through the valley
Of the shadow of death
I will fear no evil
Thy rod and thy staff
They comfort me

</blockquote>

My Literary Critic and Adviser clapped his hands and said with a wide grin and twinkling eyes "Well done." Then He offered an inscription:

<blockquote>

He said to me
I will never leave you
Or forsake you

</blockquote>

Our eyes caught each other's for a moment. Then he jumped to his feet and offered a hand to hoist me up and said, "We have a walk to take and I know just the place we need to go,"

His voice and our sudden movement frightened the flock of Pink Flamingoes and they rose into the air and circled, then returned to the pond.

We watched the birds for a moment and then walked over the top of the hill and down the other side to the edge of a swamp.

We stopped on the edge of the now gloomy looking swamp. It was as if a dark cloud had obscured the sun. "Remember Bart, faith changes things, faith makes a way."

Tall cattails swayed in the breeze as a midday darkness settled around us. The way was rough, with patches of slime and water. It was getting hard to see. We stumbled over sharp rocks, and jumped from dry spot to dry spot. Then it became pitch black.

"Put your hand on my shoulder," my guide said. "I know the way and you must follow me. I will guide your feet."

The darkness was like the inside of a cave and the same gut fear that that had touched me long ago, was taking hold of me now. I tightened my grip on the Guide's shoulder and trusted him. As my trust deepened the way was easier.

The ground became firmer, dim light returned and grew stronger as we emerged from the swamp. The day brightened, the sun returned, and by the time we reached the top of the next hill it was full daylight, and I was thirsty.

"Let's sit down and have a drink of water," my Swamp Guide said with a chuckle.

"You have water?" I asked. I hadn't noticed any water bottle but he handed me one that was cold to the touch. This was strange stuff. I had been thinking of drinking some of the swamp water so I was pleasantly surprised, but also perplexed.

I drank the water slowly and handed the bottle back to my Water Provider, Guide, Keeper, etc.

"This is special water," he said. "It comes from the spring of life. Don't drink too much or you may live forever," he said with a belly laugh.

"I believe that I will have another drink," I said rather seriously. I was thinking so many things that I couldn't say much of anything. "Does it do anything for temporal life? I'm a bit more worried right now about that. Or am I already on the eternal side?"

"This evening," my now Old Friend said to me, "I am going to take you back to the entrance of the tunnel that you came through when you first arrived here. Just take your time and remember those inscriptions that you and I thought up—even if they did seem a bit familiar. I wouldn't spend any time thinking about the one you found in that country cemetery.

It's true but it's rather dreary. Just work on the two you came up with and the one I mentioned." As he spoke he placed his hand on my shoulder and looked into my eyes.

"Why must I go back into the tunnel?" I asked the Master Gardener, the Faithful Shepherd, and the Gentle Leader. "I love this place, wherever it is, and even though you won't give me even a clue."

"You have things to do, son, and so do I."

"I am really enjoying this place and your company. I want it to last forever. Why don't we find two great women and invite them here? With all the stuff you have to do you could use a good helpmate. And believe it or not, I would like to hear a woman talk. I never thought that would happen."

"This time is for you, Bart. It's your time of reflection I don't think you want a girlfriend right now. Later is fine but today is just for you. As for me, I have to help a bride who is making herself ready. I'll see to that you are at the marriage feast." He said. "Now, take a nap."

I laid down, but for some reason I tasted something like fish and it crunched when I chewed it.

CHAPTER 39

Nearing Solid Ground

"The earth is getting firmer," Buster said. "We are nearing solid land and maybe help. We can't let King defeat us now. Everyone be alert and take any opportunity to stop him. Dutch, move in close to King. Be careful, you know what happened to Kate. She may not recover without help. The time has come to end this situation. It's up to you. We will back you up."

King came into sight. A circle of dogs barred his path but he had not seen them. Dutch lay in the grass at the point. Gators smelled him and moved in, only their eyes and the top of their snout above the water.

Dutch watched the gators carefully as they zeroed in on the scent of dog. Buster moved up beside him.

"I love Leader as much as you do, Dutch. But it's your time. Maybe all these years, Him was preparing you for such a time as this. I envy you! Be a hero my friend, and if you fail perhaps, Him will send another. I would give myself for this battle if I were allowed. There is much at stake. All of us in the pack would gladly sacrifice for him but this is not our time."

King slogged on, his rifle at the ready, held by one arm with his hand on the stock and the trigger. His other arm dangled at his side. Flies and bugs swarmed over his shoulder feasting on his blood. The wounds were still bleeding and beginning to putrefy.

Sheila and Attira slunk into the circle of hidden dogs. They were both breathless as they lay down out of sight near Buster.

"There is a road to the south," said Sheila. "Mud splattered and panting."

"There is dust to the east," said Attira. "It may be a vehicle. We will go to the road and stand on it."

174

"Take most of the smaller dogs with you," said Buster. "I will issue the orders. Big dogs will stay with me."

The word went out and the defense changed.

King stopped wading. Several snouts moved around him. Buster noted that these snouts were different. Cookie sidled up to him. "Those are not gators, sir. I think they are crocodiles and they are really mean. They're new to the Everglades, let loose from fish tanks and such. This swamp is even more dangerous than my folks told me about: crocks, pythons, Paraná, and who knows what else."

Bart stood with a white dog near a palm tree on the hammock. Lady was pulling at his hand but he stood rock still, gazing toward King.

King grinned and using one hand raised the rifle to his face, the form of Bart wavering in the sights. His heart was thudding in his chest and the infusions of pheromones took away his pain. He steadied his aim and one thought hammered his consciousness. He had won! Casey was finished.

Bart's chest was in the notch of his sights, the front sight steadying, and aligning with the rear. He slowly squeezed the trigger. A spurt of flame came from the rifle barrel, but it was pointed toward the sky. King was falling backward as a large brown dog crashed into the man's chest.

Huge jaws emerged from the swamp as three crocodiles lunged. The water seethed with the thrashing crocks and the school of ravenous fish.

The brown dog rolled and leaped to his feet. A black dog rushed in behind him with teeth barred. Both Red Rider and Moose took positions to the right and left of Buster. Dutch floundered toward shore, a crocodile lunging at his legs. He tripped in the muck and a giant mouth opened behind him.

Flash zeroed in, earned his name with his speed, throwing himself into the open mouth of the crock that would have killed Dutch.

The water roiled as crocodiles slashed with their tails. Blood flooded the water from a terrible wound. Chaos erupted in the swamp as the big dogs floundered toward shore, as a school of ferocious fish surrounded them, biting at their legs. They gained the beach and the crocks and the Paraná milled in the shallows.

Flash clawed himself to the surface with Paraná attacking to his form.

He shook them off and made a frantic dash for shore. His feet found the bottom and he struggled out of the water with a smile on his face.

"Great work, Flash," Buster said. "That suicide dash probably saved the life of Dutch. Another second and the Crock would have had Dutch in his mouth instead of you."

"I knew I had the advantage, Buster, but thanks for the kind words. I think I understand the meaning of sacrifice, now."

Five dogs backed away from the water, turned, and trotted behind Lady as she led Leader to the dirt road. Igor watched for a moment as King was torn asunder as the crocks fought among themselves for a piece. Some clothing arched through the air and Igor caught it and dragged it higher on the rising land. He smiled and trotted after the pack.

The dust cloud neared and the sound increased. A green crew cab truck hove into view, neared, and stopped. A semicircle of dogs blocked the road. A man lay in the dirt as a brown Lab leaned over him and a blood-soaked Golden Retriever nudged his ribs. He sat up uncertainly.

The driver stepped out of the truck. He was a tall man with wide shoulders wearing a heavy revolver holstered on a wide belt around his slim waist. He had on a wide rim hat, Levis, a yoked back work shirt, and scuffed boots. He kept his eyes on the semicircle of dogs.

He knew dogs and he decided these dogs were no threat to him. He carefully approached the man, lifted him under his arms and looking into the man's eyes he gasped in surprise.

"Casey, Bart Casey, are you OK?"

Bart didn't answer, he just looked back vacantly.

"You been hurt bad," said Zeb noticing the gaping wound on his head.

"Let's get you to the hospital."

Zeb led him to the truck and helped him into the backseat, laying him down carefully. Dutch leapt into the cab to lie on the floor near Bart.

Kate eased herself in with whimpers as her wound stretched painfully.

Zeb smiled, gave her a careful boost into the truck, and didn't mind the blood.

He looked at the other dogs and called but no one moved. "Come on boys, I got room in the pickup bed. Come on, he said again. Still no dog moved."

He scanned them into his memory, seven basset hounds of various sizes and colors, a chihuahua, a cocker spaniel, a hog hunting hound, a big red hound, a huge St. Bernard mix, a silver husky, a black husky a glorious saluki, and the most beautiful white female collie that he had ever seen. Zeb shrugged, got into the truck, made a turn, and headed inland.

CHAPTER 40

No Tracks in the Sand

A week later Zeb returned to Bart's hospital room for the tenth time.

He had visited at least once every day.

"Hi, Bart what you doing here?" he asked as he usually did, not expecting an answer but not really knowing what to say. Bart had been mostly unconscious all week. Zeb stood near the bed, his thumbs hooked over his gun belt, looking tired and discouraged. This time Bart turned his head and smiled.

"How about you, Zeb?" Bart asked. "The last time I saw you it was up in Steinhatchee. You had some bodies on the beach and I had a sunken shrimp boat. What brings you to Miami?" he spoke in a gravelly voice.

Zeb was speechless and stood there with tears running down his cheeks. He took off his wide brimmed officer's hat and ran the cuff off his sleeve across his eyes. Then he smiled.

"I got a temporary transfer because there was short of men and overrun with drug haulers. I guess you and I are star crossed, or something."

"It's not stars, Zeb, its angels, or God. The doctor said that the road you found me on is usually flooded and no one uses it. Then there I was, about dead and there was Zeb. How do you explain that?"

"Come on, Bart. You know it's hard for me to say, but I guess you helped get me saved years ago and it was my turn."

Bart chuckled but grimaced as the smile pulled his many stitches.

"I got me a chocolate Lab and a Golden Retriever at my place. Took the retriever to the vet to get sewed up and she is fine. The vet said she looked to be shot, and it grazed her ribs, and cut her open quite a bit."

"That big one is Dutch and the retriever is Kate—both friends of mine." Bart was barely able to talk as tears ran down his face and he swallowed at the lump in his throat.

"Listen, Bart. I went back to get the rest of them dogs and couldn't find a trace of them. I know just where I found you, found your tracks, and the Lab's and the Retriever, but that's all. The dust is loose and tracks real easy, but where I saw those dogs there was nothing."

Bart smiled and more tears worked down his cheek. Zeb noticed.

"Hey, Bart. I'll go back and look again for them others. A pack of dogs can't just disappear. I'd know them if seen them. There was seven basset hounds of various colors, a Chihuahua, a Cocker, a hog dog, a tall red hound, a St. Bernard mix, a silver Husky, kind of small, a big black Husky, a gold colored Saluki, and the most gorgeous white Collie I have ever seen."

Bart couldn't answer. He knew every one of those dogs. His throat had a lump the size of a tennis ball.

"I found a wallet," Zeb went on self-consciously, "and some pieces of clothes not far from the road. Some guy named King. I told the Feds and they are all over the place, finding parts of people, empty shells, burned out boats, and camp sites. It seems that camp was a major drug distribution place. The remains of the shack and the boats showed lots of drug evidence. They knew this guy King and were real glad the gators got him. They found some parts of him and a few others, and a big beige cowboy hat. Now they are wondering where the army is that wiped out King and his gang."

Bart smiled but still couldn't talk. He just gulped and kind of made a croaking sound. Zeb understood and kept on talking.

"That man Billy, from your office got word from the Feds about finding your boat and is sailing it back to Indian Rocks as we speak."

Bart smiled again, a bit more weakly.

"Time's up officer," said a nurse.

"One last thing," said Zeb, "I can track almost anything, but I have never seen a pack of dogs that leave no sign. I've got some thinking to do."

CHAPTER 41-I

The Pack Returns

Bart awoke with the smell of grass and flowers strong in his nostrils. He lifted himself onto his right elbow, looking off to his right across the familiar rolling hills and giant trees. A low whine caused him to look to his left and there stood a half circle of dogs. He ran his hand across his eyes to clear them and then looked again. A huge grin spread across his face.

He ran his eyes from left to right as he counted. Seventeen dogs! His eyes swept back to the left to a huge white Collie, "Lady," he whispered in disbelief. "Chinook," he said with tears in his eyes. "Sheila, Red Rider, Attira, Igor." Bart wiped his eyes on his shoulder and continued to scan the circle of dogs.

Frankie, Camper, Moose, Cookie, and of course, the big lady herself, Bonnie Lass, and her husband, Harry, and daughter, Twinkles. Then the excellent Rocky, loved by Amanda, and then Penny, the delighted, Flash the grump, sorry buddy, but I loved you anyhow.

There stood Buster, his black hair lustrous and shining in the sun. His brown eyes twinkled with love: "and my beloved Buster."

"Sorry guys, I loved everyone of you but this guy had a special love for me that touched my heart. And there stands the great friend, faithful Dutch. And last, the delightful strawberry blonde, Kate who hides behind things but loves and wiggles."

"How do you like my dogs?" asked a voice from behind. The Watchman, Gardner, Shepherd, etc., stepped into the crescent of dogs.

"There have been some changes, Bart. Everyone has done battle, everyone has overcome. Buster has emerged a great leader, Rocky a compassionate nurse and soldier. Chinook is a fearless protector and Flash, known previously as the grouch, has learned sacrifice and love."

The timid Kate is now fearless Kate, and as you can see, wounded on your behalf. The giant Dutch is a steady rock, ready to meet any challenge with disregard for himself. And Lady, steadfast in her love for you. Attira, a hidden wealth of speed, willing perseverance, and obedience.

"Igor, forever youthful and spilling energy and enthusiasm in everything he did. And there is Frankie, always the spring loaded ball of energy, daring, and macho. Camper is full of loyalty and love, always ready on your behalf. Then here is Moose, the giant of them all, not the brightest, but always willing, forgiving, and loyal."

Cookie is afraid of nothing and never gave a thought to herself, only to do what was necessary. Bonny Lass, smart, and the leader of her family, submitting but remaining strong in herself. Beside her always was Harry, her husband, tall and willing to battle, and her daughter, Twinkles, a sweet blessing to all."

"You said that they were your dogs," Bart said as he got to his feet.

"They are my dogs, sir!"

"Yes, they are, Bart, but I have been taking care of them. I am also a Dog Walker, and Canine Companion."

"Why are Dutch and Kate here? They were with me in the boat when the bright light came. I don't understand at all! Are we all here to stay?

Where is this place and where is my boat, the Pelican?"

"You ask far too many questions, Bart. There are some things that a man does not understand clearly at first, but as time goes by you grow into an understanding of many things, and gain insights into things hidden to those who do not search. You have searched and you have learned a few things, and are learning more. Your dogs have believed in you, their 'Him,' and have grown to know a higher 'Him' while serving you."

"Look, Canine Companion, this is sounding kind of spiritual, and something hard to put a finger on. Are you OK?"

"Sorry about that, but you did ask about the wolves you heard howling a few nights ago. I told you they were good wolves, remember? You also kept talking about dog breath, peanut butter, and jerky. You don't sound like you are very tightly wound, yourself."

All of the dogs sat on their haunches, poked their noses in the air and let out a startling howl. Then they all smiled, wagged their tails, filed past Bart, and sat down again behind the Dog Walker.

Bart watched as Dutch and Kate split off and sat by themselves.

"What's the matter, guys?" he asked the pair.

The Dog Man answered. "They have some things to do, so they are not going with me today. The pack has learned a lot and need to be about the big business of the big Him."

"I'm still confused," said Bart, "but I think I see the light begin to dawn. I am honored to have had this time with the pack. Thanks, guys. I love every one of you. I'm sure I will see you again."

The dogs circled around from behind the Dog Man, and as they marched by Bart each stopped, slipped words and pictures into his mind, gave him a gentle lick or nibble, and passed on. Buster stopped, looked deep into Bart's eyes. As Bart looked back into Buster's eyes he saw many things in their depth—much to ponder. It was all there in great detail, from bright light to Zeb. Then Buster blinked, and the vision faded. Buster gave Bart a gentle swipe with his tongue and passed on. Dutch and Kate still stood to one side.

Bart was sobbing his feelings softly, not hiding his joy, grief or whatever it was. "Bless the Lord, oh my soul, is all I can think to say," he murmured quietly.

"And forget not all his benefits," said the Shepherd, finishing the verse.

"Bart," he said. "Lay back and enjoy what was, and is, and what will be. Use your newfound wisdom. Smell the field, the flowers, the Lillie of the valley, and the Trailing Arbutus. And when you awake, do those things that you were called to do—and then one day come and join the pack and me."

Bart lay down in trusting submission, nestling his head in the fragrance of the Arbutus. "Good night, pack, and you too, Shepherd, Pruner, Guide, Forester, Gardener, Watchman, Dog Walker, Dog Watcher, Counselor, Keeper, Teacher, Lily of the Valley . . . ," he couldn't remember all the names as he drifted off to sleep, but he knew the man.

The End

EPILOGUE

Lady, 1930-1934

Lady, a pure white collie, was given to my parents when they moved to Eaton Rapids, Michigan, from Venice, Florida, when I was an infant.

Mother was generally doing her own thing as a budding artist. Dad was working twelve-hour shifts at an ice-cream parlor.

Dad said that Lady kept track of me, especially when my mother left me laying a table while she attended to her art. She seemed to be a natural nursemaid.

Unfortunately, Lady had learned how to open milk bottles. In those days the milkman delivered the milk and left it on your doorstep. The bottles were sealed with a thin cardboard disk that snapped into a grove in the neck of the glass bottles. It had a tab protruding that was used to pull the cap out of the bottle. Lady had learned to go to the neighbor's front step, remove the caps from the bottles and lick the cream out.

The older among my readers may remember the days before homogenization when the milk separated and the heavy cream rose to the top.

The neighbor was infuriated because of losing his coffee cream and kicked Lady in the stomach. She returned home, but something had ruptured and she soon died. My father was hurt by the unnecessary death and would never discuss it. Mother was always very sketchy about the details and could only tell me that Lady had been a "gorgeous" dog with an "aristocratic nose," and that "she was always near you." I have no memory of Lady but feel a bond.

Chinook, 1935-1942

There was a radio program called "Pepper Young's Family." It was an early soap opera. The guy who played the male lead in the show lived in a small town about ten miles north of us, and badly needed a home for his Chinook breed of Husky. The show was popular, keeping him in Boston too much of the time to have a large sled dog. He brought the dog to us, looked us over, liked what he saw, and left without his pet. We were living in Sanbornton NH on a 200 acre farm at the time.

"Chinook" was the name that I gave him. I don't recall his original name but I renamed him Chinook, even though he was of the "Chinook" breed of Husky. I liked the name.

He desired to return home but we were smart enough to keep him on a rope until he settled down. When we untied the rope from his tether it would take both of my parents and me to hold him back. He was a young dog but unbelievably strong. He pulled my sled around on wet grass with the rope tied to his collar.

Chinook nearly got me arrested when I joined some friends to mess up our one-room school house, with six grades, on Halloween eve. We all hid when a car went by but the neighbor recognized Chinook near the door. When the vandalism was discovered, the sheriff was told about Chinook and the sheriff came to visit with my father. I got the frightening lecture about reform school if I transgressed again, so I lived in fear for a long time. The sheriff didn't smile much.

Chinook frequently circled the buildings, and the land within a few hundred yards of the house. One day stepped into a fox trap near the brook, and well into the woods. It was several days before we found him, and my parents said that they couldn't afford a vet to tend to his badly damaged leg. Mother was off to New York to study art, and I was shipped to a farm about ten miles away where there was a kid of my age. I really didn't understand at the time but later wondered how mother could go to New York, and why Chinook had to go untreated. I know that times were very hard, and priorities quite different than today.

After being caught in the trap, Chinook received little attention other than food and water, and slowly died from the infected leg. Dad said that for days before he died he sat in the yard looking down the road, waiting for me to come home. I returned too late.

I daydreamed that Chinook hadn't died and would suddenly appear.

When the snow melted, I went to the place where Dad said he had buried him. His tail had become uncovered and I recognized it immediately.

Chinook was not coming home. I have lost many, family members, friends, and coworkers to death over the years and don't even remember the name of most of them. I have never forgotten Chinook.

Sheila, 1940-returned to owner in 1943

Sheila really was a lead dog for a dogsled team. She and her team were boarded with us at Tall Timbers in Sanbornton NH for several years, while the owner served his time in the Armed Forces. We had her on a run not far from the house and her teammates were on runs beyond. Mother took a liking to her and the dog was loose some of the time.

She liked me, so I included her in the story as one of mine. The team owner was finally discharged from the service and returned to claim his team. Mother tried to get him to leave Sheila with us, but she was too valuable as a lead dog.

One day while we were away the sled dogs all broke their run cables and attacked our chickens. The death toll was over three hundred chickens.

The word went out on the crank telephone party line that anyone could pick up and hear or join in on the conversation. Within hours neighbors appeared to help. By midnight most of the chickens were plucked, cooked, and canned in canning jars. The dogs had simply killed for the sport of it, so the birds were pretty much whole except for the ones where a tug of war occurred. The dogs were rounded up and secured, never to escape again.

Red Rider, 1940-1942

Red was a tall, well-built hound, mostly a light red color. He was very loving and often let me crawl into his dog house with him: I was only seven or eight at the time. His owner was in the service, as was about everyone else from eighteen to thirty-five years of age. World War II was gearing up. He came home on leave and took Red back to the army for training as a helper to the medics on the battlefields.

Attira, 1945-1960 adopted

We were living at "Steele Hill, Inn," where Dad was the manager.

Steele Hill was about fifteen hundred feet high and was located in the Sanbornton Township across the lake from Laconia NH. In New Hampshire, the mountains start at about a thousand feet and rise up to five thousand feet. They look huge from a distance. Attira was a Saluki, an early Egyptian breed: a gift from Margaret Smith, wife of Nelson Smith, the owner of the Inn. Mrs. Smith was a Wellesley girl, tall, slim with a voice and vocabulary like silk. He was a Harvard graduate of course.

He owned three thousand acres on Steele Hill.

Attira was unbelievably fast and hunted by sudden leaps in the air to look around. The breed hunted by sight and not by scent. She and I were following a fox one summer day in a huge golden wheat field. Her golden color gleamed in the sun as she sprang into the air, spotted the fox, and dropped down; passing beneath the top of the wheat until the next leap.

It was beautiful to watch. Neither of us caught the fox that day.

She went on to live a very uneventful life after I went away to boarding school, grew fat and lived a long life. In the story, she is allowed to run, and to distinguish herself with valor. Surely, she would appreciate having her part in the adventure.

Igor, 1954-1964

In the *Pack Leader Down* story Igor mentions that he was found in a sink hole in Southwestern Virginia. I knew that there was a cave somewhere on the side of a mountain that was known as Saltpeter Cave.

An old duffer told me that the cave had been used by the confederates to make gunpowder during the Civil War. As a member of the spelunking club at Virginia Tech, I had done a lot of caving and was anxious to find Salt Peter Cave. My parents were living in Wise, Virginia at the time, while I attended Virginia Tech.

In my search I found what I thought was a sink hole that might have led to the cave. I went down on a rope and found a live pup along with his dead mother and siblings. My buddy hoisted him out wrapped in my shirt, and I later fed him my lunch.

Igor nearly died of exuberance when we found each other a few days later. I named him Igor, after the classical piece named the "Dances of

Prince Igor." The same tune was used in the popular song, "Stranger in Paradise." Therefore, obviously, "Igor." See, I did get an education after all.

One night I had taken a girl to a dance, dropped her off about 3:00 a.m. and headed home. Naturally Igor had gone along on the date, and was asleep in the backseat. (There is nothing like a wet, cold dog nose pressing in between kissing lovers to cool things down.)

It was a dark mountain road and a hitchhiker gave me a thumb. I stopped and let him in. A moment later I saw that he had a gun pointed at me. In that same moment Igor flew over the back of the seat. He was all teeth and claws. I caught his collar in mid air and pulled him into my lap. He was intent on having the guy for a late-night snack.

I had to struggle to keep Igor at bay. I pulled to the side of the road and told the man he was about to be bitten. He bailed out. I went to the police station and made a report but they never found the gunman. Now Igor and I were even. I saved him and he saved me.

Igor remained an independent spirit, and took on a tractor at our small pig farm in Michigan—not far from Marshall and was thrown twenty feet in the air when he wouldn't release the tread on the tire. He survived, after lying inert for twenty minutes and immediately quit chasing tractors; but found other pursuits.

In 1965, we were living Falls Church VA. One evening, a pack of dogs was chasing a bitch through the neighborhood. Igor joined the pack and disappeared. We searched for days, driving neighborhoods and calling his name. I checked with Dog Control with no luck. I was hurt as was the family. What consoled me was that Igor went out with class, in the pack, and chasing a female dog.

Here is a short poem that Igor left on the kitchen table just before he took off with the pack.

> When you speak of dogs don't think of me
> I only act dog when it comes to pee
> Just give me a holly or an evergreen
> I'll make the brownest spot you have ever seen.
> When it comes to chow I show my stuff
> If it's not from the table I'm, off in a huff
> If it was up to me and I had my druthers
> I'd have me a pound of store bought butter

Frankie, 1968-1970 adopted

I really didn't like this guy and he didn't like me. He was ten pounds of bark and fuss.

He had obviously been a woman's dog and had a natural aversion to men.

After a while we became sort of friends. I found that he liked beer, so every night I would sit in "my chair" with a bowl of beer for Frankie. It somehow cemented our relationship, drinking buddies, I guess.

We were living in Largo, Florida in a circle of homes with just one way in. The traffic was light and the neighbors mostly courteous. Frankie defended us from dozens of real or imagined threats, jumping straight up and barking, his bug eyes blazing with zeal.

I came home to a quiet house and directions to the curb down the street. Frankie was dead in the gutter, a wound in his side. He didn't like the guy down the street who was known to shoot cats, coon, and possum.

It looked like a gunshot to me but another neighbor convinced me that for the sake of the kids I should agree that Frankie had been hit by a car.

He was buried in the backyard with honors and tears.

Camper, 1972-1985

Martha (my new wife) and I went to a Christian camp at Rock Eagle State Park near Eatonton, Georgia. We had a pop-up trailer parked on the edge of a lake in the campgrounds. A scroungy, smelly little female basset hound came out of the woods and hung around. Of course, I fed her. Her belly looked as if she had recently had pups. On inquiry we learned that no one knew where she came from and they asked us to take her home.

Martha was horrified.

You could smell the poor dog fifty feet away and patches of her hair were missing. I got a large box out of the dump and put it in the backseat of the car. Then I took "Camper" to the lake with a bottle of dish soap.

Everyday for several days we had a bath—when you bathe a dog it is a mutual sort of thing.

On the day of departure Martha was still refusing to take Camper home with us. I didn't argue, simply put Camper in the box in the backseat and started the car. Martha finally decided to go home too. We were living in Largo, Fl.

Camper was absolutely no trouble at all and I kept the air conditioner on frigid with the back window cracked a bit and Martha shivering.

Camper was our first basset hound. I guess it is obvious why we named her Camper.

Camper had very little personality as dogs go, but did show love by running to the gate when I came home from work. She would bark two or three barks and wag her tail when I spoke to her. If I forget to speak she would go to the backdoor and begin to bark. As soon as I answered her she would stop barking.

Camper lived to be an old dog, blind and lame and the terrible day came when I had to put her down. She died in my arms and I cried all the way home from the vet, and choked when we did the funeral in the backyard.

Moose, 1968-1973

I am not sure where we got Moose but believe that one of the kids brought him home from a friends litter. He grew to be a huge St. Bernard looking dog. He had a sweet and placid character and was an all around good guy. He was mostly loose, but we buried an old wheel rim deep in the ground with a chain that gave him large circle for times when we were away. We were doing a lot of camping in those days. He was not a house or car, dog.

We were going camping for two weeks, so we tethered moose and put out large pans for food and water. A neighbor teenager was to tend him and keep him supplied with the essentials. At some point his chain knotted and shortened the arc, placing his dishes out of his reach. We understand that he barked for attention, another neighbor responded by throwing stuff at him and shouting at him.

Finally, the poor beast died of thirst only a few days before we returned. We harbored ill feelings toward the teenager who should have been bright enough to see and correct the problem. I still can't believe that one of our dogs died as Moose died. I hope to be able to make it up to him one day. He lived and died in Largo.

Cookie, 1973-1976

Cookie came home with the kids from a walk in Englewood, Florida, while visiting my parents. She was small enough to sleep in one of my size 13 shoes. Her parents were hog hunting hounds, always on chains in the owner's backyard.

She grew up to very protective of the family, to the point that she wouldn't let the neighbors walk past our house. We lived on an oval, in Largo, and it was the nightly practice for many of the neighbors to walk around the oval, chat, and exercise.

A few of them hollered at the dog and flapped their arms, etc. That just worried Cookie even more and caused her to growl and get ready for battle. We finally had to chain her near her dog house most of the time.

She spent evenings with us. She was a large, strong, and firmly muscled dog. We became worried that she might be mosquito bitten and infected with heartworms. She went to the vet and got a clean bill of health and returned with the pill that keeps dogs from getting the worms.

I gave her the pill.

The next morning she jumped up on me with her front feet, and nuzzled me in such an unusual friendly and loving manner that it deeply affected me.

When I returned from work she was dead.

We called the vet; he rechecked the lab report and nearly cried when he said that the technician had made a mistake, and that the medicine had killed her. It was a gut wrencher for all of us as we buried her in the backyard beside other dogs, guinea pigs, gribbles, rabbits, pet rats, and the like. The kids, Bart, Todd, Lark, and Lois, were learning more hard lessons about life and death.

Bonny Lass (Sadie), 1985-1998 adopted

An Avon customer of Martha owned Sadie, as she was then named.

Sadie was a large basset hound. She had a fenced backyard in Seminole FL, but always managed to escape, so had to be kept in the garage while the owner worked. She damaged the doors and was so hyperactive that she was impossible for the owner to handle.

We adopted her. Martha changed her name to Bonnie Lass. We put her on a leash to go walking, but she was so strong and so unruly that it made walking a difficult chore. We had a large, fenced backyard, a covered porch and a screened "birdcage" and Jacuzzi. She was free to run in the yard and had no desire to run away, and began to slowly calm down.

Another Avon customer had a large black and white basset male.

They gave Harry to us and we had two. They fell in love and after the prescribed time period we had a batch of three puppies. None of them survived. Later Bonnie got pregnant again and presented us with nine pups. In the fullness of time, which seemed forever, we had sold all of the pups except for Twinkles.

Bonnie Lass lived with us ten years or more as the queen of the dogs.

She finally stopped eating, stretched out on the deck of our home in North Carolina and began to die. It took nearly a week for her to die. She was conscious and aware but virtually unmoving. She refused food or water but seemed appreciative of the offer. We covered her at night and let her enjoy the early summer sun by day. Then she was gone. We buried her in our sideyard in North Carolina, the first of many under a stand of black spruce trees that my dad had planted in 1982.

Harry, 1986-1987 adopted

We adopted Harry from a family in Largo, and he became the father of many, including a spotted female named Twinkles. He was a stately basset with long nose and long ears. He was beautifully behaved and a real gentleman. We named him after my father, Harry, who like the dog, had an impressive proboscis. Then Harry got sick and we took him to the vet. He was returned with medicine that worked for a few days, and then he became sick and we returned him to the vet.

We wish we had kept him at home with his family, but he died at the vet and they refused to give us his body because they didn't know what had killed him and suspected some new infection. Every year for several years the vet sent us a flower as a memorial. He was such a fine dog that the vet and the assistants and office girls had tears in their eyes when I went to pay the bill.

Twinkles, 1986-1999

Twinkles, was the daughter of Bonnie Lass and Harry. All of whom lived in Largo. She was a smaller dog than either, probably because of her runt status as a pup. She was born without a knee joint in her right rear leg and it hinged back and forth, making her a cripple. She watched her siblings run and play but she was on the fringe.

Martha took her to a vet, who specialized in show bassets. He had little compassion and wanted to put her down, so that she would not contaminate the breed. Martha declined. I then took her to another vet who had heard of a similar case that was healed. He showed me how to splint and tape the leg so it couldn't bend backward.

We changed the bandage everyday to keep it tight. I believe we kept the splint on for about three months. The vet followed her progress and eventually she grew a new joint and walked with only a slight limp. By then her siblings were gone and we had fallen in love with her gentle spirit and mischievous ways.

She lived with us for many years, making the yearly trip to North Carolina in a lump with her mother and other dogs. They were completely docile on a trip, awaking only to get a drink and go to the bathroom. Some of our trips were fourteen-hours long, but the dogs slept through most of them, tangled together.

When we returned to the farm in the North Carolina Smokey Mountains the dogs would chase rabbits in the fields and follow a million scents. She was a fast runner and full of life. Once or twice the dogs left our property while on the trail of something. We found them, scolded them, and herded them home. After that no one left our seven acres or the adjacent fields, always within sight.

Finally she stretched out on the kitchen floor and refused to move.

We stepped over her for three days as she died, like her mother, glad that we were there with her and responding with a lick if we put our head next to hers. She joined her mother in the sideyard, under a pine tree and looking down the valley.

Rocky, 1992-1999

Rocky was a heart breaker. Martha, Amanda, and Tony went to Tennessee and picked him out at a well-known basset breeder's kennel and brought him to our farm in Western NC. He had a powerful stance, a beautiful body, long ears, and a large "Roman" nose. His disposition was the epitome of a basset, laid back but alert. He knew without a doubt that he was the King, but his adopted mother, Bonnie Lass, made it clear that he could play the macho bit, but bottom line, she was in charge.

For years we had a wonderful family of dogs: Bonnie, Twinkles, and Rocky. Shortly after Bonnie and Twinkles died Rocky got sick. We had gone for a few days to a convention where we met a holistic vet and mentioned that Rocky was ailing. She gave us a few ideas about feeding and using some vitamins and minerals. When we got home he was very sick. We called the holistic vet and she gave us a prescription for a bunch of stuff. Within a day or two he was much improved.

We were to keep him inactive as much as possible. One evening soon after, he seemed really strong and acted alert. When I let him out for a walk he began to run. I called but the usually obedient Rocky took off across the fields making a long swing through the pastures, feet a blur of action, ears trailing in the wind, and tail high. He circled back to us and collapsed at our feet. We carried him into the house. He was convulsing and shivering, and acting terrified.

He wanted to be between my legs or to be as close as possible to someone. Amanda spent hours laying near him and talking and stroking him. Finally he settled down and by then it was well past anyone's bedtime, so we put him in the bathroom with a rug to lie on.

The next morning he was stiff and cold. He must have died shortly after we left him. I felt like we had abandoned him and wondered why we hadn't stayed up with him. Honestly, we had no idea that he was near death.

Tony and Amanda were deeply hurt, especially Amanda who considered Rocky her dog. Martha was hurt because she was his surrogate mother. I was so full of grief that I couldn't talk, but muttered a short service and cried when we filled the grave.

Gosh, I pray that I will one day be reunited with all of our dogs. What a day that will be as they romp across the fields, returning to love, and be loved.

Penny, 1999-1999 adopted

Penny was raised in the same family that gave us Harry. One of their daughters could no longer keep the dog and asked us to take her. This was before the death of Bonnie, Twinkles or Rocky. She became the fourth basset for a few months.

She was absolutely delighted to be free and to run for the first time in her life. She had a sweet spirit and once she learned her place in the pack, she bloomed into an excellent dog.

Then one day she didn't come home. We looked and called and asked neighbors but she was just gone. I was afraid that she might have been mistaken for a red fox and shot, or that the pack of coyotes up on the mountain might have come down and lured her away.

None of that was true. Tony found her about two hundred feet from the house, pointed toward home. She had been dead several days. We called the vet and he told us it was not unusual for a Florida dog to die of a heart attack shortly after moving to the mountains. The high altitude, the thin air, and the chance to really run all added to heart stress.

Her crippled front feet referred to in the story were exactly as told to us. Her owner had a dock protruding into a small lake where a gator lived. It is claimed that her feet were damaged by the gator when he tried to drag her into the pond. We didn't ask why a vet had not fixed them. It was useless to speculate and Penny didn't seem to mind at all.

She was often the leader in the rabbit chase. We had so much blackberry cane that the dogs didn't have a chance. As Bur Rabbit said when caught by the fox: "Please don't throw me into that briar patch."

Thick cane is a rabbit's domain.

We buried Penny along with our other dogs, keeping the pack together.

Our grief was somewhat abated by knowing how much Penny had appreciated her few months of running free, and being loved.

Flash, 2002-2007 adopted

This guy lived with us a long time, mostly remaining his grouchy self. When we answered the ad of "Basset Hound, free to a good home," an obese twelve-year-old boy answered the door and the dog stayed well clear of him. The dog showed no regrets on leaving and I suspect it had not been a happy home in Canton NC.

The mother slightly hinted that there was a problem, but the man of the house was selling hard to rid himself of poor Flash. The only good thing we could say about the family was that they must have watched the Dukes of Hazard to come up with the name Flash.

You could tell that deep down Flash was happy and appreciated the new home. However, on the surface he was mostly grouchy about everything except food. He was like a failure to thrive infant, with stiff legs and a stiff body, unyielding to petting or attention. Sometimes he wagged his tail by mistake and showed a glimmer of affection.

He lived with us for several years, but mostly kept to himself and seldom showed any interest in anything except food. He finally went into his dog house and refused to exit. He died there, warm and dry and was buried with the pack. He was damaged beyond repair in this world and we hope that in the next he will be liberated from himself, and from his past, as is suggested in the story.

Buster, 2004-2007 rescue

It's hard for me to write about Buster. I truly, deeply, loved that dog.

He had a depth beyond dog. Martha bailed him out of the pound after his owner refused. He had been bailed out once before and was slated for the gas chamber in Hazelwood NC. I was out of town for some reason and Martha was a bit frightened, being alone in the country blackness.

Buster knew nothing about treats or biscuits or retrieving sticks or even of having fun or doing tricks. He was afraid to come into the house and lay near the door unmoving. We suspect that he had spent his previous life on a chain, neglected of love and caring, but he was far from having been broken in spirit.

I came home from somewhere and there was Martha and her new dog. I tried not to steal his affection but it was impossible. He migrated to me and we bonded well below the surface. When I petted him, brushed him, or just loved him he responded with a gentle flick of his tongue on my face or wrist. It wasn't a slurpy wet lick like most dogs deliver—just a very loving and inoffensive display of his affection.

After we had been playing, or wrestling he finished with a light nibble up my arm. Not like the hurtful nips of affection that my daughter's dog Dutch administers. His nips were gentle and could easily be missed if you didn't understand his gentle spirit.

We guess that Buster was about three when he came to live with us.

He was pure black with a purple tongue and pure white teeth. He weighed about hundred pounds made up of very dense muscles. His face was as broad as a bear, with small ears and rolls of extra skin around his neck and shoulders. His face was nothing like a chow, but more like a Labrador but larger and wider. I guess he looked more like a bear.

He was truly magnificent; his coat glistened in the sun. He had a fine under hair like a Husky and loved to roll in the snow, sleep outdoors, and to eat snow rather than take a drink. He came in everyday a time or two to visit, but was soon ready to go back outside, or to his house, after an hour or so.

Buster worried me somewhat when a stranger pulled up in our yard as many do, looking for their lost hunting dogs, asking directions, or selling their services. Buster would invariable circle around behind them and stand quietly but attentively. If they kept their distance or emitted the right vibes he was fine. If they approached me Buster was on their heels.

I would call him to me and he would take up station at my side.

The "good ole boys" of our area read the signs and were very respectful and put their hands down so he could approach and sniff. I guess he listen to the tone of the conversation and understood that things were going OK. No matter what, he was close by until they left.

We had some outlanders who refused to exit their cars and even some local boys that stayed in their trucks, because Buster was too still and quiet as he gazed at them. They usually spoke to me from their rolled down windows as Buster came and sat beside me, pressing my leg and ready to do the necessary.

When guests and neighbors were received by Martha and I, Buster dropped his concern and everyone complimented us on what a grand dog he was. However, he didn't like anything to get too close to me, even a tractor. One of the neighbors often graded our dirt road, and I would go out to shoot the bull with him. Buster would sit or stand at my side. If I got to close to the tractor he became nervous, slipped in front of me and made a very low and rumbling growl. When I backed up a pace he was fine.

When you looked into those eyes there was a depth, strength, and a primordial essence that made you glad that he was a friend. There was also the recognition of the potential violence that was deep within him.

You knew instinctively that he was ready and willing to lay down his life in defense of his own.

After all, he was a country dog, with coyotes living on the ridge line and bears in between. Cows and horses surrounded us, tractors and combines roamed the fields. I was glad to have a dog that understood the realities of life, and whose spark of the wild had not been extinguished.

Buster finally seemed older. He was acting out of character, more docile and needy. We took him to the vet and he gave him a week to live.

It was a massive fast growing tumor in his chest.

It was so hard! I get teary eyed when I think of him stretched out in the living room like a black sphinx with his nose on his front paws. He took the medicine without question but there was a sad look of acceptance in his eyes. He wasn't afraid; he just didn't want to leave us.

On his final night he didn't want to go out. He lay near the sliding glass doors to keep cool as the family read and talked. About every half hour he heaved himself to his feet and came to nuzzle each one of us and then returned to his place near the door. Finally, it was bedtime; we all got down near him and told him or our love. Still praying he would survive. We all went to bed.

A half hour later my son, Tony, heard a thump and went down to the living room and found that Buster had died. My son came to our room and we covered Buster and cried.

The day before he died I let him off the deck in the morning and he took off at a powerful run down to the bottom of the field, made a wide circuit through the field to the east, returning to me panting and joyous.

It was the same run that Rocky had made the day he died.

Buster's run was a run of pure joy, and as I watched I was startled by his strength, his carriage, and his powerful body. He was saying good-bye to the world he loved.

Dutch, 2005-

Dutch was our daughter, Amanda's dog. Amanda is my third daughter and fifth kid. She bought the dog in her sophomore year of college at UNCA, Asheville NC and picked the biggest male pup she could find.

He is pure bred Chocolate Labrador with AKC papers. On occasion I call him the "red dog" because his hair becomes auburn in the summer sun with highlights of red.

Every few months he would go crazy in Amanda's college room and eat her shoes, cosmetics, etc. She would become disgusted and drop him off at our place in the country for a couple of weeks. He had gonads the size of a soft ball and the manly stance to prove it.

Buster and Dutch were buddies. Buster made it a point to put Dutch down quite often and Dutch rolled on his back and surrendered. Then up they jumped and were off at top speed, shoulder to shoulder. They would grab each other's jowls, wrestle, and run for three days straight while Dutch unwound, regained his sanity, and become a normal dog.

Soon he would be picked up by Amanda and a few months later he was delivered again for another treatment by Buster. That went on for several years until Amanda married, produced a baby and was soon expecting another.

Suddenly she didn't need a canine child, especially one over a hundred pounds, who could unintentionally hurt an infant. By then she had graduated from college, married and become a social worker. Her slant on life had changed.

We became Dutch's permanent home and I became his pack leader.

He loved Martha and obeyed Tony, but mostly lay at my feet. I am kind of a pushover and dogs take advantage of it.

Our favorite time is when I take him, and Kate, over to the creek that flows through a stand of tall poplar trees. Grey squirrels live in the tree and collect nuts on the ground, leaving wonderful trails of cents. First thing, Dutch heads for a little pool in the creek and lays down in the cold mountain water. Kate walks around on stiff legs trying not to get wet.

Then they are off on a squirrel trail.

I have a lawn chair leaning against a tree and sit in a spot of sun filtering down through the canopy of trees. The dogs return from the hunt, roll in the leaves, chase each other through the giant rhododendron bushes, and then climb the step bank on the east side of the creek, to chase cows or whatever in the big field. They don't stay out of sight long, every few minutes appearing in the distance to look at me. If I give no signal they are off again. If I give one short call they appear in minutes, muzzle me, slurp me, and are ready to move on.

As I write, Dutch is still with us but is a bit too fat and is slowing down. So am I. It would be nice to be able to freeze time and just go on living the same show, over and over. I would replay those years with Buster and Dutch every morning and every evening.

They were great days, when I was capable of absorbing a two hundred-pound impact as they bounded into me with delight. I probably shouldn't say it but it is easier to love dogs than it is to love humans.

Their simplicity, their unconditional love, and their free spirits engender nothing but love. Besides, they don't talk back!

Kate, 2008-rescue

Tony, my third son, and sixth kid, brought home Kate the day before her scheduled execution at the hands of the dog welfare people of Haywood Co. NC.

She was a beautiful mess. Three years in a cage, owned by a teenage girl living by herself in a trailer; with random administrations of food and water, exercise and love. She didn't have a clue about anything. She was the epitome of a "dumb blonde."

Kate holds her tail high, her head high, and her back straight. She is alert, a sponge for affection, ready to eat anything, and dancing all the time. She peed in the house, pooped wherever, and her nose was everywhere. We live in the country, and have a large deck, a covered porch and acres to roam in. She chased cows, barked at pigs, attacked UPS trucks, and mounted Dutch. Everything done with a flourish, a smile, and the golden flag of a happy tail.

In the summer sun she is a wonderful red and my wife, Martha, gave her the nickname of "the strawberry blonde." For you younger people, there was a song way back when with the words;

"And Casey would waltz with the strawberry blonde, and the band played on. Her mind was so loaded it nearly exploded. The poor girl shook with alarm," etc., "and the band played on." Luckily, I can't sing it for you.

Kate has somewhat calmed down and her buddy, Dutch, has taught her the basics of living in a polite society, and has learned our routine.

She is still a delight with her exuberant ways but has gained bodily control and made friends with Molly, the cat. Right now her wet nose is under the side of my hand on the keyboard demanding attention.

At my elbow on the computer table are twelve socks that have been delivered one at a time by Kate. My slippers or boots will probably follow.

Dutch is sprawled at my feet, the mountains have an amethystine haze.

My wife is planning a trip. All my kids and grandkids are safe, and it is a grand evening in the Smokies. The pack and I are awaiting the sounding of the trumpet.

. . . .
. . . .

AUTHOR'S COMMENTS

Integrity

According to Webster's Unabridged Dictionary, the word *integrity* holds a lot of powerful meaning, much of which could be applied to dogs. Definitions such as uprightness, adhering to a code of values, incorruptible, morally sound, and moral grandeur, at first seem lofty for a dog. However, when you look at them from the standpoint of a dog, from a dog's level of understanding, they begin to explain much of a dogs' behavior. That was the slant of understanding that I put on them in Pack Leader Down.

Let me tell you two stories that explain "integrity." My great-grandmother on my mother's side married a man with the surname, Allen. They built up an excellent and prosperous farm over a period of years and accumulated some wealth. Mr. Allen decided to form a bank to serve his community. Because of Mr. Allen's wise loans, and investment the bank prospered.

One day his trusted assistant did not appear at work. Mr. Allen soon discovered that the safe had been opened and all of the cash had been removed. The assistant was never seen again and it was assumed he had gone to South America or Europe and started a life of ease.

Here is where integrity comes in. Mr. Allen sold his cattle, sold his machinery, sold his barns, and sold his home and farm. He borrowed some from his family and finally had enough money to reimburse every patron of his bank. This display of integrity moved his friends and neighbors to continue banking with him, and he began to rebuild his life.

Mr. Allen's son-in-law, my grandfather, took his bride on the handlebars of his bicycle to a grassy lake and tent camped their honeymoon. He then took his bike and rode around Southern Michigan, buying up the unharvested grain crops. He used the contracts as leverage to raise money to build grain elevators, buy wagons and teams of horses to move the grain.

He became rich and moved to Florida to speculate in the land boom of the 1920s. He tithed 90 percent of his income, supporting Asbury College, the American Bible Society and local needs. The family legend states that when the land bubble of inflated prices burst he was owed seven million dollars. He, in turn, owed three million to others. It took him many years but he repaid the entire three million. He never received one cent from those that owed him the seven million. His family chaffed under their 10 percent allotment.

What did these two men have? They had integrity! It was not super integrity, it was simply integrity, a word which has no qualifiers or limitations. Integrity is integrity.

When I was growing up I didn't believe that any adult would lie. My parents didn't lie, their friends didn't seem to lie, my teachers didn't lie and so far as I knew our neighbors didn't lie.

In a very tiny way I joined my forefathers in righteous behavior. Had I been willing to cheat on the eye exam for flight school I could have had my heart's desire to be a fighter pilot. I refused to cheat and went to navigator school, where I washed out because of a car accident and seven months assigned to the hospital. That decision may have saved my life, or deprived the Air Force of a pilot. Who is to say? I believe it worked out to my good.

My first exposure to truth and lies was when arguing I discovered my friend had a completely different grasp of the facts. He, of course, proclaimed that my guy was the liar. That was my awakening to the realities of life. I still don't think that those I mentioned previously were liars—rather, they were people of integrity in a day when integrity was important. In a way, they were like the dogs, living by their integrity.

When you look around today, listen to the radio, and watch television, you become aware of the volume of lies that surround us. I am into politics from the standpoint of being an observer. Now the art of deception has taken lying to new heights. One guy announces that he is pro-choice and is fighting against the evil of the anti-abortionist. His "pro" sounds very positive and the "anti" sounds wicked and negative. That's a form of deception. How about, "I am a progressive and you are a right wing reactionary." Guess who most people vote for? The deception was in the emphasis on the negative words ascribed to the opponent.

Remember the big hassle about the president who decided to go to war based on our own intelligence and the intelligence assessment of six other nations—all agreeing about a nuclear threat. Later, after no nuclear threat was found, several of my friends flatly stated that the president lied intentionally. My point is that you are not lying if there is no intent to deceive. You are not lying if the facts you based your decision on are later found to be false. Deception is the key word.

My wife and I have raised six kids. Lying was a major problem, because it made judgment of acts nearly impossible because of the lack of reliable information. It established a basic mistrust because if you get lied to three times, the forth report will be dismissed as another lie. Lying destroys the whole fabric of the family and is the process of destroying a nation.

There is a radio ad presently running on a local talk station. This woman called her boss to tell him that she couldn't come to work, because her mother was sick. The boss said, "I thought your mother died last week and that was why you couldn't come in to work."

"Oh," she said, "the doctor resuscitated her, and then she had a baby."

The employee then went "wah wah," into the phone. "See, I have to stay home now and take care of the baby."

I think those were five lies in a row—all very obvious lies, but it makes the point. The ad was for an employment agency, so the lesson was clear that the boss needed another employee to take the liar's job.

Lying destroys the fabric of a family and is presently destroying our nation. Just last night I was listening to a politician holding forth that the other side was obstructionists and against all progress. I immediately envisioned a gentleman grabbing and jerking back another man who was hurrying because of important business, and about to step off the curb in front of a speeding truck. Would you brand him an obstructionist or a concerned citizen? It is a matter of perception based on what you believe, whether true or false.

I have two last observations before you turn to stone form boredom.

First is that as I read the Bible it is obvious that Satan is the father of lies, and has been, from the beginning. The last days will be filled with his deceptions. Now, that proves to me that liars and deceivers are connecting themselves with the red-tailed guy. The New Testament clearly states that no liars will have their place in heaven. As I look around and listen to the politicians at every level it is obvious that we will have no politics in heaven to argue about, because very few politicians will be there. That also goes for advertisers and a lot of others.

Now, one last observation is a hard truth, that any attempt to deceive is a lie. The truth is that if you don't answer a question which will reveal a deception you have lied, without saying a word. On the good side, if you make an honest mistake and give the wrong information you have not lied because your intent was not to deceive.

For a bright future; seek Integrity. It may hurt at the time, but there will be rewards in the future. The best reward of all will be your own satisfaction with yourself, knowing that you are a truthful person in all circumstances. God is truth. Your adversary is a liar. Look for the truth. If you find a lie, he, or she, is not of God, whether, Republican, Democratic, Independent, etc., it makes no difference. There is just one truth.

GLOSSARY OF NAUTICAL TERMS

Abaft	behind something on the vessel
Aft	to the rear of a part of the vessel
Amidships	in the center of the vessel
Anchorage –	a place for boats to anchor
Backing Block	a thickening of the hull for an attachment
Bandit reels –	fixed reels, manual or electric to pull up fish
Beam or Beamy	the width of the vessel
Bitter End –	the end of a line that is usually inside the boat
Bobstay –	chains attached to the hull that hold the end of the bowsprit down and centered
Boom –	a spar attached to the bottom of the sail
Bowsprit –	a spar projecting beyond the stem to attach the jib
Bulwarks –	structures around deck of a boat to deflect waves or protect the crew
Bunker –	storage box or area
Cabin –	living area of a boat
Centerboard –	a drop down keel pocketed in the cabin
Centerboard pendant	a line or cable to pull up, or lower the centerboard
Centerboard trunk –	a water tight enclosure for the center-board inside the vessel
Cleat –	metal or wooden fixture for the securing of lines or sheets
Cleat down	To attach a line or sheet to the vessel

Cleaver props –	propeller blades shaped some what like a cleaver
Coaming –	a covering board on the top edge of the hull
Cockpit –	recessed area aft where the pilot steers and controls the vessel
Companionway –	entrance to cabin with a door or bards and a slide above
Deadwood –	a filler piece of timbers
Draught –	the depth a hull rests in water
Draw –	the pulling power of wind on the sail
Go Faster –	generic name for a fast boat – cigarette types
Halyard –	the line controlling the raising or lowering of a sail
Hull –	the body of the vessel
Hull down –	below the horizon
Hull speed –	theoretical maximum speed of a hull
Jib –	triangular sail in front of the mast
Jib Sheet –	the line controlling the position of the jib
Port –	left side of a vessel
Pintle and gudgeon –	a two part hinge, one male and one female. securing the rudder to the hull
Sand sprit –	a point of sandy land
Scuppers –	ports to allow overboard drainage from decks and cockpit
Sheer –	the top edge of the hull
Shrouds –	Cables which steady the mast port and starboard
Shoal –	shallow water
Shoal draft –	able to operate in shallow water
Skeg –	a shallow keel or deadwood before the rudder
Sole –	the floor of the cockpit or cabin
Starboard –	right side of vessel
Stem –	the foremost vertical timber of the bow
Stern –	the rear of a boat
Tack –	to change direction in a sail boat
Tackle –	arrangements of lines and pulleys
Through Hull –	a fitting that passes fluid through a hull

Tiller –	a bar attached to the rudder for steering
Transom –	the rear planking of a boat
Un-cleat –	take a line off of a cleat
Wake –	a wave created by the movement of a boat
Way	the movement of a Bessel through the water
Ways –	tracks and carriage for taking a vessel from the water
Whipping –	a mast arcing violently
Worry –	to shake with the teeth or hands
Yaw	to swing to either side of an intended course

www.ingramcontent.com/pod-product-compliance
Lightning Source LLC
Chambersburg PA
CBHW050323200626
46810CB00022B/1160